The Hunt for the Jade Tiger

By

Barbara Pappan/babylonia

Dreamchasers Literary Agency LLC, publisher

Copyright 2013 by Barbara Pappan

Produced with the help of bookbaby.com
First publication, Dreamchasers Literary Agency LLC, 2013

Barbara Pappan/babylonia, Facebook/Twitter/Fanstory (lilcoyote2002@peoplepc.com)
Cover art by Barbara Pappan/babylonia

Dedicated to the twelve million who died: six million Jews and six million others, as well as all of those who fought for my right to be alive today.

Special thanks to Dave Mohr of whom without him, this would be another story just told and not shown.

Table of Contents

Kfira Takes Flight

"Kfira! Come down here!" the male voice booms from the stairwell.

"I will be there in a minute, Father," I answer, from the bathroom. Honestly, how he thinks a girl can take care of her business in two minutes is beyond me. Staring into the mirror, I smile at what I see. At twenty-five, I'm not ugly by all means, but I'm not bad looking either. I definitely have all the boys at Shul looking at me.

"Kfira! Your father is waiting," Mother's voice rings out in that stern tone that says, 'I don't care what you are doing, you have ten seconds to get your tuchas to be standing in front of me.'

I brush away the black hair from my face, and pull it back into a tight bun with a large bobby pin. Sighing, I open the door, and dash down the steps to see what new crises Mother and Father are having.

Yesterday they were upset because the neighbor's cow had died. But honestly, I didn't understand. After all it wasn't their only cow, as they have three more. It didn't really affect our lives one way or another.

"Yes." I walk into the large parlor and look around.

Mother and Father are not alone. Rebbe Schmerson is sitting on the divan with Father. Mother is sitting on the sofa across from them. Everyone appears to have something weighing heavily on their minds.

Rebbe Schmerson has been the family rebbe since before my time. My grandparents, maybe even great-grandparents, went to him for all of life's special events and tragedies. For him to make a home visit, something must be wrong.

"Hello Rebbe." I take a seat next to Mother. Sweat forms in the palms of my hands, I strive not to look too anxious. Gazing over at her, I feel almost too frightened to say anything. This is quite an accomplishment for me, as I have been known to be quite sassy and talkative. Usually I pick all the wrong times to speak my piece.

For the first time, I can see the age in my parents' faces. Both are well into their sixties. I am their youngest child with the others being at least ten years older. Gray hair adorns both their heads. Today, the little lines that usually kiss their faces seem like deep furrows on their foreheads and chins. Both have their hands clasped together, firmly in their own laps.

Rebbe looks weary today. I can only guess his age since my parents are in their sixties. He must be in his nineties, but maybe late eighties, if he's a day. His thick hair on his head, and face is snow white. His wears his familiar black suit, and a soft black hat graces his head, as always. It's said that someone brought this particular hat for the Rebbe, all the way from New York City, as a gift for a baby naming. Considering most people in this little shtetl are poor, this seems very extravagant indeed.

He's still a very tall man, who is built better than most sixty-year-olds. Something keeps him going, and most men in Shul wish they had his stamina.

My heart skips a beat. It feels as if the walls are beginning to close in around me. Tears well up in my eyes. Someone must have died, but whom? Fear keeps me from speaking, and my left leg twitches several times, ever so slightly. No one else notices, and I'm thankful.

Drawing in a deep breath, he exhales out slowly. Father finally speaks. "The Rebbe wishes for you to do something, a mission." This time he speaks in broken English. His English is worse than his Russian, but much better than his Hebrew. He refuses to learn German. His Yiddish is perfect.

I wish he would speak in Yiddish. This, I can understand without concentrating on hearing his every word or watching his lips. This would put me at ease. Gulping almost inaudibly, *I hope they can't hear me. Or do they*? I'm still silent. I'm too tense to say much because when Father uses English, it's not good.

"It's a very important job," Mother says, in Yiddish.

"What can it be?" My fists relax, and my fingers rest lightly on my knees. So many things could be requested of me, such as feeding someone's animals for a while. Maybe I will be taking care of someone's children. Or maybe, I will have to teach those awful Goldborn children Hebrew, again. What can it be? Why are they keeping me in so much suspense? They have never done this before.

"You must pick up a package for me in Bangkok, Siam," the Rebbe finally states, and looks sternly my direction. His pale blue eyes betray nothing. He leans on his black walking stick, and smoothes his long beard in contemplation.

"Okay." I want to say something else, but I dare not. This is the Rebbe, not some Avram from whom I know not, off the street. There are no questions to ask except, "When do I leave?"

"You'll catch a train tomorrow morning at seven. Your Mother and Father will give you all of the details tomorrow. You are not to ask for them before then. One more thing, you must tell no one you are going, and you must pack as light as you can. Do you understand?" Rebbe asks.

Without realizing it, I feel my head bobbing yes. "Yes."

"Good, now I must go. There are many things to do before the morrow. Benyamin, please help an old man to the door," the Rebbe says, as he attempts to pull himself up from the comfort of the divan. Grasping the arm with one hand, and the walking stick with the other, he hoists himself to a standing position. Father reaches him, as he adjusts his coat.

Benjamin grasps the Rebbe's hand in his own. With the help of Rebbe's walking stick and Father, seconds later they are at the front door, speaking softly to one another.

I wish I could listen to their conversation, but I can only hear my heart beating loudly inside my ears. Lub-dub vibrates in my ears. Turning back to Mother, I'm still speechless. The only question that keeps going through my mind right now is *Why me?*

Mother stands, and wraps her arms around me. Holding me tightly, I can feel her small body shake against me, Mother is sobbing. *Oh dear GOD, please make this all turn into a dream. No, make this a nightmare. Tomorrow I will awaken to find everything just as it has been forever. Something tells me that this time it isn't a dream.* Holding tightly to her, I don't want to let her go.

Father steps back into the room.

"Come Mama, we must go to Shul now." Father walks across the room to her. He grasps her hand, and tries to pull her away. She momentarily clings to me, her baby. "It will be all right. She is in HaShem's hands now." Is all he says, as he unwraps her arms from me, and pulls her away.

Watching them walk away, I still feel as if I am dreaming. I know I'm going to wake up at a moment's notice, and will get a good laugh about this one. But it doesn't happen.

Going To Paris

Sitting at my dressing table, I look around my little room, and already I'm homesick. *Will this be the last time I ever see this room?* It became my room when my older sister Hannah had married fifteen years earlier. Mother and Father allowed me to decorate it, as I liked without permitting me to be too vain. When one is an Orthodox Jew, vanity is frowned upon. They allowed me this one mirror, and I sit before it, anxiously getting ready for my journey.

I chose pale pinks and greens, finding they complimented both my taste and dark curls. The pinks make my dark complexion almost rosy. The green matches my eye color, but I didn't let on to Mother and Father for they would have surely disapproved. *When did they become Mother and Father to me? It seems like only yesterday that I was just a little girl, dreaming of that day when I would be able to do things my way. I still called them Mama and Papa.*

My small closet holds the many dresses I have collected over the years. Many have been hand-me-downs from my three older sisters, and a few from the young women in the Shul. Despite the fact there are twenty dresses, none of them are new. It has been difficult to choose which dresses should go and which must stay. *It would be easier if I knew how long I will be gone, or what it will be like away from home. What does this Bangkok, Siam really have for me?*

It's difficult to think at 5 AM. I'm not usually a morning person. I'm lucky if I can be roused before 7 AM. Luckily, any work that has came my way has been after noon.

Mother and Father usually awaken at this time to be sure to have Father at morning prayers by 7 AM. Then he will be off to work in the local bakery. This morning is different. I know they are awake, as I can hear them pattering around downstairs, but it is not the same. The silence speaks loudly. Father is definitely a morning person. He can usually be heard singing most mornings.

His voice, so beautiful in full tune, breathes life into the walls and Mother every day.

Why? Why am I being sent to Bangkok of all places? What could be the purpose of my traveling in such a strange time? My mind races through these thoughts for the thousandth time since the Rebbe voiced his request. I have barely been away from this small shtetl for more than a day trip, and now I am to travel half way around the world. *Maybe Rebbe means for me to travel all the way around the world?*

Several times last night, I attempted to coax information from Mother, but she would have none of it. To ask questions when the Rebbe said not to, oy! So I left it to my imagination, and this is where the trouble began.

Light knocking on the door, jars me from my thoughts of my travels and future.

"Come in."

"Kfira." Mother rushes in. She touches my face with both hands, clasping it tightly, as if she is memorizing it.

"Mama, are you all right?" I reach up, and grasp her face in my hands. Softness against my own hands makes me want to cry.

14

I always thought her to be the most beautiful woman in the world, more so today.

We must look pretty silly, she holding my face in her hands and hers, mine. Staring into each other's eyes, we are silent. She kisses me tenderly on each cheek, and I can feel her heart breaking through her lips.

"Mama, it will be all right." I try to reassure her even if I myself am petrified.

"I can now tell you several things about your trip. First -- " she pulls a handkerchief from her pocket, and wipes the tears from my eyes before wiping her own.

In a way it's as if we are sharing our pain and sorrow, without acknowledging it outwardly. I know that no matter how difficult a task it might be, if the Rebbe asks it, then Mother would not dare to disobey. Even if the task broke her heart, or sent away her youngest child. It's a great honor for such a thing to happen to one's family.

Listening intently, I watch her mouth, as if to devour every word coming from it.

"You must pack one or two light dresses. You must wear

15

three if you can. Maybe we can get you into four. You must use the carpetbag I have placed in your closet, not the other that is usually used for trips to Hannah's. You won't be going to Bangkok right away."

"Where will I be going first?"

"You will go to Paris. You will meet up with a tall blonde woman wearing a red coat that matches her lips." With this Mother made a face, as if tasting rotten cabbage. The idea of a woman coloring her face with something other than what God had intended was unnatural. "She will tell you more then. Also you are not to contact your Father or me. You can only contact us through either the Rebbe or your sister Hannah. You know her address, yes?"

"Why am I going to Paris?" I can tell from Mother's eyes that I shouldn't ask.

Shaking her head, she says nothing.

Wanting to press her about Paris, I resist that desire. All the information she is willing to give is still in my ears.

"You will go to Paris as instructed. Do you know Hannah's address?"

"Of course," I answer, reaching over and hugging her. Hannah is the only one in the family with a telephone. Her husband uses it for his work.

"I want to help you pick out your dresses, may I?"

A little stunned, I am unsure what to say. Mother never asked such a question before. "Yes, of course."

I stand up, and leave my arm draped about Mother's shoulders. We walk over to the closet, and begin to pick through the dresses. The winter dresses are in the front, since it is November. The snows began in September this year, so all summer frocks are in the back.

I grab the bag from the closet, and place it on the bed.

"You must be very excited about your trip, yes?" Mother attempts to be cheerful.

"Oh, of course." I lie, as I see the tears welling up in her eyes. "Haven't I always dreamed of going to Paris?" Laughingly, I take the dress she hands me, and place it in the bag. My hand hits something hard in the bottom of the bag. Looking inside, I see another small bag. It contains three things, a Siddur or prayer book, a ladies compact and a lipstick. Looking at Mother with a confused look, I am unsure of what to say.

"Yes, I detest such things. But there are parts of this trip that will make it important for you to have these things. The lady in Paris will help teach you how to use them," she says and then begins to chuckle. "Well, she will maybe not teach you of the Siddur, but the other things, yes."

"Mama, I will need to hurry, as I want to walk by the sea before I catch the train."

"Yes, you should. Your Father and I can not take you to the train station. Be very careful, as it will still be dark. If your coat doesn't fit over your clothes, maybe you can wear Minka's from when she was with child. (Minka is older than Hannah. Minka is younger than Esther.) You know how cold the wind can be off the sea, especially this time of year."

As an adult of twenty-five, it's difficult to believe that my Mother has never said the word pregnant to me, my whole life. Jokingly, I have told others that I thought that she thought it was too sacred even to speak.

Nodding, I say nothing.

Taking one dress at a time, I dress carefully. By the third

18

dress, I'm starting to feel a little toasty. I know once the early morning air hits me, I'll be thankful for the pleasure of the warm clothes.

Watching Mother, I suddenly realize that she is the same size as me. I have always been the smallest of the children, and that did not change with becoming a woman. Smiles in her eyes tell me that she is trying to be happy for me. Handing me two more dresses, I place them in the carpetbag.

"Thank you." I reach out, and squeeze her hand. My heart is breaking, as is hers.

"You will have a good time, but not too good a time," Mother says sternly.

Laughingly, I squeeze her hand once more. This is the Mother I know and love.

"Hurry, we must get you on your way," Father interrupts at the door.

"Yes, Father."

"She is packed," Mother calls out.

"Good."

"I just thought of something. How will I speak to this woman

I am to meet? I don't speak French."

"She will speak to you in Russian. She will tell you everything you will need to know," Father answers.

Nodding, I reach down to make sure that I have packed everything I will need. Looking at the vanity once more I spy a fresh journal that I have not written in even once. Picking it up as well as several pencils, I drop them into the bag. All is done.

"I'm ready."

"We did not try the coat on," Mother cries and runs over to it. She brings it back, and drapes it over my shoulders haphazardly.

I place my arms into the sleeves. It's easier than I envisioned it to be. It fits snuggly, but it fits warmly. The buttons close just as they should.

"I have your traveling papers and passport." Father hands them to me. "Whatever you do, don't lose them."

"The lady's name is Jean-Pierre," Mother speaks.

"Are you sure?" I ask, as I want to be sure that I have heard correctly. Jean-Pierre is a man's name, or so I think. Taking the papers from Father, I place them in a small handbag that Mother has already placed three cookies and several bread rolls.

"Yes, yes," Father says, as he looks about the room uncomfortably.

I have said too much. Beaming, I lean over, and kiss him warmly on the cheek. "Thank you, Father."

"I can't go with you. I will go to Shul, and pray for you. You will be careful, yes?"

"Yes, Father." I feel as if there is so much to say, and too little time to say it in. How could I have been so blind? These are my parents. Without them, I can't me imagine being me. I love them with all of my heart.

Pulling them both to me, we hug until finally Father gathers some restraint, and begins to back away.

"Please we are acting as if we are old women! We will see each other again. The thing you do for the Rebbe is most important. We will see you when you are finished."

Smiling, I kiss him on each cheek. Turning, I kiss Mother on each cheek. Wanting to tell them how much I love them and will miss them, I say nothing. A part of me knows this is the last chance I have to touch my father. I savor the moment.

Nodding his head, Father readjusts his black yarmulka atop

his head and moves aside, sweeping his arm in front of him, he points to the door.

Silence.

Saying nothing, I grab my bag and handbag and leave, wondering if this is the last time that I will see my parents in this house.

Walking down the stairs I find myself daydreaming of being a child in this house. Every Thursday I would help Mother prepare for Shabbos, a task in itself for one person, but much easier with two. I wonder now how she will deal with it alone.

Stopping in the hallway entrance that leads to the doors to the living room and back toward the kitchen, I spy the Shabbos candlesticks sitting on the dark wooden mantle over the fireplace. Sniffing the air, I can almost feel the warm fuzzy feeling whenever Mama lights them. Turning quickly, I can take no more, and I almost run out of the front door.

As I walk down the steps, snowflakes dance in the air in front of my eyes, as my legs carry me quickly. It is all I can do to keep from turning around and running back inside. I wish upon anything that I could cry "Please let me stay." I say nothing and continue on. I must hurry if I want to get to the train station early.

The snow flurries begin to fall faster. I feel the need to race to get to the station, but my heart won't let me. It tells me I must look. I must take it all in as if something, somehow will change everything. It will all happen in a blink of an eye.

It is too early for anyone else to be stirring. I'm thankful that I don't have to chance meeting up with someone who may want to talk. Rebbe and even Mother said to tell no one where I am going or why. So it is my guess that I will appear to leave town without anyone knowing, and in a hurry. Not always easily done in this little shtetl. Papa always laughs that people know your business before you do! It is usually true.

I walk along the walkway, the sea breeze begins to tingle in my nose. Salt. Every time I get near the sea, I think of salt. The Baltic Sea has been my backyard for so long, I can't imagine another.

Loud clopping noises along the road break my concentration, as I watch to see a horse drawn hay cart on the road. Not recognizing the young man riding atop it, I turn to look as the sun begins to peek on the water. I must hurry now. It's as if I have closed my eyes to all the beauty I see before me and now they are wide open.

Walking as fast as I can, I reach the station in good time. Looking at the clock inside I see that is 6:45. I pray that the train be on time. Except for several people working for the train, the station is deserted.

Finding money in my bag, I buy a newspaper. I sit on a bench in front of the station, anxiously awaiting the train. My legs swing back and forth, as my hands rummage through the newspaper several times.

"Are you waiting for the train?" a man in a German uniform asks, as he approaches from the left.

"Yes, will it be late?" I answer.

"It has been running on time lately. It should be here in five minutes."

"Thank you."

"Very early to be out?"

"Yes, but when you have to catch a train, you have to catch a train." I giggle and shrug.

His blue eyes twinkle, and there is a deep smile on his face. As he props his right foot up on the side of the bench, he leans in to talk. His Russian is very articulate, and his boots are almost too shiny.

Suddenly, a whistle from a distant train begins to break the almost deafening silence, startling the man. Flinching, he straightens up and looks away. "Have a very nice trip," he says, and he is gone just as quickly as he arrived.

Shrugging, I stuff the paper into my bag, and pull out my ticket. Seconds later, I'm boarding the train, and heading for my seat. Staring out the window, I suddenly realize that I'm trying to memorize the tiniest details of my homeland. Shaking my head, I look around to see that there are many people on the train. They are from all walks of life. They all seem to be engrossed in their own affairs.

Taking a cookie from my bag, I begin to munch on it. It tastes good. It tastes like home.

The Train Ride - Meeting Deborah

Leaving home, I am really leaving home. Staring out of the window next to my seat, I watch as no one else gets off the train and no one gets on.

"All aboard!" A deep, male voice booms over a loud speaker in several languages including German, Russian, Yiddish and English.

People wander about the small building, but no one is tempted to make a journey.

Although once a part of Russia, it is now considered East Prussia, my homeland. Many of the older people still refer to it as Russia. This parcel of land was fought over by the Germans and Russians during the Great War. Some like my Papa, refuse to learn German. They claim that some day Mother Russia will come back, and take her cub home again.

My German is only from the words of Yiddish that are similar. This only makes me more apprehensive about leaving my little shtetl. Everything here is familiar, safe.

Looking around, I see there are many couples, and I assume

they are married. I feel the dark seat cover, and wonder how many others have ridden on this same seat. It can easily hold three grown people. The seat across from this one faces me. Maybe if I am lucky, I will be the only one in my seat. Usually I am Miss Hospitality, but not today.

I wonder if Mama is cleaning the house right now, or if Papa is at morning prayers. Has he spoken with the Rebbe? Has he let him know that I am fulfilling my job? I pray that he is even though I'm not really sure what sort of sacrifice I am making.

Glancing back out of the window, I notice that the train is moving slightly, hesitantly, as it builds up the power needed to roll down the tracks. My first train ride, and I'm alone. I would rather be with my parents, or even my sister Esther. Esther is the oldest, and she never lets me forget it. She is forty now, fifteen years older than I am.

"If you don't agree to a marriage soon then the Rebbe will not be able to find anyone for you. You will have to take care of Mama and Papa." It is not a threat. I love Mama and Papa very much. Until last night I would have never thought about leaving them for any reason. They are not just my Mother and Father, they are my Mama and Papa. I'm their scared little girl once more.

The train begins to pick up speed. Pulling my ticket from my bag, I search through it to see what stops will be made. It says there will be a short stop at the capital, Konigsberg. Then the next stop will be in Poland, Warsaw. The next big stop is Prague, and finally on to Paris. There are many little stops along the way. *No stops in Germany. Is that strange? How long will this journey take? Will I be home for Chanukah?*

Peering out of the window, I see the trees begin to blur together until there are no trees.

###

Snapping the back of my head against the seatback, I stare at my surroundings, a little disoriented. *Where am I? How long have I been asleep?* The sound of the train, as well as the vibrations of the cars motoring down the tracks, bring me back. I'm on a train going to Paris. Soon enough, I'm going to be in Bangkok. *Doesn't that seem like a long way to go for one trip?* In my sleepy state it does.

A young woman sits beside me. She is maybe twenty-one.

Her blonde curls tightly frame her smiling face. Her bright blue eyes almost light up the car. She is wearing a very smart burgundy suit, and she too is carrying a carpetbag and a small purse.

"Hello!" she says in Yiddish, as she puts her bag under her feet.

"Hello." I smile. Apprehensively, I want to try to ignore her, but the old me says no. I must have a conversation with her. If we were in another place at another time I would think nothing of starting a long conversation with her, maybe even becoming friends with her. So why should things be different now?

I reach out my right hand, "My name is Kfira and you?"

"My name is Deborah," she answers gleefully, and takes my hand warmly in her small one.

"Are you having a good day?"

"Yes, it's a very good day to travel." Deborah points to my bag. "I see you have a newspaper. May I look at it for a minute?"

"Of course." I pull the newspaper from my bag, and hand it over to her. Spying the date, I shake my head subconsciously, November 7, 1938. What a day to be traveling! Chanukah is quickly approaching, as well as winter. I love snow. I wonder if I will see any snow in my travels.

"I don't mean to be so forward. I was just hoping to see if they have any idea what the latest fashions are in Paris," Deborah speaks. There is an excitement in her voice.

"Are you going to Paris?" I ask.

"Yes, I'm meeting my aunt there. We are to take a boat to the United States. I have another aunt and uncle who live in New York." Deborah hands back the newspaper. "I forget there isn't much in these little papers."

"I only picked it up, as I thought it might help me kill time. I've never ridden on a train before. How long does it take a train to get to Paris? Will we be in Paris by sundown?" I ask, hoping with all hope that she will say we will be there tomorrow, but feeling pretty doubtful. Placing the newspaper in my bag, I will look at it later.

Laughing, Deborah lightly pats my leg. "You are so silly! I wish! I could have been in Paris last week. If we are lucky, and there aren't many delays, we will be there in three days."

Eyes wide, I don't know what to say. *All I have to eat are a few biscuits and cookies? How will I survive three days with so little food? If I had known, I would have asked mother to pack more food.* Fear encircles my heart and squeezes.

"I know what you are thinking."

"You do?"

"You're thinking that you might get hungry before then, am I right?"

Nodding yes, I say nothing.

"They feed you in the dining car, silly."

My eyes widen, and my cheeks flush. But of course, they feed us in the dining car! I hadn't completely looked at my ticket, so when I turned it over there it was, a free meal pass. Thank you, HaShem.

"I must look so naive."

"Believe me, I did the same thing when I traveled the first time. I was twelve and my parents took me to Amsterdam. I kept thinking I would starve, or wet myself before we arrived until my mother very politely pointed out the possibilities."

Smiling, I feel warm all over. "I am so thankful you sat down next to me."

"You look like you could use the company, and I hate traveling alone."

"Thank you."

"Are you Hannah's sister?"

"Yes, I'm her youngest sister."

"I thought I recognized you. I have babysat for her children. I think one time you two came in together after Hannah's shopping. That was a few years ago so you probably don't remember me."

Thinking seriously, I try to recall her. "I'm so sorry I don't recall you. I'm still a little nervous about the travel," I confess. My mind moves back to several years back, but still nothing comes to mind.

"Don't worry about it. We only talked for a couple of minutes. I couldn't even tell you why I was there. I just remember the babies were very young, and she was pregnant at the time. Her husband was out of town, and the children were ill," Deborah replies.

"You said she had two at the time?" I frown.

"Yes, and she was close to delivering the third," Deborah

remarks.

"Yes, she came and got me to stay with her. She was very anxious as Josef, her husband, was away on business. She had a baby girl two weeks later. She had a baby boy the next year." I laugh as I recall Mama's loving nickname for Hannah, her baby-making machine. Unlike the Hannah in the Torah reading that is read every High Holy Days, this Hannah easily becomes pregnant, and has many children.

"They were beautiful children. I should only hope to have such beautiful children as hers." Deborah lightly pats her hands together.

"She does have beautiful children," I agree.

Walking up from behind us, the conductor stops in front of us.

"Be sure to have your tickets ready. We will be stopping in ten minutes," he says and moves on.

"We must have reached Poland," Deborah voices.

Saying nothing, I pull my ticket back out. Out of the blue it dawns on me, she spoke Russian to me. Without acknowledging the change, I decide it would also be safer to speak Russian as well.

"Maybe as soon as they look at our tickets we can go to the dining car. I am famished."

"That does sound like a good idea." I glance out of the window to see the station in the distance. The train is starting to slow down a bit. Many men in uniforms, German uniforms, stand around, everywhere. They are waiting, and watching, almost like ghouls. *Are they waiting for us? I can't think right now. Maybe I shouldn't. Maybe I should stay calm and pray.*

We can hear the conductor and his friend, a German soldier walking down the aisle. "Tickets please," they ask. Sometimes they ask, and seconds later they ask again. Rarely, they take a few minutes more, and then they proceed.

Trying to remain calm, I want to turn around like a meshuggah and get? I don't know. *What are they looking for? Why do some people need extra time?* Anxiety fills me until I am almost blind with fear.

"Kfira. Take a deep breath in and out."

Without thinking or questioning, I do as she says.

Whispering softly, she says "Follow my lead."

Not saying a word, I smile at my new friend. *So her being*

34

here is not just a lucky coincidence! But who made her take this trip? And why?

Just as the men stroll up next to us, Deborah pulls out her compact and lipstick from her purse. She is chatting almost non-stop about something.

I can't understand half of what she is saying. I just smile. I turn to pull my lipstick and compact from my bag. Watching from the corner of my eye, I see how she applies the red stick to her lips and follow suit. It feels like I am putting cold, red wax to my dry lips.

"Yes," she remarks to the men standing beside us.

They stand silently for a few seconds before both say "tickets please" at the same time. It is more than a little obvious that these two are enchanted with Deborah's beauty.

Giggling, Deborah pushes a curl out of her face with her left hand.

"Here." She hands them first her ticket, and then mine.

The men barely look at our tickets, as they stamp something on them. "Thank you," they say simultaneously. Their cheeks turn crimson, and they are gone almost as quickly as they arrived.

Thank you I mouth to her when she glances back to me.

She shrugs.

We both know this isn't a time to talk of such things. I can't even ask her if I applied the lipstick correctly. It's time to eat, or do anything, that would make us appear to be regular tourists out on holiday.

"Are you ready to eat?"

"Yes."

Looking at the men, I listen intently to their words now. They have been asking for people's passports! They didn't ask for ours.

Getting up, we pick up our bags, and head into the direction that the men had just left.

"It's just the next car over."

It isn't over so we can talk openly about what is going on. I feel a little more than lost right now. I wonder if my parents know the risks I'm taking by being here right now. I pray they are not as scared as I am. I keep reassuring myself that it will all be all right if I'm patient.

"You will love the food."

"I hear it is very good," I brag, and realize that lying isn't my strong point. Actually, the people I have known who have taken the train did not eat in the dining car. They preferred to eat their own food that they had brought from home.

Despite the fact that we have only met once, we make small talk as if we have been old friends from childhood.

The Train Ride - Warsaw

When we get back from the dining car, I am stuffed. I didn't think I was that hungry, but the pastries looked and tasted wonderfully. Wearing three dresses and under things, I found it difficult to eat too much, but somehow I managed.

I wish I could talk to my companion, let her know that I know something about what is really going on, and why she is here. But then maybe it would be better to play the naive girl instead of the knowledgeable woman. Keeping my eyes wide open, I am now more aware than before of my surroundings.

"We must get some sleep," Deborah is saying now.

I only nod in agreement although I am unsure how I will be

able to do so. Sleep seems so very far away.

"They will wake us if they need anything from us."

Shutting my eyes now, I find it very difficult to fall asleep. My mind is racing back and forth between now, and the moment I saw the Rebbe in our living room. How quickly life changed, and I am scared, but I want to be brave.

Closing my eyes, I can feel the vibration of the train car as it moves forward. Looking around, I notice many empty seats. *They are probably in the dining car or the necessity room as they are not here in their seats.* Placing my left ankle inside the loops of my bag, I push it behind my feet. Resting them on it gives me a secure feeling. Laughing inside my head, I am not sure what sort of security, or why, but that it does. If someone really wanted my old dresses, I would easily give them up, but not my Siddur.

As for my money, Mama had instructed me on how to keep it close to my body, and only keep a small amount of change in my bag. She had taught me this when I was very small. Being a little Jewish girl, I have been the target for many bullies in my day.

I had never seen so much money, as the money Mama and

Papa had given me to take on this trip. I wonder how they could let me part with such an amount. My guess is that the Rebbe gave it to them. I have a little money as well, from several small jobs that I perform for the Shul. All of a sudden I frown, *who will do my jobs now that I am not there? The Rebbe probably has people taking my place with Hebrew classes and such.* Still, I am a little sad. I did not get to say good-bye to my students.

Sensing that my companion is already asleep, I try to think happy thoughts to ease me.

Mama and Papa. Just saying their names in my head conjures up fresh vivid, good memories. Being a child and being held closely to Mama's bosom, as she said the Shabbos prayers with Papa. Most wives did not do this but Mama insisted that she learn and say them, as if she were a man. She then taught them to her children, all eight of us.

Papa always made a warm fire during the cold winter nights. One could find him singing his daily prayers as he chopped wood. Once, one of the others had asked if the Rebbe would approve. Papa simply replied that he wasn't praying to the Rebbe, but to HaShem. He figured HaShem understood that everyone needed a little inspiration to keep up the good work of providing for one's family.

Thinking about this makes me realize why Mama would risk putting that small book in my bag, to give me hope for whatever task I might need help with. Suddenly, I begin to feel my eyelids droop in the heaviness of sleep, and not just the "pretending to be asleep". Smiling, I feel safe.

###

Feeling a small hand on my shoulder jars me awake. "Hello?"

It's Deborah. "We are almost at Warsaw."

"How long have I been sleeping?"

Chuckling, "long enough," she answers.

Sighing, I try to move my legs, but it feels as if they are not a part of my body anymore. Searching around me for a way to stretch and awaken them, I find a small space between the seats. Sticking my feet into the space helps me to flex my toes inside my shoes and pull my legs. Small cramps in my calves make me wince in pain. My toes curl up awkwardly, pushing out on my shoes. I thrust them back and forth, and side to side. Slowly, the pins and needles of the pain subside, and I feel like I have feet and legs again.

Studying the way Deborah is stretching, I attempt to follow her lead. We both stand, and reach for the ceiling, and then the floor. It's easier for me to do this than her, as I am shorter.

"Are you awake?" Deborah asks, as she yawns. Quickly, she covers her mouth with her hand, so as not to be rude.

"Am I dreaming?"

"Not likely," Deborah answers, as she stands and wiggles her hips as if to jar them awake.

"I didn't think so, but I thought I'd ask." Smiling, I pull the bag from my ankle so as not to trip over it, and place it in the seat next to me. I take the compact from my handbag, and look at my reflection. Never have I seen my face in such a tiny mirror before! I know there is probably not one other woman on this train who can honestly say the same. As Mama would say 'I look a little tired.'

"They will be calling for the tickets again soon."

Nodding, I say nothing. I have already begun to figure out part of the game.

"Do you want to go to the washroom first?"

All of a sudden, I realize that it's the only thing I can think of doing.

"It's right next to dining car. You can't miss it."

I have been to the washroom since boarding the train, but I'm thankful for her directions as I feel slightly disoriented. Picking up my bag and handbag, I head in the right direction. I wish to splash cold water on my face, as I am starting to feel warm. I had taken off my coat when I had boarded the train, but the cold in the middle of the night made me slip it back on sometime in my sleep. Cupping my hands to make a small bowl, I can drink several times before I finally splash the cold liquid on my face and neck.

Taking down my hair, I comb it as best I can in tight quarters and pin it back up. Drinking a few more bowlfuls, I dab my hands and face dry on one of the dresses clinging to my body. Mama always said, wash your hands but be weary of communal towel sharing.

The seats are starting to fill back up again. People from all compartments, return to their seats. People are gabbing, as if it is a beautiful day and everything is wonderful, instead of the fact that German soldiers are everywhere. They cluster in small groups, here and there. Occasionally you can hear their conversations and laughter.

Never in my whole life have I seen so many soldiers. We live in East Prussia that was actually part of Russia until the World War, the Great War, or whatever one wants to call it. It was there that Germans and Russians fought mercilessly for such a tiny piece of land, or so Papa would say. Although it is claimed by Germany now, so many Russian influences abide in it. It might as well be Russian. Even our passports still have our identity as Russians.

We live in a very isolated part of East Prussia, so we aren't as easily accessed as other parts. Occasionally the soldiers came to town. I only know of once or twice when a large group came, and it was over a ceremony of some sort. I wasn't allowed to attend. Papa said, we are Russians and we are not to support Germany.

Seeing German soldiers scare me, and I am not certain why. Deborah grasps my hand. I look into my companion's face and smile.

Just as excitedly as she had been the moment I met her, she says, "Can you believe we are really going to Paris?" Pulling her hand away, she clasps her hands together against her bosom, and looks up into the sky. "No parents to spoil our fun. It will be a wonderful holiday."

"Yes, I believe so. There are so many things to see and do. Where does one begin?"

She giggles loudly, as if she hasn't a care in the world. She closes her eyes and smiles. "I love PARIS."

Laughter is definitely contagious, as I find myself giggling, even though I'm not finding this to be funny. Not at all. I'm just thankful to be this far into the journey, and still be alive.

Abruptly the train begins its slow descent into the station.

Butterflies attack my stomach like it is the best tasting flower in the field. Taking a deep breath in and out, I make an effort to keep myself calm. I struggle to keep from looking out the window, and seeing all the German soldiers on the platform, waiting.

Are they waiting for us? Or are they waiting for me?

Deborah must sense my apprehension, as she smiles at me

44

and reaches over to squeeze my arm. "I must take you to my most favorite dress shop. The dresses there will make you look stunning."

"Do you really think so?"

"But of course you will. You have such a darling figure. I saw you eat. I know you are not shy. We will get you a few new dresses and you will feel like a new woman."

Several soldiers walk by our seats barely noticing us. They seem to be looking for someone.

"What color do you think would look best on me?"

"Well I hear that black and white is in this year, but personally I think they are much too drab. I would think you deserve a bright pink or maybe some other pastel color. No sense making you look like an old woman before your time."

"That would be nice," I agree. I know it is just a conversation and this is just a dream idea, but for a moment I saw myself walking down the streets of Paris, wearing a pretty pink frock with a pink parasol in one hand. It is a sunny day, and I'm basking in the sunshine, as I look into all the shops.

Shaking my head no ever so slightly, I know that this is a

dream. The reality is that I am on a train to Paris, and German soldiers are going through here like it is a parade. *Just keep talking, laughing and smiling,* I say to myself every few seconds.

The conductor is making his way down the walk with another German soldier. Serious expressions cover both of their faces.

Snatching up my purse quickly and sitting back down, I patiently await my cue to take out the lipstick.

"Hello," Deborah says, as they stand in front of us.

"May we see your papers, please?" The conductor puts out his left hand limply, almost apologetically.

"Why of course," Deborah gives him her best smile. Pulling from her purse what looks like a small bundle, she hands them to the conductor. "Silly me, sister," she turns to me. "I am afraid I have been a naughty girl. While you were sleeping I took your papers from your purse, and put them in mine so you needn't look in your bag." Turning back to the men, "She is a very sound sleeper, and I didn't want to wake her if you came and asked for them before now." Again the wide smile of almost perfect teeth appears.

I say nothing. I know my real papers are safely tucked away

in my handbag. I checked while I was in the washroom.

"Oh, thank you sister for being so considerate." I clasp my hand onto her shoulder, and smile at the men.

Looking over the papers, the German smiles and hands them back to the conductor. "Everything seems to be in order," the soldier says.

Handing the papers back to Deborah the conductor grins. "Thank you, miss."

The two men walk to the next seating compartment to repeat the process.

I don't know what to say. The butterflies are now in my throat along with a small lump. Oh how I wish we could be in Paris in an hour. I wish to ask many questions. Never in my life have I held my tongue for so long! Mama would be so proud.

"As soon as the train starts we will go get something to eat. I am starving."

"Okay."

We're off to the dining car once more.

The Train Ride - Prague

As we go back to our seats, I start to feel a little strange. Something crosses my mind, and I'm not sure of what to do about it. It's as if lightning has struck my heart, and knocked me off my feet. I feel so disoriented now.

"How are you feeling?"

"I am fine."

"You don't look well. You didn't eat very much. Are you sure you aren't just hungry?" Deborah leans in closer to touch my forehead with the back of her hand.

"I miss Mama and Papa," I whisper in Yiddish in so low a voice I am sure no one can hear. Sighing, I want to cry. I want to go home. I want to be with my family. The uneasiness is building, and every fiber of my being says I must scream, but I don't. I mustn't attract attention to myself.

Turning away and looking out the window, I take a deep breath in and out. Deep breath in and out, and all the little things will be better, thank HaShem.

Deborah touches my shoulder, and pulls me to face her. She

mouths, I understand. "It takes a few trips to get used to sleeping and eating on a train. Sometimes it just takes a day or two to get used to anything."

"Maybe it will be better after the next time I sleep."

Deborah's eyes burn with a new brightness. "They will be all right," her lips say without sound. "They are in your heart."

Nodding, I glance back out of the window. "What day is it?"

"I think it is November 9th," Deborah answers.

A man across the way is reading a newspaper. Sitting beside one of the largest women I have ever seen, he seems to be very engrossed in the writings in the middle section. The woman and the man are opposites in size, where she is large, he is thin. She is tall and he is short. They wear the clothes of German distinction, well tailored traveling suits of charcoal gray. Her hair is thick and red as fire, and his is white and thinning to almost nothing. What a pair these two make. I can only imagine what they might look like walking down the street together, and I have to stifle a laugh.

"Excuse me sir," Deborah says, as she turns to face the man, "my sister and I have been on the train a while. Can you tell us what today's date is? Her birthday is November 15th, and she doesn't want me to forget it." Deborah giggles and tugs at her curls.

"It is November 9, 1938," the man replies with a huge smile, as he leans a little closer to her.

The large woman elbows the unsuspecting man sharply in the ribs. He glances at her with a smirk on his face, before he covers his face with the newspaper once more.

"Thank you."

It's always good to be polite even if it falls on deaf ears.

The conductor walks down the way, and I expect him to say that we will be pulling into somewhere soon, but he is just looking.

"Sir," I say, as he walks close to us.

"Yes."

"How long before we get to Prague?"

"We should get there in the wee hours of the morning. We are running a little behind, as there has been a large herd of cattle on the tracks up ahead."

"I didn't notice us slowing down," I say without thinking.

"It was probably while we were in the dining car. You know how when we start eating and talking, you don't notice things." With that Deborah tosses her hair back and beams.

I smile. I'm a little more than irritated that "sister" Deborah is always giggling and tossing those blonde curls around.

"It will go by quickly," the conductor reassures me, before he goes to check on the others.

Nodding subconsciously, I turn to look at the others on the train. I realize that until this moment I could have been watching a black and white movie show. Nothing seems real. I'm in it, and participating, but not really here. Crazy as it sounds to me, I feel as if it's the only truth I do know.

I am on a train to Paris. It's November 9, 1938. My parents and whole family aren't with me. I pray it's a dream, and that I will awaken soon.

"Let's go get you something to eat."

"Maybe that would help."

Standing and grabbing our bags as have become our custom, we look over to see two more Polish soldiers walking down the aisles. They are asking people for their paperwork again. After inspecting the papers, they return it to the rightful owner.

Smiling at me, Deborah pulls the paperwork out from her bag in preparation.

"May we have your papers please?" the older one asks. He is tall and blonde probably around twenty-five. Little spikes of a faint moustache look almost comical on his upper lip.

His blonde partner is shorter, maybe sixteen. If the boy loses much more weight he might disappear. He stays close, almost on the coattails of the older fellow. Never once does he look up from the other man's hands.

"I have ours right here." Deborah hands them over. She is giving him her best smile with the twinkling eyes.

Trying not to make eye contact, the older soldier shakes his head no several times. It's as if he is unsure of what he is seeing is real. Looking back at Deborah and then at me, he sighs. You two are going to Paris?" he asks, in a thick German accent.

"Ya," is all I can say. I only caught the Paris part, but I'm pretty sure I understand the rest.

Twisting his lips around, he says nothing.

Deborah takes his arm and smiles again, trying to get his

attention. "Have you been to Paris? It is the city of love!"

"Ya, I have been," turning to the younger man he says something I didn't understand till I say what the young man did.

He took our papers, and pulls out a stamp. On each of our papers, he marks one word ... Juden.

My heart sinks. I'm not sure what that means as far as our trip goes, but something tells me it isn't good. Papa has often talked about the Pogroms that the Russians have enforced from time to time. It didn't take a fool to know that such a marking on one's papers may be ... I dare not even think of it now.

Smiling, I say nothing. This is what I have feared the whole time, and now that it has happened, I feel relief. This is the thing I had no name for ... being stamped Juden.

Handing back the paperwork to Deborah, he says nothing more. She takes them, and smiles weakly. No more attempts to flirt or distract, only submission.

"Thank you," I say, as I realize the spark has left my friend. Putting my arm around her shoulders, I pull her closer. "It will be all right. HaShem will take care of us."

Reaching her arms about me, we hug for what seems like an

eternity, but it's only a few seconds.

Pulling away, Deborah looks down at her feet. "I am sorry."

"Let's not talk now. Let's eat." Grasping at her arm, I attempt to stand her up.

Looking weakly at me, I know she wants to protest, but she doesn't. Taking my lead, she stands and we grab our bags. With our heads held high, we walk to the dining car.

Feeling harsh stares on my back, I glance over to where the eyes may be coming from. It's the couple with whom we had asked about the date. The woman snickers, and a look of contempt crosses her lips before she peers out of the window as if nothing has happened.

"What do you think they have to eat now?" I ask cheerfully. I refuse to look at this as something bad. I have been called worse. I'm not afraid.

"They should have those lovely pastries you drool over," Deborah says with a lilt in her voice. It's as if someone has turned a key inside her, and brought her back to life. She is the same happy girl she was when we first met.

\###

Looking over the menu, I am unsure of what to eat. I'm not even sure I'm hungry. I find myself staring at the people in the dining car. They all seem so happy. Their clothing is bright and colorful. Recalling the moment I caught this train, I only saw people with gloom around them, most were wearing blacks or dark grays. I thought I was at a funeral, or that they had just returned from one.

"I think I will have the roast beef," Deborah is saying to the waiter.

"And for you miss?"

Juden ... "Huh?"

"What would you like to eat?"

"How about the pastries?" Deborah taps the back of my hand.

"I think I will also have the roast beef."

"Very good." He takes the menus, and leaves us to the small talk that this room is famous for.

"Roast beef? Aren't we being daring?" Deborah chortles.

Smiling and nodding yes, I feel like my old self once more. "You only live once." Shrugging, I pick up my water glass, and take a big gulp. *I don't know why I was chosen for this trip or why I met Deborah. I don't even know why those soldiers put a*

label on me. I only know there must be a logical explanation, and

I hope to hear it some day. But for now I will eat roast beef and

maybe then I will have a pastry or two. Who knows?

###

Once we are back to our seats I notice that the little couple

with the newspaper are gone now. Several seats in front of ours

as well as behind us, are empty.

"So we have the measles now," I say to Deborah in a soft

voice. In the old days I would have said it so loud everyone

would turn his or her head to see who said it.

Shaking her head and lightly chuckling, she says, "You are

something."

"What are you talking about?" I rearrange my bags on the

floor beside me.

"Are you ready for Paris?"

"The better question is ... is Paris ready for me?"

Smiling and laughing once more, Deborah lays her head back

against the seat, and watches the train scene.

Everyone seems to be resting now even though it is quite

early. *Maybe when I get to Paris I can get a small watch so I can know what time it is. Did I say maybe? I mean when I get to Paris I will get me a small watch so I too can be a slave to it.*

"Kfira."

"Yes."

"You must try to get some rest now."

Taking in a deep breath, I let the in and out of the air ease the pain of what is left for us in the future. Nodding, I place the bag back on my ankle. Try as I might, I can't get comfortable. Eventually, my eyelids begin to droop, and I start to feel myself drift off.

\###

CHOOOOOOOOOOORRRRRRRRRRTTTTTTTTCCCCCCHH HHHHHOOOOORRRRRRRRTTTTTTT!

Awakening with a start, I kick my bag several times almost knocking it off my ankle. I slap Deborah with my right hand. Jumping to my feet, I trip over the bag and fall into the seat across from us. Thank HaShem it is empty. *Are we in Prague? What is going on? Are there more cows on the tracks?*

My heart beats hard against my breasts, filling my ears with the rhythm of my fear. My mouth is to dry for me to speak, and I feel lightheaded. Fear grips my being, and my hands tremble against my legs. Licking my lips, I try to calm myself.

I turn to Deborah, but she is still asleep. Clutching her handbag, she leans over into the area I was sitting in only a few seconds earlier.

I attempt to see through the darkness outside of the window. I sit back down on the seat across from "our" seat. Others are also gathering around their windows, trying to understand why the train whistle screams so loudly over and over again. I can barely hear the others whispering, but I watch as they point.

The conductor appears from out of nowhere, and he looks scared. "Sorry about the confusion ladies and gentlemen," he states in several languages, as he walks up and down the aisle. "Is there anyone who was to get off the train in Prague?"

No one answers.

"Due to circumstances beyond our control, we will not be able to make our usual stop in Prague. We will also not be able to stop in Germany. We will stop once we reach France. We are so sorry for the inconvenience. Hopefully all delays will be minimal as we will be in France ...."

... As speedily as we can be, I want to finish. *What could possibly make a train not stop at the appointed destination? Is it because of me? Is it Deborah? So many questions race through my mind, and not one has an answer.*

Everyone is still crowding around the windows, but the darkness only blinds them. Suddenly, we all see it all at once. The night lights up like the sky is on fire. Several buildings are aflame near the station. Bright oranges and reds dance along the way while bodies' race towards and away from thcm.

A collective "ooh!" goes through the crowd.

Sighing, I sit back down. No, this isn't just about me. No, it isn't just about Deborah. It's about everything and everyone, on the train or not. Life is changing. Life will never be the same for me again. I have a choice ... will I let it make me better or not. Either way, I get the feeling that I can never go home again.

Kristallnacht

"What is going on?" People start murmuring amongst themselves.

Looking over at Deborah, I am speechless. *Do I wake her so that she can view this horrific sight or do I let her rest?* Knowing there is nothing she can do, I turn to watch as people scramble all around in the distance. They are doing the same inside the train car, and it is very frightening to witness. I hope that at least the people on the outside are attempting to put out the fires, and maybe save the lives of those inside the buildings.

It looks as if there is a huge screen up instead of the train window, and I'm watching a picture show. I lean forward, so I can capture all of their images in my mind. A few people race toward the railroad cars, turning back and pointing, as if to make sure we know. They want us to witness this horror. All of us.

The beating of my heart in my ears begins to calm, and I can hear the others speaking. Some are speaking in German, some French, some Russian and a few in Yiddish. They are all saying the same thing, "What could have caused such a commotion? Where are we? Are we close to Prague? Have we crossed the border into Germany? No, we must still be in Prague. What is going on here?" Voices speaking softly and some loudly, all want the same things, answers.

Pausing to look at my fingers as they caress the windowpane, I can feel the heat from the fires. For a moment I am transcended to the warmth of the fireplace at home. Papa might affectionately ask if I wish to have a few potatoes placed amongst the coals for a toasty bed. He had found an old bed warmer on one of his few trips to his parents' homeland in Russia as a boy. He would place the half-cooked potatoes in the bed warmer, and put it under the covers, making for a very toasty bed.

But this is not home. It is a train full of strangers, and soldiers with big stampers at the ready to mark you, Juden.

Stirring slightly, Deborah watches through half open eyelids at me now. "What is the matter now?" she asks irritated.

"I don't know." I turn back to watch the scene. I really don't know how to answer her question.

We are rolling past the station. It's shut down. Parked next to it are two large trucks, and a small group of German soldiers are lined up around them. Others are running back and forth between the station, and another building not too far from the tracks.

"Maybe you can tell me." I turn back to Deborah who by now is also seeing the flames.

"Oh my," she says, and shivers almost violently.

"Are you cold?"

Shaking her head, she whispers, "no."

Someone is saying something about an invasion. Another person is talking about the peace agreement and the return of the Sudetenland to Germany. A young woman asks if this means she won't be able to go to Paris.

People from the right side of the train switch with the people on the left, and back and forth. From what I can tell, with the exception of the station on the right hand side, there is no difference. Soldiers and fires decorate the countryside.

"I don't know what this means."

I say nothing.

"Maybe the Germans finally did something to the Jews," someone says, in a loud whisper in a very distinctive Russian.

Mumbling can be heard, as well as grumbling about everything. So many voices.

I realize that unlike school or home I am on a train, and there is nowhere to hide if these people decide they don't like us. I also know that Deborah and I are not the only Jews on this train.

"Calm down everyone," the conductor says, as he begins his descent down the aisles to where large conglomerates of people are looking out the windows.

"What is going on?" many ask.

"Do you know anything?"

"The Germans have secured the train station for today as a reason of national security. That is all that I know. We will stop as soon as we get to France. Please people, please find your seats. There is nothing here to see," he says, almost begging the people.

Snapping of pictures, as people take their cameras from bags. No one seems to know how to deal with the countryside on fire.

Sitting back in my seat, I think about Mama and Papa. *Are they safe? They have been dealing with this sort of insanity all their lives. Surely this will seem like a piece of baklava to them, easy to handle. But still I fear for them.*

Sitting back down, Deborah attempts to speak. "We must try to get more rest."

Smiling, I nod, but I know that I won't be able to until we're in France. Then we can get a newspaper, and solve the mystery of the fires in the night.

"Do you speak French?" I whisper.

Nodding, Deborah motions for me to sit next to her.

Moving back to my original seat, I lean in closer to her so I can hear Deborah's every. She won't have to talk over the crowd. They aren't extremely loud, but it feels as if they are screaming in my ears. I wish I could cover them with my scarf, but realize I might miss something important. I wish to disappear, and never recall this night again. But I know this wish isn't good. Swallowing hard, I know Deborah is about to say something I won't like.

"Sleep." Deborah leans back.

Nodding, I understand. Maybe I should pretend to be asleep.

Closing her eyes, Deborah says nothing.

Eyeing the little group, I see that most have returned to their seats. Turning to the window, I can see that most of the excitement is gone from our sight. People are whispering amongst themselves, but they aren't as visibly upset as a few minutes earlier.

Lying back in the seat, I place the bag back on my foot, and cradle my handbag for a pillow and security. Saying several prayers in my head, I have no intention of falling asleep. The lull of the train is too much, and I'm aware of my heavy eyelids.

###

Awakening with the sound of the train whistle, I glance around to orient myself once more. I'm still on the train. My bag is still on my ankle, and Deborah isn't by my side.

Where can she be? I wonder. She is probably in the washroom I conclude. I find myself needing to use the washroom as well. Standing and yawning, I stretch and move my arms from side to side, as if to awaken them.

Others are also doing the same. In a way it's as if the excitement of the night before never happened. People are laughing and joking, making small talk.

Walking to the washroom, I also notice that no one is treating me any differently than when I boarded the train ... was that a hundred years ago or ten hours? I feel a little confused but push it to the back of my mind and trudge on.

The cold water feels good against my warm skin. I can't wait to get the newspaper, and see what the commotion was all about. *Why did it seem as if the night was on fire?*

Returning to my seat, I find that Deborah is still missing. A young man walks through carrying a bag full of newspapers in one arm, and a single in his left hand.

"Newspapers," he calls out in several different languages.

"Newspaper?" I ask, in English.

"Yes," he says, with a smile.

"I will take one," I say. I unsnap my purse, and begin to look through my purse for change.

Handing me one, he smiles and shakes his head. "No charges pretty lady."

"Thank you," I say, taking it and giving a slight bow.

"You are welcome." He heads back down the aisle, peddling his newspapers to the others.

Opening the newspaper, I see that it's written in French. I

can't read it, but maybe it will have some sort of explanation of the night before. Maybe even pictures. Maybe Deborah will translate.

The headlines hit me in the face almost knocking me down.

Kristallnacht. A small caption in English and French say that Germans gathered up a group of Jews in Germany, thus causing a backlash in some surrounding countries by resistance fighters. They say known Zionists are also in the area, as speculated by the local police. All was seen to the rest of the world was a night of fire and hate. Several pictures show buildings on fire.

Zionists, where have I heard that name before? I ask myself. Nothing comes to mind. I vow to ask someone later.

Thirty minutes later the train begins to move once more. Deborah isn't here. Pulling Mama's cookie from my bag, I take a bite of home.

I'm unsure of what this means for me, I honestly know it isn't good. *Papa used to tell me to be wary of times like these least they turn on the Jews. Where is Deborah? Why is she not here? Maybe I should look in the dining car?* But my heart says don't. It says pretend. Pretend to be alone once more. Even though my heart beats hard against my chest, as fast as the train moves

across the tracks, I tell myself not to panic.

The Train Ride - Joe the American

I watch out of the window, as we move along the track. I hope

that this part of the trip won't take long. Many people continue

on the train ride despite everything that happened last night. I

glance around, and notice everyone seems to be preoccupied

with going to the dining car or resting. Some are even reading the

free newspapers.

I'm tempted to ask someone what the stories mean, but

don't want to appear stupid. I look back at all of the pages, the

only portion not in French is the small story to the Kristallnacht

picture. I sigh, and wish I could have learned French, but then

how many languages is one person supposed to know?

It feels like I stepped into another world with the drastic

change in people's dress and mannerisms. A few people are

wearing the dark traveling suits of the Germans or the

mismatched, heavy clothing of the Russians. Even more are wearing gay colors of wonderfully styled outfits. It's a joy to see.

I listen to the others, as they are all excited about one thing, seeing Paris. I'm thankful that I'm not the only one on this train who has never been to Paris. I wish that Deborah was still sitting beside me, I feel a little lost without her company.

Upon hearing a rumble in my stomach, I realize the cookie that I ate not too long ago isn't enough to keep me full. Maybe I should go to the dining car, and see what is on the menu. I'm starting to like going to the dining car. Since I was ten-years-old, I haven't eaten a meal that I didn't help prepare.

I laugh out loud, and then glance around quickly to see if anyone noticed my silliness. No one is looking my way. I know I shouldn't worry, but there's a part of me that still feels the sting of the stigma of 'Juden' being stamped on my papers by the soldiers. Wait a minute ... pulling my papers from my bag frantically, I begin to search through them, front and back. Nowhere on any of my papers does it reveal the big red stamp of the soldier. But of course, they were placed on the papers that DEBORAH had in her bag. Deborah's gone. I don't know what to say. A part of me feels relief. My stomach says it for me, 'feed me'.

I stand, grabbing up my carpetbag and purse, I head for the dining car.

It looks very crowded except for one table with four chairs. A young man sits, facing my direction.

I feel uneasy, as I know I must eat soon. I feel a little lost. A single woman is to never eat alone with a single man. It would be even worse if a married woman ate with a man who isn't her husband or relative. But this isn't my little shtetl, is it? I'm not married. I can't wait until someone leaves.

I take a deep breath in and out, as I approach the table with a smile. I hope I look confident, as I really feel like a small child.

"May I share this table with you?" I ask, in broken English. I'm anxious, as I realize if he says no that I will have to leave. I know that leaving without food isn't good for me.

"By all means," he says, with a big smile as he stands to pull out a chair for me. He is much taller than I. He wears a dark blue suit that is tailored to his form. His hair is light blonde, but it's slicked back in such a way that it makes it look almost white. His eyes twinkle a sea blue that a girl can swim in.

I feel enchanted, and I find him handsome. Men in my world would never dress in such a way.

He scoots the chair and me into the small space, and takes a seat across from me.

"Thank you."

"You are brightening up my day," the man says, in English with almost no accent at all.

"You are American?"

"Yes, I am. I came to Europe for business and decided to see some of the countryside. My name is Joe, Joe Dexter," he says, and holds out his right hand to me.

I take it, and try not to let my hand become too limp. He stares into my eyes, and I find myself unable to move or speak.

"Your name?"

I laugh and pull my hand away quickly, I feel a rush of color kiss my cheeks. Inside, I can't stop giggling at my embarrassment. "I'm so sorry."

"Just tell me your name, and we will call it even," he laughs.

"Kfira."

"What a lovely name," he says, as he reaches for his water glass. "What does it mean?"

"It means the lion in Hebrew," I answer without thinking. Then glancing down quickly, I try to decide in ten seconds or less if I have made a blunder.

"It's as beautiful as are you." He fails to say anything about the mention of Hebrew.

Now I'm sure that my face is as red as Deborah's suit, and I wish she were here now. I'm glad he didn't mention the Hebrew. I'm not sure I want to advertise I'm a Jew. I'm not ashamed, but afraid. If Deborah were I, she would be flirting shamelessly with such a man. While I have never dared.

"Are you going to Paris?"

"Yes, yes I am," I say, as I realize that embarrassment will not kill me, at least not today.

"So am I. I have a few more days of work before I head back to New York. I was thinking of spending a few days of vacation there as well."

"Paris is a nice place to visit."

"Have you ever been to Paris?"

I giggle and eye the small white plate and silverware as if they might have flaws, I begin to fuss with them. I want to distract my body, to keep from blushing every time this man speaks to me, although it is quite difficult since he is so handsome. I'm also finding myself unable to stop laughing at the wrong time, I have always done this when I'm afraid. Today is no different.

"This is my first time away from home."

"You will love Paris. Of course there are so many things to see that a person would almost have to live there to see everything."

The waiter walks over to the table, and refreshes Joe's water glass before he turns to fill mine. It's the same man who has served Deborah and me since the beginning of the trip. I wonder if he ever rests.

"What would you like?" he asks, with a big grin on his face.

"I will have the soup," I say, without thinking. I had intended on ordering the roast beef, as it had been quite good the last time I ate it.

"I will start with the soup as well." He grins at me, "I hope my date will be eating more than just soup today."

Did he really just say what I think he said? A smile is on my face, but it feels as if it is on fire.

The waiter doesn't seem to notice, as he walks away.

Please, someone, please put the fire out on my face! I pick up a small card from the table, and begin to fan myself. I actually find myself sweating. My palms are so damp that it soaks the paper immediately.

"Are you all right?"

"I have never been on a date before," I manage to say before I realize I really will die of embarrassment. I think for a few seconds, as I try to calm myself, and look back into Joe's face.

"Your secret is safe with me," he leans in and whispers.

"I see you have a newspaper as well," I say, looking at the one beside his plate.

"Yes."

"I don't read French. Can you tell me what the headlines say?"

"I am fluent." He picks it up, flipping it back to the front page. He scans it quickly. "Let me see."

"I can read the caption but ..."

"It says that they are calling it Kristallnacht. German soldiers rounded up many Jewish men who had thriving businesses in Germany. They are being detained until further notice. The Germans burned books, businesses and synagogues. They say that the fires were so hot that the glass from the windows were blown out in a wave of splinters ... making it Kristallnacht or the night of the broken glass. It goes on to say that it happened in Berlin. People in other areas began to retaliate in fear that their communities might be next. A group they are now calling the Resistance might have set fires to distract others. Germany has been causing problems for other cities and countries, some as far as Prague. Only recently it took back Sudetenland." Joe puts the paper down before he takes a drink from his wineglass.

I watch him, and I'm not sure of what I am waiting for, but I know this does explain last night. I now understand the night of fire I wrote about in my journal earlier. My heart quickens, as what he has just read sinks in. Jewish men were detained. Jewish men. My pulse races, as my head goes numb. I find it difficult to think. My mouth is dry, but I can't make my hand move to grasp my glass long enough to get a drink.

"Are you all right?"

I wrinkle my nose at him, as if he was my favorite cousin, and I was trying to make a joke. "Yes, I will be all right." Finally, I take my napkin from the silverware and place it along my lap. I'm lost in my thoughts. *What does all of this mean for me? And for Mama and Papa? Several brothers-in-law work out of Germany. Are they all right? I pray they are home with their wives.* I shake my head, and attempt to push such thoughts from my head. My heart sounds like a drum, beating wildly in my chest. I can barely hear the others around me.

The waiter returns with our soup.

"I think the lady and I will be having the roast beef after our soup."

"Very good sir," the waiter says, as he pivots around, and is gone.

I laugh, as I find myself starting to relax with this man. Tears come to my eyes. As I wipe the away with my napkin, I put the new information aside. I will ponder on it all later. For now, I will eat my food, and have a conversation with a man on a date. Oy! If Mama could see me now! I hope to not do anything too shameful or embarrassing.

The Train Ride - Paris At Last

I watch Joe eat, and notice he does this so gracefully. I feel clumsy and awkward, and still a little shy about being here with a strange man with no family to chaperon us. I just know I will do something that is awkward.

"Aren't you hungry?" Joe asks, as he watches me.

Pushing the food around on my plate, I am unsure of what to say. *Should I blurt it out as I do home? Or should I try to be coy and sweet, and not let on that I'm worried?*

I touch my handbag and feel the small Siddur I placed in there sometime after I discovered Deborah gone. Bravery wraps itself around me, and makes me want to tell him what I am feeling. *Well, maybe I can tell him some things. A woman has to leave some mystery.*

"I wonder whom the people are they rounded up." I take a bite.

"Oh, the newspaper article," he says, and then takes a bite of meat. It's as if his chewing will help him find an answer I will understand. "It doesn't really say. I suppose with it being a border paper that it might not give all the details. Plus, it only happened hours before the newspaper was put to bed so to speak. They will have more information tomorrow."

I nod and take another bite. I wonder what put to bed means but don't want to look stupid asking questions all of the time. Papa would say that nothing will be revealed, and soon people will go on as if nothing happened out of the ordinary.

"Do you have family in Germany?"

"Yes and no," I say, and giggle. How does one explain my family's idea of what country they live in. "I'm from a small village close to the Baltic Sea. It's a part of land that was fought over between the Russians and Germans during the Great War. One day we are Russians, and the next day Prussians. Or are they calling us Germans? I forget."

"Let me guess, your father declares himself to be Russian," he answers for me.

"Yes," I say enthusiastically. It's as if this man knows my story, but how?

"It's the same old story with countries or pieces of land that are constantly being fought over. People live there so long, and see so many new governments."

"And this happens everywhere?"

"Pretty much, didn't you study about it in school?"

"I probably did but when I got older I was so busy helping Mama, and my sisters with their babies. I work as well. I know how to read, write and do math. I'm supposed to be married with babies of my own by now." *Instead I'm on a train a million miles from home, doing GOD knows what, for the Rebbe,* I tell myself.

Chuckling, he smiles at me before taking another bite.

"What do you do?" I ask, hoping to take the attention off of me.

"I am a reporter," Joe replies, as he reaches for a roll.

"In New York?"

"Yes."

"Did ..." I want desperately to ask him about the fires. I want to know if he had been at Kristallnacht, or maybe one of the places mentioned in the newspaper. Why does he not seem more concerned? So many questions have gone through my head since I saw the Rebbe sitting in the living room with my parents, and no one has ever given any answers. Another scary thought trudges before my eyes, *he's probably not Jewish so of course none of this affects him. How would he feel if he knew about me?*

"We can talk about serious matters later," Joe says, as he pushes the bread basket toward me.

"When will we be in Paris?" I take a roll from the basket, and dip it into the roast beef juice. I take a bite, and it almost melts in my mouth. I look around at the people, and wonder if their lives are as mysterious as mine.

"We should be there soon, depending on the train. We will be there at least by this evening."

I'm feeling quite full and sleepy. "This meal has been very lovely, but I think I must go back to my seat and rest before Paris." Reaching for my glass, I take a big drink of water.

"That sounds like a good idea. I want to give you my card. I will put down the hotel and number I will be staying at. Please call me, and we can dine in Paris with style," he says, as he quickly writes the information done on the back of a small card. He hands it to me.

Taking the card, I hold it in my hand as I rise. "Thank you so

80

much for a lovely time." A part of me says to tell him I will call him, and another part says that if I do I may be lying. I say nothing at all.

Standing and walking around quickly to my side, Joe pulls the chair out so that I might rise. He gently touches my hand. "I have had a wonderful time. Please call me."

My heart skips a beat, as I melt in his eyes. "I will," I promise. I have never broken a promise, but I have never been on a date before either. Picking up my bag, I head back to the other car and my seat. I carefully conceal the card in my Siddur.

Passengers I have come to recognize throughout this trip, talk softly to one another. We are all anxiously awaiting Paris. Placing my bag back on my ankle, I find myself drifting to sleep almost immediately.

###

Running feet behind me, someone is chasing me through the field. I must get home to Papa. I must reach safety.

I glance around to see if there are any familiar trees to climb and escape. *Why is this crazy boy still chasing me?*

Mark Heinen hates me. He teases me mercilessly, and a

month ago he gave me a black eye. He calls me "that Jew bitch".
I never tell Mama and Papa or they would take me out of school.
Now, he is pursuing me, and even when I reach my street he
follows. I pray that someone will see us, and stop him. No one
does.

We race through the streets. They aren't really streets, but
more like paths through fields. We call them streets, as the
animals are always walking up and down them, tamping down
the grasses.

"Leave me alone!"

"You come back here you Jew bitch. I'm going to teach you a
lesson."

Ducking down into the tall yellow stalks of wheat, I try to
make my way carefully through without hitting something, or
making a sound. I can't hear him. Maybe he went home, but I'm
scared. Once before I thought he was gone, and he was three
meters from me. A black eye was my reward. I told Mama and
Papa I tripped on the steps at school.

"COME ON, LITTLE JEW BITCH!"

Where is everyone? Surely, someone can hear him, and will

82

try to stop him. Silence. It's as if everyone else disappeared. The only noise is my heart beating in my ears, making my temples throb. I try to control my loud breathing, but it's difficult. I gasp several times.

Getting up, I try to race across the field. Suddenly, something slams against the back of my head, and knocks me down. I fly through the air for five seconds before landing hard on the ground, face first. Blood trickles from my nose, and a small cut on my left eyebrow. I scramble to my feet, and lose my schoolbooks. My heart is beating so hard, I know it will fly out of my chest if I breathe, so I try not to.

THUMP! Knocked down again, I sense a sharp pain in the middle of my back from his second blow. I'm so dizzy that it feels like the world is spinning out of control, as my stomach churns in the opposite direction. I feel queasy. I try to stand, and run again, but my arms and legs refuse to cooperate. I'm sure I'm already dead.

"Please stop," I hear a voice say, not realizing it is mine. I voice this over and over again, as I thrash about.

A soft touch on my shoulder jerks me awake. "Huh?" I say

with a start. Looking up and around, I slide my body back onto the seat, and grab at my bags. *Where am I? Where is that meshuggah boy chasing me? Please don't let him catch me.*

The boy isn't here. Joe stands in front of me. He is grasping my arms in his hands. A look of concern on his face scares me almost as much as the boy in the dream.

Tears roll down my cheeks, as I realize I'm not in the field at home. I'm not twelve years old. I'm on a train to Paris, a never-ending train ride. I catch my breath, as the loud thumping in my ears slow down. Sweat pours off my face, and I reach for my bag and a soft cloth. My hands are so slick that my bag slips out of it several times.

"Are you all right?"

"I didn't know where I was," I mutter, half coherently.

"You are on a train to Paris. It's November 10th, 1938. I came looking for you because we will be in Paris in a half-hour, and I wanted to help you find whoever is there waiting for you."

Sighing and putting my feet back on the floor, I still feel a little disoriented and scared. I grasp my purse, and open it. Pulling out my handkerchief, I dab at my face and neck. In minutes it's soaked with my fear. I place my bag back down on the floor. I want to speak, but my mouth is too dry.

"Drink this," Joe says, as he sits beside me, and pulls a silver flask from his coat pocket.

Not even asking, I remove the lid, and take a long drink. It is delicious, cool water. Taking a smaller sip, I put the lid back on it, and hand it back to him. I'm able to speak once again. "Thank you. I was having a nightmare. Did you hear me from the dining car?"

"How long have you had these nightmares?" He takes the flask, and places it in his coat pocket.

"I haven't had one I was twelve and left school."

I wipe the tears from my eyes, and fumble with my hair. Taking in a deep breath, I blink several times to get the anxiety out of my eyes. I don't know whether to be embarrassed or afraid. Joe blocks the view of the people around me. Their whispers of a few minutes ago are gone. Their voices return to normal, chatting away as if nothing happened.

"May I help you?"

I have no choice. I know I can't do this alone, just as I couldn't fight off Mark alone.

"Yes."

"Good." He takes a cloth from his other pocket and wipes my face and hands. "Are you sure you are all right?"

"Yes."

"Paris in five minutes," the conductor speaks in several languages, as he makes another descent down the aisle.

I realize that I will miss this conductor's voice when I'm off the train.

"Who will be picking you up?"

"A lady by the name of Jean-Pierre," I answer without thinking. I probably shouldn't be so forthcoming with the information, but I don't want to be scared. The fear in my nightmare begins to subside. I'm not still dreaming, and I'm a very long way from home.

"I will take you to her. She is an old friend," Joe says enthusiastically.

"Do you know her?" I ask, as Jean-Pierre still sounds like a man's name to me.

"Yes, I know she loves having family stay with her. Are you

family?"

With this question the whistle blows, and the train stops. The brakes make a soft hissing sound as the smoke billows from its smokestacks.

"Let me take your bag." Joe lifts the carpetbag, and takes my arm.

Together we walk into the aisle, and toward the door.

Won't she be waiting for me outside? How does Joe know this woman? But of course, he is a newspaper reporter, he knows everyone. Well, in my shtetl that is how everything works. Wouldn't it work this way in real life? I ask myself.

We walk down the steps, and the first thing I see is the Eiffel Tower in the distance. It's not a dream. I'm in Paris.

"You aren't saying much," Joe chuckles.

"I never thought Paris real."

People are everywhere. Huge buildings adorn the walkway. Street lamps as I have never are scattered everywhere. Cars. Yes, there are cars at home, but not so many. I try to take everything in but it is all so overwhelming.

"Come quickly," Joe says, as he half drags me to an area away from the station. It's behind the station.

My little legs try to keep up with his long ones, but it's difficult, especially after my nightmare. I hadn't even looked around at the other passengers to see if they saw it. I was too busy having Joe take care of me. Now he has my bag, and is making me almost run on stone feet.

"Here she is," Joe says, as he stops in front of a woman, an older woman.

I stop and look from Joe to the older woman, and can't help to notice the resemblance in the two. The woman's once tawny hair is now silver but the eyes are the same blue. She is almost as tall as Joe. A turban covers her hair with a jewel-encrusted broach affixed to its middle. She wears a full-length red coat with her full lips matching in color!

"Jean-Pierre?" I ask.

She smiles, and extends her hand to me. "You are Kfira, yes?"

"Yes."

"I see you have met my grandson. Welcome to Paris. Let's get you home, and into a hot bath. The train ride must have left you exhausted."

With that Jean-Pierre, Joe and I walk across the way, and off to her home.

I feel dizzy from all of the excitement. *Nothing to this point has been a coincidence*, I tell myself with a sudden realization that I'm not alone.

Paris

"The house is not too far from here," Jean-Pierre says, as she walks on.

I notice her hands as she speaks. She constantly waves them about, as if to emphasize everything she is saying. Her English is broken, but easy to understand. The lines on her face tell a story, and if I were to guess her age, I would say she is at least seventy.

"Are you hungry dear?"

"No, ma'am."

"You will be after your rest, I am sure. You're very fortunate to have met my grandson on the train. I was unsure of what you looked like, as they did not send a picture of you."

I don't know what to say. Until this train trip, I had never thought much about pictures or cameras, I'm sure that no one has ever taken my picture.

The walk is not so far and before long we stand in front of a long row of houses that are so close together they look as if they are kissing each other.

"This is it," Joe says, as he opens the door. Holding it open, he patiently waits as Jean-Pierre and I walk through before entering himself.

"Be sure to take her bag to her room," Jean-Pierre says to Joe. "Come, come my dear. We must go into the parlor so I can have a good look at you. Then off to the hot bath I promised to help you relax from your long journey."

We walk down the long, well lit hallway. Tile flooring makes our shoes clip clop along, and echo back. In the middle of the hallway is a large chandelier that shows off a grand staircase on the right. To the left are glass double doors that I would later learn are called French doors.

Never before have I seen such elegance. I feel out of place in my basic cotton dresses and coat. I want to protest Joe's taking my bag to my room, but I'm speechless in such elegance. Maybe this trip is a blessing. Never have I been so quiet in my life, as I have been on this trip.

Jean-Pierre opens the French double doors and steps inside.

"Into the parlor," she says, and pushes the doors wide open.

I peek inside, as if I'm a mouse lurking about in case a cat might see me.

A young woman wearing a green suit is standing at the large bay window with her back to us. Turning around, she smiles. "Hello Kfira!"

"Deborah!" I rush to her, and wrap my arms around her. It's as if she is a life preserver, and I'm drowning. Tears cascade down my cheeks, and I look over at Jean-Pierre with amazement in my eyes before giving my attention back to Deborah. "Where did you go? I must know. I was so scared, and I tried to be so brave. I wanted to ask the conductor about you, but was afraid. What if I had made you up? I convinced myself you were a dream," I say, and move from her grasp. Wiping my eyes with the back of my hand, I search in my pocket for another handkerchief.

Deborah holds out her hand. In it is a pink lace one. She grins from ear to ear.

"Thank you."

"I had to go."

"Why?"

"We can't tell you everything right now, but it was better that Deborah leave you when she did. She sent Joe in to keep an eye on you. You did very well by yourself," Jean-Pierre said confidently. Her delicate hand reaches into a small box and produces a cigarette. Lighting it with a gold embossed lighter, she inhales deeply and turns around.

"I know this is all confusing to you right now, but it will make sense some day soon ... I promise," Deborah says, as she takes my hand and squeezes it tightly in her own.

"But for now you are to take a hot bath, and get ready to go out. I promised you a nice dinner," Joe says, as he enters the room.

"Are her things in her room?" Jean-Pierre asks.

"Of course, Grandmother."

"Deborah will take you, and show you around. It's a very large house, and one can easily get lost," Jean-Pierre chortles.

Taking me by the hand, Deborah leads me away. I know that I will have time to look more closely at this room as well as others, later. As for now, I am just so excited at seeing Deborah. It's like she is an old friend I haven't seen in ages instead of less than a day.

"We have so many things to do. You will just love the bath. I picked out the bath salts myself," Deborah says, as we walk up the stairs.

"Is this place safe?"

"Yes, this place is safe."

Sighing, I'm still unsure if I'm having a dream instead of reality. For a second, on the train, I had begun to think that Paris is a dream, and Mark is not.

"Kfira."

"Yes." I give her my full attention.

"You will be taken care. You are safe. Don't worry. I know this isn't so easy to hear, but everything will be all right."

"I just ... I just ..." I try to say something, but nothing comes out.

"We will explain everything in time."

Nodding, I'm silent. I realize I'm too drained to persist.

"Do you know how proud I am of you? When I learned you didn't panic after I left I was thrilled? I was so afraid you would start asking people if they had seen me. It was very important that you didn't. I am very pleased that you were willing to do what the Rebbe asked."

"But of course I would do what the Rebbe asked." I began talking rather quickly, but by the time I voiced 'I', my voice began to slow down. "You?"

"Again, we will talk more later." Smiling brightly, Deborah leads me to the first room on the right after the stairwell. "This is your room."

She opens the door, and steps inside. Never have I seen such a room as this before! In the middle of the room is a huge white framed canopy bed with dark pink covers and light pink bows on green silk sheets. A dressing table sits across from the bed. A large white closet is against one wall, and glass, double doors to a balcony on the other. Close to the bed on the left side is another door.

Running to it, Deborah opens it. "This is your bathroom."

"Mine?" I ask, feeling as a child might upon requesting knowledge of ownership.

"Yours, with a hot bath waiting just for you."

Walking over to the door, I peer inside speculatively. It's the largest bathtub I have ever seen. Bubbles are floating up, and over the white porcelain.

"I don't know what to say."

"Say nothing. Take off those dirty traveling clothes, and ease your troubles away. I will bring you something to drink and eat, maybe a little fruit."

"I don't know what to say".

"Are you modest? I can step out." Deborah points to the bedroom door.

"No, not necessary." I walk over to the bathtub, and reach down to touch the downy softness of the bubbles. The water is quite warm, and gentle against my hand. *Maybe I'm dead and this is heaven*, I think, as I begin to take off my many dresses and underclothes. If it is then Deborah, Joe and Jean-Pierre are my guardian angels. Sliding into the water, I immediately feel all my fears and tension float away.

Time

"I am back." Deborah walks into the room, carrying a tray. She places it on a small white table sitting next to the tub.

I try to take everything in, but I'm feeling overwhelmed and tired. Blinking several times, I look down at the fruits on the plate. Two glasses of water, as well as two more that appear to have wine also adorn the tray.

"Thank you." I reach for a glass of water, and taste the wetness with parched lips. I feel like I'm in a wonderful dream of luxury, and I hope I don't wake up.

"I know you must be thirsty from the long trip. I always am."

I pick up a piece of fruit. Fresh fruit is a luxury for the summer time in the shtetl. *How do they have fruit now*? I say nothing so as not to look naive. I take a bite of the orange red flesh, and the sweet juices run down my chin. It's sweeter than candy or sugar. I want more. Making a face, I hope I don't look silly, as I wipe at it with a small, wet cloth.

"Never had an orange before, have you?"

I want to be embarrassed, but I can't be. I'm too hungry for the fruit.

"Kfira, I was really afraid for you back on the train. I know I said it before, but I have to let you know that what you are doing is .... I can't even imagine a word for it."

"Deborah, is my family safe?" I ask earnestly. I don't care so much for myself, but my family is everything. Mama and Papa have been through so much.

"Yes, I think they are for now," Deborah answers. The stern look on her face makes me want to believe her.

"You aren't going to tell me much, are you?"

"Not now."

"What is in these other two glasses?"

"Wine, it will help as well."

I frown. I only drink wine on Shabbos once or twice a year.

"It won't hurt you. It's much better tasting than the water."

Did I travel hundreds of kilometers just to drink wine and take a bath? I lift the clear glass with rose colored liquid to my lips. I have nothing to lose. I want to be able to rest, and I fear the nightmare of the train will come back when I lay my head upon the pillow. I take a sip and almost choke. This isn't Shabbos wine. It tastes cool going down my throat, not the fruity flavor of the Shabbos wine.

Taking a piece of fruit, I eat it and then sip the wine.

"See, you are a Parisian already."

I smile, and take another bite.

Getting up, Deborah walks back into the other room, then quickly returns. She carries a large thick, pink dress. "This," she holds up for closer inspection, "is a dressing gown. When you are done with your bath, dry off and put this on. You can lie down and take a long rest. I will awaken you in three hours. We will dress you up, and take you out."

"Really, I will be just fine without going out," I protest, thinking they must be going out of their way to do these things for me.

"Yes, we have to."

Again the mystery.

"I will be back after your rest." Deborah leaves.

As I eat a few more pieces of fruit, I begin to relax. After I sufficiently wash my hair and body, I rise from the tub. A softness to the towel is something that I could have never imagined. It feels better than kitten fur. I wrap the robe around my body, and feel as if I am a queen. I'm tired. I drink the last of the wine in the first glass, and go into the other room.

I lie down on the bed, and suddenly realize that I am naked under the robe. Knowing I should rise and dress, I find myself unable to move. Lacking real sleep from the train ride, I sense it has been days since I had any real rest. I close my eyes, and everything goes numb.

############

I glance around. I'm in the field, running for my life.

"Come here, you little Jew bitch!" Mark screams in the distance.

Nowhere to hide. Why are there no people on the streets? What did I do with my schoolbooks? Didn't I have them in my hands two seconds ago? I can't remember.

My heart is beating so hard, I know it will tear a hole right through my chest. Blood pulses through the veins in my neck and arms. Panting ever so softly, I try not to make a sound. Mark is like a hawk, he hears and sees every move around him.

"I have something for you, Jew bitch!"

Mama! Papa! Someone ... please hear him screaming at me and help me, I pray.

"I'm going to get you. I have a present just for you!"

I close my eyes and pray. I try to crouch down and crawl along the yellow wheat stalks almost ready for harvest. Surely, he won't see or catch me here.

Something hits the back of my head. Pain screams in my ears, and I feel dizzy. Lunging forward, I try to catch myself with my hands. A sharp object hits my back. My air filled lungs gasp loudly. Everything goes black, as I feel something wet and sticky in my hair and clothes.

When I wake, I find that I'm on my back. Dried blood on my forehead makes it difficult to move it. Pain from the tips of my hair to my legs, and back again, makes me want to scream. I feel lost even though I'm not far from home.

Mark stands over me. "Yeah, you Jew cunt. My father told me about girls like you."

I say nothing. I can't feel my arms and legs despite my head and back agony. I try to lift up my head, but each time I do the earth comes up to meet me, swallowing me.

I look around to make sure I haven't just hit my head. No dream. Mark stands over me. He pulls my arms up by the wrists across my face, keeping me from fighting him off.

Leave me alone I want to say, but it's all I can do to breathe.

Mark moves my wrists from my eyes to my forehead, so I can see what he is doing in the small space between my arms. I watch in horror, as I realize that he is taking his pants down. His shmeckie is dangling in front of my face, and I try to shut my eyes.

He lets go of himself long enough to slap the top of my head, forcing me to open my eyes. "Look good at it. You know you want it. I'm going to give it to you."

"Noooo!" *Did I say that out loud*? I feel my legs tighten, as his other hand pries my knees apart.

"Don't fight me, bitch." Sensing the muscles tense, I try with all my heart to keep my knees locked together.

He digs his fist into my left thigh, and then my right until they go numb.

Please GOD ... please make him stop. Please ... someone ... help me.

His grip on my arms doesn't falter, but tightens. It gets hard to take in air as he presses his mouth down on my nose, forcing my mouth open. I can't scream, as I can barely breathe.

THEN the agonizing pain, as something rips through my body. Tears course down my cheeks, as I hear him grunt above me, satisfied that he is inside of me. His hand and arm are slick with sweat, as it attempts to keep me defenseless. Salty water drips across his forehead and drips on to my face. It tastes salty in my mouth, and burns my eyes. I feel sick, but dare not throw up for fear I will choke to death.

"You fucking Jew bitch. You love it and you know it." The mantra that echoes out of Mark's mouth, as he pushes himself in and out of me.

It feels like he slams into me a million times, and this will never be over. I open my eyes, and see the expression on his face change. His breath quickens, as he lurches harder and faster.

I try to scream with the intense pain, but nothing comes out even though the grip on my arms has loosened.

He crinkles up his face, and closes his eyes, as his grunts sharpen. Almost as if his head might explode he thumps hard against my pubic bone. He cries out, and his body goes limp.

He covers my body with his, and .... I .... feel .... so far away.

###

Screaming, I thrash and fall against the floor trying to scoot away from him. What just happened to me?

"AAAAAAAAAGGGGGGGGGGHHHHHHHHHHHH!"

"Kfira! Kfira!" Deborah shakes my shoulders. "Please wake up."

"AAAAAAAAAGGGGGGGGGGHHHHHHHHHHHH!" I jump up on the bed, and look around. My breathing is so shallow, I can barely feel the air fill my lungs. My heart beat pulses through every centimeter of my body, making me feel as if my skin will climb off and walk away. My privates ache with a pain that seems so unreal.

For several minutes I don't know where I am. Everything is frightening.

Deborah sits next to me, holding my hand in hers.

I look around and frown. I'm twenty-five years old, and I'm in Paris. I think of this room, but not from today. I recollect Deborah.

"Kfira, hold me." Deborah she grabs me up in her arms, holding me with all her might.

"I ... I ... had a nightmare. But it wasn't a nightmare, was it? It was real? I have been to this house before, haven't I?"

Deborah nods.

"I was raped thirteen years ago. I left school because of it. No one will marry me because I'm not a virgin."

Sweat pours down my body bathing me in the fear and pain of the past. Tears soak my cheeks, and my hands tremble. Mama and Papa know, and that's why they have protected me all these years. I face so many answers to my questions. *Would I have asked if I were home? I doubt it.*

Reaching over and brushing the hair from my face, Deborah holds my chin in her hand.

"You will be all right now."

I take in a deep breath, and exhale slowly.

"You will understand, but for now drink this and rest." She picks up the wineglass, and brings it to my quivering lips.

I push the glass away several times. My throat is so dry and thirsty. I finally grab it and gulp down the strange liquid. It tastes

sweet, and slides down my throat easily, warming me instantly.
My eyelids feel heavy, and I find myself rolling back over to
rest.

Shabbos

I wake with a start. A heavy green and yellow blanket covers
my body, and I feel toasty warm. Stretching my body across the
bed, I suddenly realize that I'm not at home. It isn't a dream. I'm
in Paris, and in the home of a lady with the name of Jean-Pierre.

"Good afternoon sleepy head." Deborah sits in a lounge chair
set beside the bed. She is reading a book, and looking quite
bored.

It's a small brown, yellow and green sofa, with only half of a
back

"How long have I been sleeping?" I focus on the room around
me.

"I would say you have slept a good eighteen hours or more.
You were exhausted, especially after your nightmare." Deborah
looks at her watch. "It's nearly three o'clock in the afternoon."

"What day is it?" I pull the covers off sharply, and realize with a start that I'm still only wearing the pink dressing gown. Feeling the red rise in my cheeks, I'm thankful that it completely covers my nakedness. I move the cover aside, and let my legs dangle over the edge of the bed. Never have I slept so long and not been ill.

"Why it's Friday, of course," Deborah says with a smile.

"Shabbos!" I clasp my hands against my cheeks and wrinkle up my forehead. *What am I going to do?*

Laughing and shaking her head, Deborah swings her legs over the side of the lounger to face me.

"It's not Shabbos?"

"Tonight."

"How will I celebrate Shabbos here? I look forward to Shabbos every week. We have such celebrations at home." I need to feel something familiar and Shabbos is it.

"We will have a very special dinner tonight. We will celebrate.

I take in a deep breath, and exhale slowly. *It will be all right*, I repeat over and over.

"We washed your dresses, but to be honest Jean-Pierre has a

few dresses that will fit you that will look better than these hand-me-downs." Deborah rises, and struts over to the armoire and opens both doors.

On one side are the six dresses I own. On the other side are six more dresses that even from a distance look exquisite.

"They are new," Deborah entices me. Opening several drawers under the closet area, she adds, "and there are new unmentionables."

"I don't know what to say. Are the dresses modest?" I rise, and try not to race over to the other side of the room. I want to see new dresses. I yearn to feel them close to my skin. I can't imagine wearing something that no one else has worn. I feel pretty silly even thinking about them at this point, but I do. A lady is supposed to be modest and thrifty at all costs.

"Try them on," Deborah encourages, as she pulls one out.

Reaching into one of the drawers, I grab a few things I will need and head for the bathroom, dignity and bashfulness intact. I know that Deborah is a woman, but Mama always says it's important for a woman to maintain her self-respect when she can.

I put on the new clothes, and walk out to where Deborah is

sitting.

"You look stunning." She marches over, and grabs my arm. Pulling me over to the dressing table, she points at my reflection.

I sigh and then turn toward the woman in the mirror. I can't believe my eyes. It's a beautiful light green dress. It's not too tight and yet very comfortable. A V neckline reveals nothing, and the length is a few inches longer than most people might wear, but it works well for me. At the hem is a two-inch ribbon of black. Black buttons adorn the front, and down the middle.

"Let's fix your hair." Deborah pulls a chair out.

I take a seat, and turn to face Deborah. "Why are you being so nice to me?"

"Because I'm your friend."

I glance in the mirror. The terror from the night before stares back at me. "I had such a horrible nightmare."

"It will all be explained at dinner," Deborah says, reassuringly.

I turn back around, and she brushes out the tangles in my black curls. I pray that I will understand. Right now, nothing is making sense.

###

Dinner is promptly at seven with everyone dressing.

Deborah helps me find my way to the dining room. The table, like the family table at home, is huge. A white cloth covers the dark wood. Beautiful china and crystal make for an elegant table.

Jean-Pierre is already in the room. She's also wearing a tailored, green dress suit. Her white hair is pulled into a tight bun on top of her head. "Come, come." She stands by a young woman dressed in a black dress with a white apron and scarf on her head.

I ease over to Jean-Pierre, feeling more anxious than I did when I saw her after the train ride. My palms go warm and clammy, and I'm short of breath.

"Good evening," Deborah says, as we stand before her.

"Good evening," I repeat like a parrot.

"Good evening. You look very dignified," she says, with an air of contentment in her voice. She turns to the young woman, "Catana, this is Kfira. Kfira this is Catana. Catana is my personal maid. If you need anything, please let her know. Please tell the cook that dinner should be served in fifteen minutes."

"Yes, ma'am." Catana exits to the right. I notice her black dress goes down to her ankles. Her dark, brown hair is pinned in a bun on the top of her head.

"I trust you had a good rest," Jean-Pierre states.

"Yes ma'am, I did. I -- " I want to say something about the nightmare, but I don't. *Should I apologize for calling out? Did she hear me? Or for being a burden?* I'm not really sure how to handle this situation. I say nothing.

"I know about the nightmare." Jean-Pierre takes my hand in hers, and looks deep into my eyes. "I will explain everything, as soon as the dinner starts. Right now we are waiting for two more guests."

"Who are we waiting for?" Deborah asks.

"We are waiting for ... oh hello you two," Jean-Pierre says, as she swerves to watch Joe and a young man enter from the big doors on the right.

I spin around quickly to see Joe and Elijah enter the room.

Elijah? What is Elijah doing here? He is Esther's son. He is twelve, and already looking like a man. Both men are dressed in handsome black suits. Elijah is almost as tall as Joe.

110

"Elijah!" I dash over to him, and grab him up in a warm embrace. "My nephew, my sweet nephew, I haven't seen you in so long!"

Smiling, he hugs me tightly. "Mom said you would be here. I'm so glad to see you."

"How did you get here? Where is your mother and father? Is Esther here too?" I stare behind him to see if others are coming through the door, but no one does.

"I hate to break up the party, but don't we need to start Shabbos?" Jean-Pierre asks, at the head of the table.

"Yes," I say, pulling away from Elijah. I reach for his hand, and squeeze it before I pull away once more.

"This is a night of surprises that even the great HaShem will want to bless. Tonight, Kfira you will light the candles again." Jean-Pierre points to two large candlesticks on a table against a wall.

The long tapers are snug in the polished silver candlesticks. A box of matches rests next to it. On the table are several silk scarves placed to the other side. I pick one up, and place it atop my hair and slightly cover my eyes.

I grab up the matches and strike one. The instant flame illuminates my face. Holding it to first one wick and then the other, I light them. I wave my hands above the flames three times, and then cover my eyes with my hands.

"Baruch atah Adonai, Eloheinu Melech ha-olam, asher kidshanu b'mitzvotanu v'tzivanu l'hadlik neir shel Shabbos."

"Amen."

I turn and walk back to the table.

Jean-Pierre points to a seat next to Elijah. I'm so thankful to see my nephew, someone familiar on this crazy, mixed up journey. I can't help, but to keep looking at him, and notice how handsome he is becoming. His white hair, an oddity for our family, makes his golden skin stand out.

"I'm so glad you are here," I whisper, leaning closer to him.

He beams.

"It's wonderful celebrating Shabbos in this house once more. When I'm alone, it hardly seems worth the effort. I go to Shul occasionally, but not as often as I should. It's also good to see young people here."

Catana walks in carrying a tray with a serving soup bowl and ladle. Stopping at Jean-Pierre first, she begins the walk around the table.

"I'm afraid you will have to ladle your own soup here. Catana is one of the few servants I have retained over the years. By the way, the soup is always good."

I ladle some into my bowl, and then fill Elijah's, as Catana stands between us.

"Thank you." I put the ladle on to the tray.

The others follow suit.

Once Catana leaves the room, a quiet falls over the room.

"Would you like to say the blessing over the food Elijah?" Jean-Pierre asks.

"Yes, ma'am. Baruch atah Adonai, Melech ha-olam, ha-motzi lehem min ha-aretz." His voice squeaks several times before the words are out. Smiling over at me, I wink at him.

"Thank you so much. We have challah in the bread baskets before you. Everyone has their own small one. Don't fill your tummies with just soup and bread, as there are many goodies to come."

I take a spoonful into my mouth and realize without asking

that it is Mama's chicken soup. It melts in my mouth. The challah is soft and warm. I'm hungry, and without realizing it I have dunked half of my bread into my soup to allow it to soak up the juices.

"Are you hungry?" Joe asks, as he chuckles.

I glimpse around, and realize everyone is watching me, except Elijah who is doing the same thing.

"I guess I'm a little hungry." I wrinkle up my nose and smirk.

"I'm glad to see you eat. You scared us all last night when you had your fright." Jean-Pierre picks up her wineglass, and takes a drink.

I stop in mid sip. I look over at her, and try to grin but can feel the frown. I had almost forgotten it all when I saw Elijah standing in the room. I nod.

"We don't have to talk about all of it," Jean-Pierre began "but we can talk about why the Rebbe and HaShem sent you here."

"I want to know."

"Good. Don't be frightened by what you hear tonight. It's all going to be told because there can be no secrets in a time like this with unrest in our midst."

Out of the corner of my eye, I observe Deborah swallowing hard and looking down. She puts her spoon in the bowl, as does Joe. Elijah keeps eating, unaware of what new thing will be thrust upon us.

"Do you remember what happened? The part after your dream? I don't want to go into any messy details about the dream itself. You and I, or Deborah can discuss it later. No, I am talking about how you were found, and the other details?"

I shake my head no. I don't want to think about the dream, but I do want to know what happened afterward. In the past two years, I have tried to think about what happened for two years around the time of my leaving school. It's always a blank. I try asking Mama about it, but she sighs and says it is better to leave the past behind us.

"This is where I come in," Joe volunteers, as he takes a sip of wine. "I was visiting my Uncle Havner in a house not far from the field. I heard a lot of commotion in the field. I thought that one of the calves had gotten lost, and was wondering around looking for his mama. I walked into the field and saw it." He looks away. Picking up his wineglass, he takes large gulp this time. "I ran over, and hit the young man across the back of the head with a solid wooden cane. He didn't hear me, or I probably wouldn't have been able to knock him down so quickly. I thought I hit him hard, but apparently not as he just jumped up, and cursed at me, 'What the hell did you do that for?'" Joe's voice rises softly.

I stare at my soup.

"He runs off as if his pants are on fire. At first I wasn't sure what he was doing. I couldn't see that there was someone else in the field or so I thought. I looked down and there you were, Kfira. Your face was as white as a sheet. Your dress had been pulled up to your waist. Your legs and dress were covered in blood from your head and lower -- " Joe took another drink.

I glimpse over at Elijah, and with relief I see him still eating. In a way it feels   as if he isn't in the room.

"And then?" I ask. I sigh, I'm not sure I want to hear everything, but know I must.

Joe's voice softens as he begins to unravel the mystery. "I picked you up and carried you to my uncle's house. He knew you and your family. He sent me for them and the doctor. Your parents came first, and they wanted to take you home. My uncle convinced them to let you be examined. The doctor looked you over, and said that you were hurt. He wanted them to put you into the hospital, but your parents said no. He told your parents what to do for you, and they took you home. They refused to speak of it."

"You were in shock. You had this glazed look in your eyes. When you looked into my eyes it was as if you were a million miles away. I felt like my heart would break. The boy who hurt you never got into trouble."

"I begged my uncle to make sure you were all right. I wanted to call the police but your parents forbade it. Your father said it would only cause trouble. So, I went home, but I couldn't stop thinking about it or you."

I feel memories start to flood my heart and mind. I remember Joe. It all makes sense. My parents wouldn't let him see me, but once or twice, but I do recall he was always polite to them.

"Joe and I are cousins." Deborah takes a large swig of her wine. "Joe asked me to let him know how you were when he returned home. Being several years younger than you, I wasn't

117

sure how I would do that. I found out that your Mama often taught some of the young women how to cook. I asked her if she would teach me, as at the time my own Mama was very sick. Everything you're eating today is your Mama's recipes. I made it."

Deborah gazes into my eyes, and I see the tears streak down her cheek, smearing her makeup. "When they found out you were pregnant, your parents panicked. They were afraid of the embarrassment of having an unmarried daughter with child. How would it look to the congregation? I told them of a place that you could go, and have the baby and get better. By then my Mama had died. I was also sent to Aunt Jean-Pierre's."

Clearing her throat, Jean-Pierre looks from Joe to Deborah, and finally rests her eyes on me. "I knew Deborah was keeping an eye on you. Deborah needed help coping with her mother's death. The Rebbe and Deborah's family arranged for the two of you to come to Paris. You were here almost two years. At first you had a bit of trouble with your memory. The doctors said because of the trauma that you suffered, your mind just wasn't able to handle everything. You got better and gave birth to a beautiful baby boy. At first you were able to love him, but then the nightmares came. Your sister agreed to take the boy for her own. Her own son about his age had died several weeks beforehand. No one knew about the baby's death."

The food tastes like ashes in my mouth. *How awful that I should have a child that I couldn't take care of. Who is my child? If Esther took him then ... I try to count the years and children.* My eyes grow wide, and I stare first at Deborah, then Joe, and Jean-Pierre and finally rest on Elijah. Of course!

"Elijah?" I almost shout.

"Yes," he says, coming out of his food trance to look over at me.

"You, he?" I ask, looking over at Jean-Pierre.

"Yes." Jean-Pierre sits up straight, rearranging the silverware by her plate.

"I, I ... is that why Esther has been so hard on me?"

"Your family didn't want to believe the rape at first. With the baby, it became difficult for them to deal. Esther thought it would be safer this way until Elijah began to ask questions, and the world began to change."

"I ... you are my son?" I ask, as I swivel around to look at him. In some ways he reminds me of Mark. Elijah's features are just like Marks's, all but his eyes, they are mine.

"Your brother-in-law could no longer understand the deal, and so he pushed for the ... for lack of better word ... truth." Joe picks up his bread, and pulls off a small hunk. Stuffing it into his mouth, he is unable to say anything more.

"Is this why I'm in Paris?"

"No, not completely, but that is for another moment. As I said before, with what you must do ... we all must have more trust. We knew the only way that trust could be built would be if some of your questions of your past were finally answered."

Catana enters, breaking the silence. "Are you ready for the next course Madam?"

"Yes dear, please serve it right away."

Catana clears away the soup dishes.

"May I keep mine?" I ask, as I look down and see that the bowl is half full of bread and soup. I would never want to waste good soup.

"Catana, leave Kfira's bowl for now. You can get it next

time."

"Yes, madam," she says, and begins to pick up the empty bowls, avoiding mine.

She exits the same way she came in.

Shaking my head, so many things I want to say come to mind. All I can do is stand, and grab Elijah in the biggest hug I have ever given.

"You know?"

"Yes."

"For how long?"

"Last summer, I overheard Mama and Papa arguing over you and me. At first I said nothing, but then in September I had to ask other questions. Papa had gone out of town, and he had said he wasn't coming back until it was taken care of. That is when I ..."

"... told me he wanted to change things," Deborah continues the story.

I feel as if I'm the only one here who is lost. My thoughts bombard me like sparks from a fire. Everything is light and everything is dark. I understand so much, and yet so little. I'm more confused than before I walked into this room tonight.

I know one thing ... this is my son. Elijah is my son.

"Kfira, I wish things were a little easier for you," Deborah voices softly.

"We all do," Joe remarks.

"I'm not looking for easy," I reply.

"It did make it easier when you started recalling the truth on the train," Jean-Pierre breaks in.

Deborah pushes her chair aside. She runs over to embrace Elijah and me. Before I know it everyone is hugging us.

"This is the grandest day, to see a mama and son united at last," Jean-Pierre says, chokingly.

Yes, it is. I would have never guessed it would be Elijah and me.

Order to Life

"Deborah," I say, over the music of the Big Band on the stage.

"Yes." She leans in closer to me and smirks.

"Why did you talk me into coming here?" I look around the room cautiously. So many things I have never done in my life, and now here I sit, in a dance hall or party or something. I don't know if it's the right thing to do.

Couples are on the dance floor dancing cheek to cheek to a slow song as the band plays on. A huge dance floor holds at least fifty couples are more singles are milling about, dancing. All the women are all dressed in their finest dresses with little hats atop their tightly coiled hairdos. Most are form fitting. Red cheeks and lips make them the painted ladies Mama says they are. The men all wear some form of tuxedo. I had to ask Deborah about their clothes, as it isn't the usual attire for men in the shtetl.

So many things in my life have changed that I feel like I'm watching someone else live for me. Although everyone keeps reassuring me, I still feel very frightened and confused. I'm feeling a little more comfortable, and I'm thankful for the Shabbos celebration last night. I wonder what mama would want me to do.

"Would you like to go home?"Joe asks, coming up beside me.

He watches me, as I try to put my coat on and then take it off again. Scratching the side of my face, I feel my forehead wrinkle up and a stern look crosses my face. It's nice in here, but this is not a place for me.

"We promise not to let you have too much fun," Deborah giggles, as she lifts her glass and takes a sip.

"Are you sure this place is safe?"

"Yes, tonight it's safe. Tomorrow, maybe not," Deborah replies.

"I promised you a nice supper. Would you like to go to the dining area?" Joe strolls over to me, and hunches down beside me.

Feeling an unmistakable roar in my stomach, I smile and nod a yes. I tried speaking above the band earlier, but it only made my ears ring. I need a little peace and quiet, as my headache has doubled in the last hour.

"Will you be safe?" Joe turns back to Deborah.

"Tom is here." She points over to a young man who is checking in his coat and hat.

"Does Grandmother know he is here?" Joe asks protectively.

"She arranged it." Deborah giggles, and waves over to the young man so that he will see her.

Walking over, the young man bows before her. Falling to one knee, he reaches up and kisses her hand.

"Always one for the drama." Deborah grasps the young man's face. "Kfira, I want you to meet Tom. Tom, this is Kfira. I told you she was coming to visit."

"Oh yes, I'm so happy to meet you." Tom stands, and extends his hand to me.

"Hello, Tom." I reach my hand out for his warm one.

He kisses it lightly and winks.

I am unsure what to do. Pulling my hand away quickly, I feel my cheeks grow warmer by each passing second. Looking up, I can see why Deborah would want to see this young man. He is as tall as Joe with light brown hair combed back softly against his tan skin. His hazel eyes reflect a blue light from the brighter ones above us. They go with his blue suit.

Deborah is also wearing a long blue formal.

I realize they match.

They managed to get me into a soft pink one that I am sure is a little too revealing at the top. Already many men have said you look beautiful to me.

"You are too modest," Deborah said, as we dressed tonight. It's easy for her to say that she doesn't have a Mama like mine. I know Mama would not approve of this dress or nightclub.

"Tom, Kfira and I are going to have a nice dinner, and maybe a stroll along the river. Will you make sure Deborah gets home safely?"

"Sure." Tom reaches out to shake Joe's hand.

Pulling out my chair, Joe grasps my hand, and leads me away. I gaze back at Deborah who is motioning me to go with both hands. She wishes to be alone with Tom. I pray that Tom is a good man.

"It is a lot quieter in the dining area so people can talk," Joe says, as we attempt to break through the crowd.

Did everyone pick this night to go dancing?

Finally, we reach another entrance where a man in a black and white uniform stands. I'm amazed at the tie with red and white striping and white gloves. His black hair is slicked back and he is handsome.

"Two?" he asks, as he steps aside.

"Yes." Joe takes my arm, and leads me inside.

The man in the uniform leads us into a huge room with many tables. Picking one to the far corner, but near a bay window, he nods for approval from Joe.

"This is great." Joe pulls out a chair for me, and I allow him to seat me.

"Thank you." I realize his hand has brushed against my tucas. My face reddens even though I know no one else is aware.

"Someone will be here with a menu shortly," the man speaks, and he is gone.

"This is a very nice place." I peer around the room.

At least thirty round tables of all sizes are scattered about. Each table has several white linen tablecloths with silverware of all sizes. Preset plates and glasses give the place a homey feel.

Oh so many things to wash runs through my mind.

"Do you think Elijah will be all right?"

"Of course, Grandmother has a wonderful new radio to listen to, and if that isn't entertaining enough she might bring out her old Victrola. She'll have him dancing around the room with her." He grins.

"Oh, you are so silly. I know I have just learned that he is my son, but I have always taken care of my family." I look toward the big bay windows next to our small table.

The scenery is breathtaking. It's as if night is day with all the lights. Some of the houses where I live still don't have electricity, and mine is one of them. Here, everything has electricity, and everything is alive with lights and colors.

"I'm so glad you decided to come here," Joe says, as the waiter crosses to our table.

"Would you like something to drink?" he asks.

"How about a couple of glasses of Chianti?"

"Fresh bottles came in from Italy only this morning," the waiter replies.

Laughing, Joe shakes his head, "I hope they aren't freshly

made this morning."

"No monsieur, they only arrived here this morning." The waiter snickers and avoids eye contact with Joe. He keeps glancing around the room, and out of the window as if looking for an escape route.

"Okay, two glasses it is."

"Very good sir." He turns and leaves.

Joe turns back to me.

"He doesn't like you much," I say, and realize I didn't answer his other question. "I am glad, too."

"I want to tell you something."

"You aren't a lost brother or something, are you?"

We both chuckle.

"No, I'm not related to you at all. When I saw you in that field, something happened."

"What?" I stare at my napkin. Picking it up, I fold and refold it. *What if he says he ... I made him sick. What if ... I'm so scared of what he might say next.* I gulp several times, as the palms of my hands dampen. My heart skips a beat.

"I fell in love with you. You were hurt, and I had to help you.

When your parents pushed you away, I was so angry with them. I couldn't understand. I was twenty years old at the time. I couldn't imagine my parents doing that to me, but more importantly, I fell in love with you because you were beautiful." He peers at his empty water glass and looks around. Pulling his silver flask from his pocket, he takes several sips. He sets it on the table beside us.

I can't believe my ears ... *he fell in love with me? But how?*

"I don't understand." I stare at my hands now.

"I was in Paris when you were here. I was in school. I lived at Grandmother's."

"Why didn't you go to school in the United States?" I eye him.

"I wanted to be near my European roots. My father left after the turn of the century thinking he could find an easier life there. He died that year, so I decided to come here. Grandmother was very happy to have me. She taught me so much."

The waiter interrupts, carrying the two glasses of wine. He places them before us. "Would you like to order?"

"Two roast beefs," Joe says, with a smile to me.

We both break out in grins when the waiter walks away. Roast beef, just like our dinner on the train.

He reaches over, and takes my hands.

"Kfira, when I saw you on that train it was all I could do to keep from running over to you, and grabbing you up. I wanted to kiss you. You're just as beautiful now as you were thirteen years ago."

"Why haven't you married?" I take a sip from the wineglass. It's not as sweet as the wine I have been drinking since arriving in Paris, but it's tasty.

"Because there would never be another you." He kisses my hands.

I don't know what to say. A few beads of sweat break out along my hairline despite the coolness of the room. I hide my eyes, so he can't see my embarrassment. I don't know what to say.

"I don't understand -- " I want to say I'm ruined. I'm not a virgin, and what man would want to be with a woman who isn't a virgin.

"I have waited so long to say these things to you. I want to be with you for the rest of our lives. I know this is quick for you, but for me it is thirteen years in the making."

I peek into his eyes, and the warmth and love I see in them is strong. *How could I have missed that look, but then I have never really looked, have I?*

"Do Mama and Papa know?"

"Yes, they do now. Rebbe promised he would talk to them after Shabbos. When Rebbe makes a promise ... " Joe begins.

".... he never backs out," I finish.

"Yes."

Suddenly, a different waiter appears with our plates. He sets them in front of us, and says nothing as he moves away.

"Thank you," Joe says to the man's back.

"I don't know what to say. Where I come from marriages are arranged. Everyone from many generations back allowed the Rebbe and the matchmaker to arrange a marriage." Looking down at the plate of food, I'm unsure if I'm still hungry although it looks quite delicious.

"I have something for you." He pulls out an envelope with my name on it. It's in the Rebbe's handwriting.

I take it, and slip my finger through the opening, and slit through the seal quickly. It's written in Yiddish. I can hear his voice, as I read it.

"Kfira,
When you read this letter you will know many truths. First, you will
know that Elijah is your son, and the circumstances around his birth. You will also know that Joe is in love with you. I give you my blessing, my child. Marry this man, and make him a happy man.
I have another request for you and it's in another letter that Jean-Pierre will give you in the morning. For now you are to celebrate your son, and your forthcoming wedding.
Blessed Love,
Chaim"

I can see him wiping at his forehead, as he looks over this letter to check for mistakes. Maybe even to contemplate what he is doing, and if it is God's will.

"Kfira, I want to marry you. If you will have me." Joe pulls a small box from his coat. Opening it up, inside is a small ring with a large rock, no a diamond, set into it. Diamonds I have seen many, but mostly they are ones that have been hidden, and yet still managed to be handed down, generation after generation.

My eyes widen, as I realize that this isn't a joke. I'm not dreaming this time. It's all real.

"Are you all right?" Joe caresses my cheek with his fingers.

133

"Yes." I beam at him.

"Yes, you are all right or yes, you will marry me?" A look of concern flashes in his eyes, as if fear has taken hold.

"Yes, yes, yes." I look deeper into his eyes.

"Now, I know that you have to go to Bangkok on a mission, and you will still do that but I want to know ... if you will still be my wife?"

I had almost forgotten about Bangkok with everything else going on. Only a week ago life was the same day after day. Nothing new ever seemed to happen to me. Now, life is one big chaos with my name on it.

"Yes, I will do my mission as the Rebbe asks. Yes, I will marry you."

Without thinking, Joe jumps up, and grabs me into his arms. Holding me as close as two people can get, he moves his face toward mine, and gives me my first kiss.

It is light and feathery and tickles my lips. My heart skips a beat, and I giggle like a schoolgirl at the prospect of getting more such kisses.

"I have waited so long for you." He swings my small body

around.

I'm thankful the restaurant is empty because we might have bumped into someone. Sitting me down in my seat, Joe takes his chair. I feel breathless, as my heart plays inside my chest. "I have to tell you that I'm not as quiet as you have seen me these last days."

"As I recall you can be a real chatterbox." Joe grins. "And a nice little yenta!"

"You -- " I point at him, and make a face.

"I know you don't remember all of those two years, but I do. I know that some things probably didn't change. Naturally Elijah will come to live with us once we are married. For now he will stay here with Jean-Pierre."

Elijah! "Does he know about this?"

"Yes, I told him before the Shabbos meal. He's very excited for us, and can't wait to get some brothers and sisters."

"'Whoa! Hold the horses big fella,' as Mama would say to me ... 'I see no wedding ring on this finger'." I hold up my wedding ring finger.

"No, but you do see an engagement ring." With this he pulls

135

the ring out of the box, and slides it onto my finger.

Gasping, I can't believe how beautiful it really is on my hand. How can all the tragedies in my life give me so much beauty now?

The Jade Tiger

"The evening out with Joe was so spectacular I felt almost like a princess in disguise. We ate the roast beef, and it tasted better than manna from heaven. Then we danced around the dance hall. My feet almost left the floor several times. I can't believe he wishes for me to be his bride." I write this on a blank page of the journal.

I wanted to write something in it every day when I first found it, but I never could until now. I peek down at the ring on my finger, and realize that there are so many things I need to ask Joe. I realize that the questions in my mind might also be the same ones that Mama and all the other women must have of their men.

Walking over to the French doors, I open them and step out onto the balcony. From here I can easily see the Eiffel Tower and the river. It's so beautiful. Did I really wake up, and see this every day for two years? Already I am remembering the streets and how to get around the house without help. I couldn't do this if I had not been here before.

Staring at the stars, my eyes start to cross, and sleep wishes to overcome me. I walk over to the rail, and hope that I might see Deborah being escorted home by Tom. I wish I could talk to her, but know it's better to speak to her tomorrow. I only pray I can sleep.

Surprisingly, as I lay on the bed and wrap the covers up to my neck, sleep is instant.

###

"Good morning everyone!" I walk through the doors into the dining room.

Catana is already setting up breakfast on the buffet table on the east wall. Jean-Pierre is sitting at the head of the table, and Elijah as well as Deborah, are already enjoying their food.

"Good morning," Deborah sings across the room.

"I trust you slept well." Jean-Pierre pours herself another cup of tea.

"Yes, I did." I lean over, and kiss Elijah on the forehead.

He smiles shyly and continues to eat.

"Did anything interesting happen last night?" Deborah asks, before she bites into a piece of bread.

"I don't know." I reach across her with my left hand, into the breadbasket on the table in front of her.

"He did it!"

"Yes!"

"You said yes?"

"Deborah." I giggle and playfully push her right shoulder with my left hand. "You knew all, along didn't you?" I take a bread, and sit down beside her. Smiling at them, I hold up my left hand, as if it's an object to display.

"Congratulations." Deborah pulls my hand over to admire the ring. "He told me he was going to ask you to marry him, but I didn't think he would. He was so nervous last night. He almost talked himself out of meeting us there."

Eyes wide with fright, I look from Deborah to Jean-Pierre. *Does he not love me? Is he marrying me because of some guilt? What does she mean?* I don't want to say anything as to jinx

138

everything.

Grasping my hand, Deborah leans toward me with a smile on her face. "He loves you. He was afraid because he thought you might say no."

Sighing with relief, I smile once more. "I was afraid you were going to say this was another part of the plan, and that has to marry me so I can go to Bangkok."

"Actually, it was the last thing I was thinking would happen when I knew you would be going, there. But now that it has happened, it might actually be beneficial for you. You could marry Joe before leaving for Bangkok. You would have American papers. It will be easier for you to travel," Jean-Pierre says with a bit of practicality on her side.

"But then my Rebbe couldn't perform the ceremony," I fuss. I had never dreamed of having anyone, but Rebbe say the prayers for the ceremony.

"You can have a second wedding when you come back," Deborah encourages.

Looking between them, I'm unsure of what to do. At least if I had a second ceremony, then Mama and Papa could also be there. I'd been worrying about the prospect of traveling to Bangkok alone. It feels like since I left home, I have done nothing alone.

I nod and sigh at the same time. "You're right of course. It would make more sense with the marriage before the trip." I stand and walk over to the buffet table, thinking about the letter from Rebbe in my carpetbag with my journal.

"I have another letter for you." Jean-Pierre pushes it toward me.

Deborah picks it up, and hands it to me.

With stiff fingers I open it, ever so careful to not tear it or smudge the writing. I read aloud

"Kfira,

I know that in your heart there are still many questions. Will I still need to go to Bangkok? What is so special about this place? Why was I chosen?

Jean-Pierre can now give you all the details. You must listen to her. You must learn. This trip is not without danger. I wish you all the luck in the world. Special prayers for you and all your family."

It is signed as before "Chaim".

"Tell me, Jean-Pierre, tell me my fate." I put the letter down, and look intently into Jean-Pierre's eyes.

She closes them, and then opens them again, as if to dismiss her role in the journey. She can't, it's her fate.

"I can tell you everything now. Yes, you will still need to go to Bangkok. Your job is to pick up something special there, and take it to Palestine. But first you must go to Morocco where you will receive a special something to take with you to Bangkok. You will then catch a boat to Bangkok. A Buddhist monk is holding something that only you can pick up. The people that you will need to meet with will always have a small jade tiger with them. It may be a broach or a little statue. Anything. Or if they speak to you of a jade tiger, you will know they are safe."

"A jade tiger?" I ask, wanting to be sure I heard correctly. *What can be so great about a jade tiger?*

"Yes, a jade tiger will find you throughout all of your travels. People have to mention the jade tiger or show you one," she reiterates.

"Will Joe be with me?" I search their faces for answers.

"Sometimes, and sometimes I will be with you," Deborah answers.

"I'm still unsure I understand." I feel anxious to know what they have in mind. My heart races as fast as my mind between the questions sitting on the edge of my brain.

"We're part of the resistance, a Zionist group who wishes to make Israel a real homeland once more," Deborah continues.

"Already Kristallnacht has caused good men to be arrested, and taken away to where we don't know. Jews will never be safe until we have a homeland." Jean-Pierre watches me, as she speaks.

"Who was arrested?" I whisper. In my heart I already know two that might have been arrested. My mind wants to hear their names spoken out loud. Confirmation for the inevitable.

"Your brother-in-law Josef and your brother-in-law Samuel," Deborah answers.

Hannah's and Esther's husbands names, I shrink back. Poor Hannah with all the children. How will she cope?

"Don't worry, Hannah and the children are safe. In fact there are safe escape plans for all of your family should it be necessary." Jean-Pierre takes a sip of her tea.

"What about Mama and Papa? Papa is very head strong. He will never leave his home," I protest. Papa, who refuses to be called a Prussian, hiding from the Germans? Almost seems too crazy now to even speak out loud.

"I know this is hard to hear but it's the truth. If you were there ..." Deborah shakes her head. "Your being here will help your family. This trip you will make will help our people, Jews. Are you willing to do it?"

"Of course," I answer without stuttering. "I just wish I knew why I was picked."

"Because of all of the people in your village, you are the only one they can depend on to complete such a task." There, it's said.

It still doesn't completely explain why, but in some sense I do understand. I'm the only one who ever talked about leaving the shtetl as a little girl. I was the only one who did it except Josef and Samuel. They sit in a prison somewhere having GOD knows what happen to them.

"When do I leave?"

"We don't want to cause suspicion. We will have the wedding, and you two will leave for a honeymoon. We can do this in a week," Jean-Pierre answers.

"A week?"

"You have something better to do?" Deborah giggles.

"No." I shake my head for drama. "Can you tell me what I'm to pick up in Bangkok?"

"I guess it wouldn't hurt. A thousand years ago or so, maybe longer, a very old Torah scroll was taken to Asia and hidden. No one really knows how old it is as few have seen it. It's possible it's one of the original works. We don't know all the details. We just know that it's said in some circles that once that Torah scroll makes it home then Israel will become a strong nation once more." Jean-Pierre takes a sip of tea.

"Why Asia?"

"Because that is where the Torah is," Elijah says joining into the conversation.

"Oh, you." I giggle, and wink at him. I turn back to Jean-Pierre, and give her my best serious face. I really want to know the whole story. I have kept my tongue till now, but no longer.

"As I said I really don't know the whole story. I do know that the Monks at this particular place has kept a written and oral tradition, and they will tell you more when you take the treasure," Jean-Pierre replies. Sitting there in her chair, she looks so regal.

I decide there is nothing I can say to get any more information from these two. "Well, I guess we have a wedding to plan." I beam.

"Hurray for weddings!" Deborah claps her hands together.

Jean-Pierre and Deborah both show a look of relief to not have to answer anymore questions. I allow this time of leisure, as I know that soon enough I will ask more questions. I hope they will give the answers.

"I know nothing about weddings. I don't even have a rabbi," I cry, as I rise and walk over to the buffet table to pour myself some juice.

"I have the rabbi," Jean-Pierre responds.

"We will need to go shopping," Deborah says excitedly.

"I have no money," I wail all of a sudden, as I realize that I have no dowry except for the small amount of money that I have in my bag upstairs.

"Catana," Jean-Pierre calls out.

Catana quickly appears at the door. "Yes, madam?"

"Please bring Kfira's dresses," Jean-Pierre remarks.

Catana races out of the door and quickly returns, carrying five of the six dresses I was wearing or carrying from home.

"Give them to Kfira," Jean-Pierre orders.

Without saying a word, Catana drops the dresses in a chair beside me.

"Thank you, Catana." I lightly pick through the dresses. "I don't understand."

"You should know this one Mama," Elijah says, as he stands and walks over to me. "For as long as there have been a Jew alive, someone has hated the Jew. Jews have been forced to flee their homes, and homelands, at a moment's notice. They are always only allowed to take what they can carry on their backs." He says this as he grabs one of the plainest dresses, and begins to pull at the seams and hems. "We have always had to be resourceful. Doesn't mean we aren't always caught, but we do try." With this Elijah releases paper bills from the hem of the dress.

"You mean all of these dresses have money sewn into them?" I grab one up, and begin to follow his lead.

"Yes," Elijah answers.

"But don't think you are going to be spending your money on a wedding dowry, young lady," Jean-Pierre speaks in a very matronly voice.

"No?"

"No, I am financing this party. Joe's father left a tidy little sum for a dowry for his only son." She chuckles lightly. "He was so afraid Joe would never marry."

"Apparently, he kept telling his father he would never wed if he couldn't marry you," Deborah says.

"Okay, but Deborah you will have to help me with whatever I will need. I don't need anything fancy." I open another seam, and more money falls out.

"Look at her." Deborah glances back at Jean-Pierre. "Nothing fancy, when I get married I want extra fancy. I want to be a princess."

I already feel like a princess, but how can I tell them this. Would they even understand. Two honors to fulfill and I'm the one to do it. I must bring the Torah home and save my family,

maybe even my people. I must marry a man who loves me, and

somehow deep inside I know I love him.

In my mind's eye I see a jade tiger sitting lonely on a rock

above the valley, anxiously awaiting the return trip home. A

trace of fear laces inside my heart like a spider web, but it's so

small right now I can't see it. I'm ready for the surprises ahead of

me.

Preparing for the Wedding

"Kfira, we just have to go shopping," Deborah says as, I look

at all the money sitting before me.

"As I said before, you save your money, and I will take care

of everything. You will need your money for your trips," Jean-

Pierre says, with a lilt in her voice.

"When can we go shopping?" I gather the money into a pile.

"We will go as soon as you are ready." Deborah gets up, and

walks over to help me with the money. "We will put this in a safe

place."

"If you will let me, I will see which currency is best to exchange it into for your trip," Jean-Pierre suggests.

Thinking about it for a minute, I suddenly realize that of course exchanging it would be necessary. I feel so silly for being afraid to let them touch it. After all, it is pretty obvious that they have more money than I do, and aren't wanting to steal mine. I'm afraid. I don't know anything about the money system in other countries. *How will I know if someone is cheating me. I will just have to have faith that they won't.*

Elijah looks at me and winks. He too, knows the money laying before us seems substantial to us, while to Jean-Pierre and Deborah, it's but a pittance.

"I agree." I make several small stacks. I try to count it all, but have a hard time keeping track.

"The dresses will have to be put in the rag barrel." Deborah picks each one up and folds it.

"Wait." I touch one of Hannah's darker ones with large pink flowers on it. She last wore it before she had babies. It's worn out, but still carries memories for me.

"Are you okay?" Deborah asks.

"I ..."

" ... need to throw these away. You can't take them with you. Wearing dresses like this will cause suspicion. We have to get you newer, more modern clothes. We want you to come back alive," Deborah remarks.

Until this very moment I never thought of my life as being in danger. I know that Josef and Samuel are in danger, but me? Surely no one would really want to hurt me. Looking at the old dresses, I push them toward her and sigh deeply. It's a link to home and its being taken from me.

"Maybe I can have Catana do something with them," Jean-Pierre says softly.

I smile at her.

Deborah picks up the dresses, and takes them to the kitchen. "You just have a bite to eat, and we will hit the streets of Paris with its willing shops!"

"Mama would never believe this." I look over at Elijah.

"Bubbe would approve," Elijah states. Standing, he walks over and gives me a quick, firm hug. "Are you hungry?"

"Yes." I peek over at the buffet table once more.

"I will fix you a plate." He moves over to the table, and grabs a plate. He places some cooked bread called French toast on it. Next to it he places fresh strawberries and orange slices. He ambles over, and places the plate before me. Leaning down, he kisses me on the cheek.

"Thank you, my son." I reach up and touch his cheek. I'm so thankful he is my son.

"We will have the wedding in two days," Jean-Pierre states. "Yes, I will have everything ready for you, including a rabbi" she reassures me with a smile.

I pour the thick syrup on the French toast, and dream of the day when I will be married to Joe. Is it really going to happen to me?

###

Pulling me from shop to shop, Deborah leads me through the best places in town.

"I don't know. They just don't have my style," I beg off.

"It's just because you are used to wearing everyone's hand-me-down Bubbe dresses. You're in the fashion capital of the world, and you don't even have to worry about money. Humor me, please." Deborah looks at me with big, droopy eyes and lips. Her hands hold onto my left wrist, and she is trying not to crack laugh.

"All right, I will try to see what you see," I agree. Even unmentionables are different in this new world. Saturday night Deborah had introduced me to a bra. I still find the contraption slightly more comfortable than strapping my breasts down with knotted ropes!

"Let's go in this shop, they have bridal gowns." Deborah says, as she pulls me to the door.

Conceding to the idea of a new wedding dress, I walk in calmly, still letting her hold my arm. I turn to see some of the display mannequins when something catches my eye. I pull away from Deborah, and walk over to what is the most beautiful dress I have ever seen in my life!

"May I help you?" the tall, red headed woman with green eyes asks, as she approaches from the left. She has a pencil dangling from her left ear, and glasses on a rope around her neck.

"Huh?" I ask twisting myself around to see who is talking.

"Do you see something?" Deborah asks, as she walks over to

me.

"This is so beautiful." I reach out, and finger the silky cream colored fabric between my fingers.

"Yes, it is," Deborah agrees.

The neckline comes down in a V with a small teardrop hole cut out at the V. The sleeves are puffy but not too much with small pearls laced around the hem and forming delicate flowers here and there. They stop right above the elbow. The waist is tapered with a small bow in the front that is also encrusted with more baby pearls and lace. Strips of lace hang from the belt around the waist. On the hem of the dress are more baby pearls with an occasional tiny blue rose, alternating with little red ones.

"Do you like?" the saleswoman asks. "I think I have one just your size."

"Oh Kfira, it's so beautiful." Deborah caresses the soft fabric. Reaching out, she touches it to her cheek, as if it's a fur.

"Here you go," the saleswoman says, returning quickly with the dress.

"Let's go try it on." Deborah pulls me toward the dressing rooms.

I have never been in a dressing room in a store, and fear makes my heart skip a beat. *Will these people be able to see my nakedness?* Feeling my heart beat ever faster, I suffer like I am twelve years old. Yes, I did this before when I was twelve! Deborah and Jean-Pierre took me clothes shopping. Deborah sits in the dressing room with me, to calm and reassure me.

I laugh at my silliness back then and now. "I will be there in a second."

The little dressing room is smaller than I remember, but there is enough room for both of us. I remove my dress, and Deborah takes it from me. We say nothing, as if by talking, it will jinx the magic of the dress and its beauty.

Sliding it on, I find it easily fits into place. Deborah zips up the back and steps aside to take a look.

"You aren't going to believe this," she says.

"How does it look?" the saleslady asks from beyond the curtain.

"We will be out in a second." Deborah pushes me out into the open.

Stepping out of the curtained room, I catch a glimpse of

someone in the dress I'm wearing. She is very beautiful. No wait, it's me. I'm ... I can't express my feelings. I'm a woman.

"Oh mademoiselle, the dress looks exquisite on you," she coos.

I can't take my eyes off my reflection, as I look in the full-length mirror in the corner. The dress fits perfectly. A full-length mirror in my neighborhood would not be kosher unless it is in a store frequented by goy. If I or anyone else is caught doing such we would get such a tongue lashing about vanity, but here, no one cares.

"We can fix the length if you like?" The saleslady points to the hem, which reaches the bottom of my ankles.

"No need, this is going to be her wedding dress," Deborah states matter of factly. Turning to me, she walks over and squeezes my arms together. "Joe is going to love you in this one."

"Do you think?" I ask a little unsure. I can't take my eyes off all of the little details on the dress. I can't even imagine how much such a dress must cost. I dare not ask, or I know I will be frightened away from getting it.

155

"We will take it," Deborah says, to the saleslady. She chuckles, as she pulls me gently away from the mirror. "We have a whole trousseau to gather for you. This looks like the place to get it."

In the dressing room once more, I remove the dress carefully, ever mindful of the delicate details. I put on the dress I was wearing a few minutes before, also new and start to feel a little more relaxed. So this is what a pampered life is like. Mama used to laugh at some of the wives of the richer men in the community. She would say they wouldn't know hard work if they were bitten on their tucas' by it. Here I am having someone else do my bidding. I'm a little confused about it all, but will have to think about it later.

"Are you ready to shop?" Deborah asks, as I come out of the dressing room. She takes the dress, my precious dress, and hands it to the saleslady. "Please wrap this up."

"Right away. Let me know if there are any others." The saleslady walks over to a large desk set in front of a small curtained-off area.

"Let's look at these dresses over here," Deborah says, as we

156

walk around the room.

Other women are milling about the store as well. Some are speaking French and some English, and I'm glad that Deborah and I agreed to practice our English while shopping today. They all seem fashionably dressed as well, and I don't feel out of place wearing a new dress Jean-Pierre bought for me before my arrival. It all makes me sense that I'm home.

"Here we go," Deborah says, as we look at several rows of dresses.

I glance around at everyone enjoying themselves as they pick out different dresses. Holding them against their bodies, they laugh and dance around at times as they talk with their friends.

"I like this one." I pick out an emerald green, cotton one that is the same style as the wedding dress.

"Good choice," Deborah says, as she checks it over. "I think it will fit. We must make sure you have something nice for the honeymoon." She winks at me.

I sense my cheeks turn a brighter shade of red, as my eyes stare at the floor restlessly. In all of the excitement I had forgotten about that! Oy Vey! A honeymoon, too? I'm a little lightheaded, and hold onto the pole the clothes are hanging on.

"Are you all right?" Deborah asks, as she turns to face me.

"I think I'm getting a little thirsty," I confess.

"Come over here." Deborah grabs my wrist, and leads me over to several chairs by the mirrors. "Sit down, and I will bring you something to drink." With this, Deborah disappears. She returns rather quickly with a small glass of wine. "Drink this."

I eye her suspiciously, as every time she says drink this, I go to sleep.

"It won't make you go to sleep, I promise." She smiles.

I nod and take a sip. It's a light grape juice. It tastes nice and sweet in my throat. I feel almost normal.

"You sit here, and I will bring dresses to show you. If you like, you get."

"Okay." I take another drink and let the coolness of the juice coat my dry throat.

Deborah leaves, and I take another sip.

Just then the saleslady approaches from the other side. "I have something to show you," she says, with her hands behind her. "I understand that you're getting married," she says, in a very discreet voice.

"Yes, in two days," I answer.

"This will make your honeymoon." She pulls around a beautiful, light green negligee.

Holding my breath, I reach out and stroke the silky fabric. A part of me says I should be embarrassed but I'm not. I'm to be a married woman soon, and it's time to think about the reality of my life.

Deborah strolls up from the other side, and sees the negligee. "That is so exquisite. You just have to have it."

"Yes, I do." I smile, and look back and forth at the two eager faces before me. They really are happy for me.

I pick out a few more dresses and shoes to match, all while sitting. The saleslady refills my glass several times before we are done.

"I think we should go for a snack," Deborah voices, as we leave the store. Deborah gives the saleslady our address, and makes sure the things are delivered to Jean-Pierre's later today.

"Are you sure it's safe to do this?" I ask, thinking about the dress going to someone else's house.

"Yes, you will have your dress."

We dine at a little restaurant close to the Arch d'Triumph. It feels like old times. My memories of the two years are slowly beginning to trickle back, one by one. I find it easy to get back into the lifestyle I had back then. No wonder there were times when Mama claimed she just didn't understand some of the meshuggah notions that crossed my mind. Of course, she has never left her world.

When we get back to the house, we observe Jean-Pierre busy making arrangements for everything. Everyone is caught up in the hustle-bustle of getting things ready for the big day.

"We will have a big dinner tomorrow for many people," Jean-Pierre says, as she walks into my room.

"But for who?" I look over the dresses I picked out at the store.

"Many of the people Joe knows, and many you have met years ago," Jean-Pierre replies. "Also I wish to talk to you now before everything happens these next two days."

She sits on the chaise-lounge that Deborah had left in here from the first night. She takes in a deep breath, exhaling slowly.

I sit before her.

"When I met you so many years ago you were so naive about the ways of the world. You were scared like a frightened mouse for the first six months. But then as it came closer for the time of the baby you started to be less nervous. You brought HaShem back into this house."

I stare deep into her eyes, and see little tears edge to the surface.

"I knew Joe had feelings for you even back then, but I discouraged them as I thought 'no, no grandson of mine would marry a mixed up peasant girl, ever.' He will marry a rich American girl like his father, but then I got to know you, and I started to love you. When you walked back into our lives it was like manna from heaven. We are all so blessed for it."

"This thing that you do, HaShem will guide you through it just as before. The Torah will be back in Israel and HaShem will help us all, so will we."

I don't know what to say, as I lean closer, and reach out to hold Jean-Pierre. I know that no matter how difficult my mission may become, I have to fulfill it. I must help my family, all of my family to survive.

"Thank you."

"Thank you, Jean-Pierre, for making me whole again." I squeeze her shoulders.

I realize that we are both crying. Wiping each other's tears away, we smile.

"Time to finish getting ready for the wedding." Jean-Pierre pulls away and stands. "I hope you are ready."

Giggling and wrinkling up my nose, as if I'm five, I nod. "Yes, I am ready."

The Wedding

Sitting at the vanity, I know I should be getting ready for the party, but I feel so nauseous. The big party the day before the wedding is a big step toward my becoming Joe's wife. I have watched this happen with my sisters and brothers, but I never dreamed the day would come when it would happen to me.

"Knock, Knock." Deborah opens the door slightly to peek inside. Walking in, she closes the door behind her.

"Come in." I pick up the hairbrush, and tug at the rats' nest in the back of my hair. I laid down for a short nap earlier, and when I awoke this is what I found, knotted hair. Although I can't look back upon what happened in the dream, I know I must have tossed and turned during it.

"Here, let me help you with that." Deborah takes the brush from my hand, and starts detangling the hair beneath it.

"I'm so scared." I wince, as she struggles to gently undo the mess.

"There is nothing to fear." Her hands work deftly, as the hair begins to smooth out.

"I don't know these people."

"Some of them you have met before."

"When I was here before?"

"Yes, they will understand if you don't recall their names, after all they only have to know your name. You can't possibly recollect everyone from thirteen years ago. I promise, they will understand."

The hair is detangled, but Deborah keeps working on it. "I'm going to fix your hair. You're going to get dressed, and we are going downstairs to greet your people."

I nod. *My people? I have people?* It sounds so strange to my ears.

"But," I turn around to object.

"Do you want to marry Joe?"

"Yes."

"He's waiting for you. He's afraid you aren't going to show."

I can't believe what I'm hearing. "Okay, fix my hair."

"That's the spirit. I will help with your makeup. You are going to wow the crowd. Honestly, you act as if you've never been in front of a group of people before."

'It's true, if I was at home now instead of in Paris, I would still be teaching." *It's always a small class of five or six, but there have been times when as many as twenty children came for lessons. I teach anything from Hebrew to Jewish history to whatever is needed. I've even taught a few wives how to cook. How can I let a silly thing such as fear get in the way?'*

Deborah talks about the fashions in the stores, and what she and Tom plan for next week. I try listening, but I soon find my mind wandering through the past. I never thought of myself as

164

the bravest in our shtetl, but here I am.

"You're done." Deborah she looks at my reflection.

"You did such an exquisite job!"I turn around, and gaze into Deborah's eyes. They are beaming. She curled the sides into tight rolls, and made a small bun at the nape of my neck. A few of the shorter strands are little ringlets cupping my face.

"You're going to take Joe's breath away. Hurry up and get dressed."

I go over to the wardrobe for the green dress. I change quickly and return to the chair so Deborah can apply my makeup.

Deborah chats, and I catch most words, but not all. Occasionally I give an uh-huh in reply, as if I'm listening.

Every inch of my body is tingling with excitement. My mouth is dry despite the fact I keep drinking water. My palms are so damp, I'm afraid to touch anything for fear it will be stained with wetness when I move my hands away. I keep swallowing, and listening to the pounding in my head. It's like a drum.

"Just relax." Deborah applies the last of the makeup.

"I am trying."

###

We walk down the stairs fifteen minutes later, and I feel like a princess. Excitement quickly overtakes trepidation.

Joe and Tom stand at the bottom of the stairs, awaiting our arrival.

"You look so lovely tonight," Joe whispers in my ear, as he takes my hand, and leads me into the ballroom.

It's huge with people of all ages and sizes milling about, gabbing in several languages. They are intent to make their point known and believed.

I giggle after hearing someone with the same ideas as my father.

"I have several people you must meet." Joe guides me over to three people standing by a baby grand piano.

"Joe, is this our Kfira?" the lady of the group asks. She reaches over, and takes my other hand.

"All grown up." Joe flashes a white, toothy grin.

"You filled out quite nicely. I always thought you were a looker," she whispers into my ear.

"Thank you." I let Joe guide me back to him.

"Miriam, Aaron and Moshe," Joe nods to each, as their names

are said.

Miriam is about Mama's age. She wears a red woolen suit with a red hat topping her grayish white hair. She is a little plump, but would be considered small in shtetl world. Her eyes are bright and smile almost as much as she does.

Aaron is Joe's age. He's tall with wavy, jet black hair and olive skin, and soul piercing eyes the color of dark wood. They somehow make me feel safe.

Moshe is older, maybe in his forties. He contrasts with the other two men. He is pudgy with light brown hair and gray eyes. He sports a full beard and moustache already showing signs of gray.

"We haven't seen you in so long," Aaron he reaches for my hand.

"Did I know you when I was here before?" I ask.

"Yes, you probably don't know this, but I had a crush on you, too. Joe just reached you first."

Feeling my face burn with the heat of the blush, I close my eyes for a second, and open them quickly to see the three still standing before me.

"We're so happy for you and Joe," Moshe speaks.

"Thank you." I watch as the three begin to look a little uneasy.

"Can we take a few minutes to talk alone?" Aaron asks Joe.

"Sure, come in here." Joe grasps my arm, and leads us to the dining room.

Moshe closes the door behind us, and we huddle close to the table.

"These three are a part of the Zionist group," Joe speaks.

"You are the ones who ... ?"

"We're going to help you fulfill your mission," Moshe answers.

"How?"

"We don't know all the details, and even if we did we couldn't say right now. It would be too dangerous for all of us. True, we are in Paris but things happen. This mission is too important to take any chances."

"You're still willing to do this, aren't you?" Miriam looks deep into my eyes.

"In the name of Abraham, Moshe and Elijah; I will do it." I watch as all three sigh with relief.

"You will travel to Casablanca with Joe. At some point in Casablanca Joe will have to go back to the United States on business," Aaron whispers.

"I will be alone?"

"No, not really," Miriam answers.

I nod. I have yet to be alone throughout this whole trip, I understand this won't change. "It won't look suspicious?"

"Not if you have family wherever you go?" Moshe answers.

Aha! So that's how it's going to work. I will travel, always to seek family members who might not be true family members. I can reach Bangkok and then Palestine.

"She knows about the Jade Tiger brooch she is getting from her Aunt Leah." Joe puts his arm around me, as if to trigger my memory.

"You know?" asks Moshe.

I nod affirmation.

"Good, one of us will keep in constant touch."

"We better get back to the party before anyone misses us," Miriam laughs. "I saw Gershon heading for the buffet table. There will be no challah or lox when he is finished."

Everyone laughs.

I'm not sure who he is, but I did see a few rather large man standing around talking to others, as Joe and I met up with the trio. *Maybe I could call them my three musketeers.* Laughing to myself, I feel safer with each passing moment.

The night is filled with gay music, laughing, dancing and eating. I hardly know where to begin with meeting all the new people. Joe is constantly by my side, making introductions.

"Kfira, it's getting late. We don't want you to be late to your own wedding," Jean-Pierre speaks above the music.

Looking at the mantle clock, I see it's almost midnight.

"I don't want to seem rude to the guests."

"I'm sure the guests will understand if you retire early, dear. The wedding is tomorrow, and you will have a full day."

Feeling like a little child being forced to bed early, I sigh and nod in agreement.

"People, people," Jean-Pierre calls out loudly.

Suddenly, the music and dancing stop with all eyes turning toward us.

"We want to thank all of you for coming tonight. The bride

must retire for tomorrow ... " Joe begins.

" ... is the big day," someone calls out.

Everyone chuckles.

"I want to thank everyone for coming tonight. I hope you will be here tomorrow for the wedding. I will see you then." I turn and walk out.

Immediately the music begins to play.

"I will go upstairs ahead of you. You must say good night, as you won't see each other again till the ceremony." Jean-Pierre stands on the first step. With this she turns and walks away.

"You have pleasant dreams." Joe kisses my hand.

I smile and sigh. "You too." Turning to go upstairs, I don't look back. It would only break the romance of it all.

###

I awake with a start the next morning, but it's not fear I feel today but exhilaration.

Deborah runs into the room, we almost collide in front of the bed. She clasps my hands in hers.

"Oh isn't it just the loveliest day?"

"What are you talking about?" I look around the room hastily.

171

Maybe something happened that I didn't know about?

Letting go of my hands, she dashes over to the big bay doors leading out to the balcony, and flings them wide open. "Smell the fresh air. Feel the sun bright and shiny, on your face."

"Deborah, are you all right?" I slip on the dressing gown, and head for the balcony.

"Yes silly, it's your wedding day. Aren't you excited?"

"Yes, I am. I actually slept last night without taking any special medicine. I didn't have any bad dreams."

"Then this is truly a fantastic day." She bounces back into the room, and grabs my arms. Laughing, she tries to get me to dance around the room with her.

"Why are we dancing?"

"Because we're happy."

Sounds like a great reason to me, and I follow her lead until I look over at the clock. The wedding is set for three and it's one o'clock now!

"Don't panic." She lightly pushes my shoulder before pulling away. "We can have you ready in an hour and a half easy. First, I will bring you some food, and run your bath. You will clean up and dress. I will fix your hair and makeup, just like last night."

Yes, it will be like old times. "That sounds great to me," I answer.

Deborah barely hears my answer, as she turns the water on in the tub. As quickly as she arrives, she departs. In a way it feels like the first day all over again, but this time I'm not apprehensive about being here. A serenity that I have not known in a very long time, settles inside me. I'm thankful. I thank HaShem.

Returning with a tray of fruits and toast, Deborah places it on the table she used before. I'm already sitting in the bubbly water, contemplating what will happen after the wedding.

"The party is all set up for after the marriage vows. The same crowd from last night will be here."

"Have you seen Joe? Is he here?"

"He is, and he is overjoyed to be marrying you today."

"Are you sure?"

"Yes."

"He isn't marrying me just so ... " I begin, but I'm unsure if I should even dare ask.

"So what?"

"So, I will go get the Torah?"

Giggling, Deborah pushes at my shoulder lightly. "No, he would still be marrying you no matter what." She shrugs her shoulders and announces, "he loves you". She jumps up, and goes back into the other room.

Instead of her idle chatter, she is singing. Her melodies are so lovely, and sweet that I can think only good thoughts. I dream of the moment the rabbi will announce us man and wife, and Joe breaks the glass.

###

"Are you ready?" Jean-Pierre steps into my room.

Deborah has only seconds before finished with the hair and makeup on both of us.

"Yes." I pivot about in the chair and stand.

"Oh my." Jean-Pierre gazes at me, searching up and down for flaws. "You're breathtaking."

"Isn't she?"

"Deborah." I try to prevail an air of modesty. I can't, I feel like I could command many men with my looks, or something like that. I think I read that in a book about someone in the past.

"I have something for you," Jean-Pierre says, as Catana enters the room.

Catana carries a long cream colored lace.

"Thank you, Catana." Jean-Pierre takes it from her and Catana leaves. "This is for you. We can't cover our faces with a veil, but we can cover our heads." Jean-Pierre places the cloth on my head.

It was something my own Mama would have done for me. I wish she and Papa were here to see me marry.

"Don't cry or you will smear your makeup," Deborah warns.

"Okay." I turn to and give her a wink.

"It's time," Catana says, as she pops her head back into the room. She is gone again.

"Let's go." I grasp an arm from Jean-Pierre and Deborah, and stroll toward the hall. I know I'm walking, but it almost feels as if I'm floating. Everyone has their best faces forward. I feel the sunshine on my face even though I know we are in the house, and not facing any windows.

At the bottom of the stairs, Catana is holding a bouquet of

flowers. It's as if I'm not really here, but watching from upstairs. My eyes blur, as my palms sweat. Catana places them in my shaking hands. My palms are so wet that I fear the flowers will take root and grow around them. I try to notice the others, but the next thing I know we are standing next to Joe, in front of the rabbi.

"Are we ready to start the ceremony?" The rabbi asks.

"Yes," Jean-Pierre answers.

Deborah transfers the flowers into her hands. Jean-Pierre and Deborah step back. She winks.

It's hard to believe that last night there was a party in this room. It's set up for a wedding with everything including the chuppah!

I'm terrified, as I become conscious that this is real. I glimpse Joe in the corner of my eye, and his grin tells me everything. The rabbi seems like a nice enough fellow. He's Joe's age. Short with dark hair and eyes. His yarmulka slides down his balding head several times. After each instance, he gracefully catches it, and places it squarely back in its rightful place.

At one time I knew the prayers for the marriage ceremony by

heart from going to so many weddings; but today it's as if I'm hearing them said for the first time. I try to listen, but it feels as if the blood is rushing into my ears. I'm so warm and happy inside, I know that at some point it will bubble to the outside. I will gush.

Joe slides a ring on my finger, and saying words of love to me and HaShem loud enough for all the room to hear. I do the same for him. Looking deep into his eyes, I feel a love that I have only dreamed of.

"Now you must break the glass so that your family will forever be in peace." The rabbi hands a small white cloth to Joe.

Joe positions the cloth covered glass off in an area where no one might accidentally step on it, and smashes it.

Clapping and yelling "YYYEEEAAAHHH!!!"

Joe leans over, and grabs me in his arms, kissing me. His lips are soft and moist against mine.

"I love you," he whispers.

"I love you too."

"Let's have a party," someone calls out.

The Road to Casablanca

The band plays on.

"Would you like to dance, my sweet wife?" Joe pulls me

aside.

Wife, I am a wife, everything is happening so fast that I can

hardly believe it's true. I'm afraid that at any point I will wake

up and be back home. Or worse yet, having a nightmare of the

rape. My heart quickens, and I remind myself to breathe. "Yes, I

would love to dance with my husband." Joe picks me up, and

carries me over to one of the two chairs that are waiting for us in

the middle of the room. Placing me on the chair, he takes his spot

in the other.

From out of nowhere, eight large, well-dressed men hoist the

chairs into the air. Everyone sing boisterously, as the men dance

us around the room.

I can hardly catch my breath from laughing so hard. It feels as

if I'm on top of the world. My stomach muscles begin to ache,

and despite painstakingly trying not to mess up my makeup with tears, they flow naturally from all the belly laughs. It feels as if the music is playing directly into my ears.

I watch as Joe waves his arms around, and gracefully moves his shoulders in a dancing motion. Klezmer music plays in the background. A grin never leaves his face even when the men almost drop him by the buffet table.

We dance around in circles for several dances until my head and heart spin faster than the men twirling the chair. Everything whirls past me, and I dread falling to the ground in front of all these people. I know I will land on my tucas with my dress over my head. I tap one of the men on the shoulder, and point to the floor.

"Are you all right?" he asks, a worried expression on his face.

"I'm getting a little dizzy, maybe I should have something to drink," I try to speak over the music.

He gestures to the others to put me down. Quickly, my feet touch floor once more, and I'm thankful. No one prepared me for a ride such as this one, the room starts to spin again, and I blink several times to refocus.

Looking over at Joe, I observe him telling them lower his

chair as well.

"Are you okay?" Joe runs to my side, and he puts his arms around me.

"I think I need to eat or drink something. It ... " I smile, "took my breath away."

Joe beams and pulls me closer. "That's what marriage does to you, makes you dizzy. Let's get something to eat." With this he pulls me to my feet, and helps me to the table.

I sit down, and look around at all the people. Tonight, more people are milling about than last night.

"I will get you a plate. You stay right here, and someone will bring you a glass of wine. Don't say no, I know you will like the wine and the pampering. Enjoy it while you can because after the honeymoon you will get to pamper me." Joe winks and gives me a soft kiss on the cheek.

I touch his cheek, and it feels so warm against my hand. I nod, and think about all the work expected from an orthodox married woman. I pray I can do it all.

He steps away.

"Was that a fun ride or what?" Deborah pops out of nowhere,

and takes a seat beside me.

Taking a deep breath in and slowly exhaling out, I giggle. How do I explain what all this excitement is doing for my imagination? In a way I feel like a fish out of water, but in other ways, not.

Eyeing Deborah up and down, I notice someone has placed little flowers here and there in her hair, making her stunning. "I have watched and helped but never ... "

"... had the ride?" Deborah finishes.

"Yes," I answer.

"Jean-Pierre has written a note to your parents, and will send them a picture of you with Joe. They'll get it in a couple of days. They know you are safe and sound," Deborah states, as she watches the others. She pretends to make small talk when anyone ventures too closely.

"I tried to write them a note yesterday. I didn't finish it, but could you make sure they get it?" I ask.

"Oh yes, I think Casablanca will be quite lovely this time of year. With the French influence anything can be made elegant," Deborah says, as several large women in dark blue walk by.

"I agree and it's so near the ocean. I love the ocean, don't you?"

"Yes, I'll see it many times this summer."

The two women move on.

"I will make sure that Jean-Pierre gets it."

"I have no idea what is going to happen next," I state, as Joe places a plate full of food in front of me.

"Why you get to go on a honeymoon with me." Joe sets a plate in front of the chair beside me. He takes a seat, and leans over to kiss me.

"I know that silly, but I know nothing else."

"Well, after we leave here tonight," Joe begins.

"We leave here tonight?"

"Yes, it will be rather late when we go," Joe answers.

"How are we going to get to Casablanca?"

"A driver will drive us to Spain. We will catch a boat that will take us to Morocco, and from there we will drive from Tangiers to Casablanca. I know a nice little place to stay, as I have stayed there before."

"I haven't even packed."

"I have done it for you." Deborah picks a strawberry from my plate.

"When will we leave?"

"Probably around 1 A.M. when all the other guests are leaving."

"Doesn't Kfira look exquisite tonight?" Deborah asks, as a couple of tall men in black suits walk by.

"I have never seen a more enchanting bride than mine." Joe reaches down, and takes my hand in his. He kisses it with his supple lips.

Looking dreamily into his eyes, I believe I can melt into him. My breathing calms, but I can still feel my heart beating faster than the drum of the band.

"Eat, I want a healthy wife."

I look down on my plate to see some very non-French foods such as challah, roasted lamb, potato blintzes, baked vegetables and fruit. Everything looks so good. I try to take small bites, as people roam by and offer their congratulations. I find it difficult to talk to someone while I'm eating, but it's all part of the wedding.

The room becomes clearer to me, and I'm unsure if it's the food, or just the realization that I might not see this room for a long time. The colors the people are wearing come alive. It's easy to get caught up in the swirling motion as their owners' dance around in front of us.

"I'm going to go find Tom." Deborah stands to leave, her eyes never stop scanning the room. "I will talk to you two later."

"Are you nervous? Because I am?"

"A little."

"I promise everything will be fine."

"I know it will, with you."

###

It's one in the morning, and people are leaving. At times it seemed like the night would go on forever. People sing at the tops of their lungs, as they take off to their cars.

"I have the note," I say, to Deborah, as she helps me put on my traveling clothes. Pulling it from my handbag, I hand it to her. "I finished it when I excused myself to use the bathroom."

Shaking her head, Deborah touches my hair, and pulls my face toward hers. "You're starting to become the clever girl I used to know."

I giggle. *Was I ever a clever girl?* It seems so long ago that I boarded the train that changed my life. It started my journey to becoming a clever girl. Maybe I was all along, and just didn't know it.

The bags are already in the car, and the driver is waiting for us. Slipping my coat on, I can hear Jean-Pierre giving instructions of what to do with the wedding dress. "We must hurry and get you out of here as the traffic can't die down before you leave."

I nod in understanding.

"I have this for you to put on your coat lapel. You must wear it at all times somewhere on your body. Joe has your papers. He will let you have them when he must return to America. Keep them safe. I want you to be brave. We hope to be able to help you if something bad happens but who knows? Take care and I expect to see your babies crawling up and down those stairs just like Elijah did." She pins the brooch to my lapel.

It's an emerald colored tiger with black stripes and gold eyes. It is big enough to catch an eye, but not big enough to attract attention.

Elijah! I tried several times to talk to him, but people would stop to talk to me. He kissed me on the cheek after the ceremony, but that seems like days ago.

"May I see him?"

"You will."

"We must go." Joe enters the room.

We all stroll down the hallway and stairs, acting as if this is any other day, and November 16, 1938.

Joe helps me into the car. I notice someone sitting across from me, Elijah.

"I'm so glad to see you." I reach over, and kiss his cheek.

"We will be traveling as long as we can, or until the driver becomes sleepy. Then we will find a place to stop. For now I think all of us should get some rest," Joe suggests.

I want to protest, but I realize that with all of the excitement I'm getting sleepy. Snuggling up into Joe's waiting arms, let the hum of the car ease my mind.

###

"Wake up darling," Joe whispers in my ear.

Jumping up, I tumble into the floorboard. I glance around, and realize that I'm in a moving car.

"Where are we?" I ask.

"We are near the border of France and Spain. We're going to stop, and find a place to get something to eat. Another driver will take over. We must keep moving," Joe answers.

"We're near Lourdes," Elijah volunteers.

"And the Pyrenees mountains," adds Joe.

"Is this why my head feels so stuffy?" My ears feel as if they are full of wool, and about to explode. I shake my head to relieve the pressure, but nothing seems to work. Clamping my hands tightly around them, I pop them several times. Nothing.

My two companions cackle like chickens, as both clutch their sides.

"Why are you laughing at me?"

"We aren't laughing at you. We are laughing with you," Joe pats my knee.

"Here we are," Elijah says, as the car pulls into the parking lot of what looks like a quaint little inn.

It's a rooming house on the third and fourth floors, with a

place to eat on the second.

"Is this the place?" the driver asks, from the front.

"Yes, this is it."

On the front is a small wooden sign hanging from a small flagpole "Le Chateau".

Seems easy enough to remember.

We get out of the car and head inside. Immediately a man walks over to us, and asks us something in French.

His slick backed brown hair and upturned moustache is larger than his small stature. He wears a white shirt with a blue black vest and a red bow tie.

"Oui," Joe answers with a hint of a French accent.

Following the man, he seats us at a table in the corner and disappears. He quickly returns with bread and water to fill the glasses in front of us.

I take a quick look at my new husband, and can't help but to know there are many mysteries between us. *How will I ever learn them all?*

"Isn't it wonderful here?" Elijah asks, as if he travels here all the time.

"Yes, it is."

"I will order for us since I don't think either of you read or speak French," Joe states.

"Actually, I know enough to know how to order from the menu," Elijah confesses.

We both stare at him with a look of shock on our faces.

"A friend of mine moved from here three years ago. He taught me French, and I taught him Yiddish. He was always wanting to know what the old yentas were saying about him," Elijah chuckles.

"And were they?" Joe asks.

"Were they what?"

"Talking about him?"

"Sometimes. He was always doing things they didn't understand, like chasing chickens. Drinking from the cows' udders when he got thirsty. One time he stole Minkava's pie off the windowsill, and she let out such a string of words even I didn't understand." Elijah's eyes light up, as he tells the Tale.

"What is your friend's name?" I ask.

"Jean-Claude."

"Jean-Claude sounds as if he might be a bit of trouble, a little headstrong." I take a piece of bread from the bread basket, and break it into bite size pieces.

"You're a Mama for how many days, and already you're giving him a hard time? His friend sounds like someone else we all know and love." Joe winks at me.

"Am I that bad?"

"Well, Bubbe says you ask more questions than anyone she has ever known."

Feeling a little self-conscious, I gaze around the room to see many people entering Le Chateau. It's very popular.

The waiter returns to take the order, and I excuse myself for a few minutes. I must find the necessary room. I'm thankful for the pictures on the doors so I won't get lost.

Returning to the table, I find the food has just arrived.

We eat our meal in silence with each of us in our own thoughts. Occasionally, Joe squeezes my knee under the table. Elijah gives me a wide grin. When we are done, Joe pays and we leave.

An older man dressed in a heavy gray wool coat and cap

stands by the car. His black pants are a little too long, but he appears not to notice.

"Ready?" he asks in a heavy Spanish accent.

"Yes." Joe helps Elijah and me into the car.

I look out the window to see snow covered tall mountains in the distance. The snow reflects the sunlight and warms the air.

"It will take a little time to get over those but we should be in Spain soon."

"It's quite lovely." I watch the timberline pass us by along the road. I'm careful because I know this is what usually puts me to sleep.

Without warning, a loud bang and pop echoes throughout the mountains. The car spins around and around. Peeking from window to window, all I can see is the edge of the mountain coming towards us. A scream leaps from my mouth. I reach out try to grasp anything that might keep me from slamming face down into the floorboard.

I can barely hear Joe yell to hold on tight, as the screeching tires, and honking horns from a passing truck deafen my ears. I roll myself up in a ball with my hands hiding my face. The blood swooshing in my ears carry out the beat of my heart. I listen to the glass shatter, as little slivers hit against my back and head.

The car shifts to the right, and tumbles once, twice and a third lands it in an upright position next to a tree. We slam together, and several times I feel someone's body collapse on top of me. I pray that we'll all survive. Someone is screaming, but until the car rests on its tires, I don't recognize it's me.

My hand is trapped under Joe. Elijah is moaning, but still moving around. I peek to see where the driver is but there is no one in the driver's seat. *Did I go blank? Where is he?*

"Are you hurt?" I ask to anyone who can answer.

No answer.

Everyone moves in slow motion. Elijah shakes his head, and attempts to stand.

"You can't stand," I say without thinking.

"I ... for a minute I wasn't sure where I was," Elijah confesses.

"Here let me help you," someone says from the outside. It's the man from the truck. He forcefully pulls at the door to open it.

It creaks and groans, metal grinding against metal until the door opens ajar. With the strength of three men, he grasps the door in his large hands. It gives way to his force, and opens all the way.

"What happened?" Joe starts to come around.

"Looks like something blew out your tire." The stranger points to one of the flattened tires. Just as he says this the other three begin to go flat.

The stranger takes hold of each of us by the arms, and helps pull us out. I steal a look to see the stranger's face as he takes my arm. He looks like my brother Isaac, and as if by instinct I say nothing about the uncanny similarities. He is a little shorter than Elijah with black hair graying around the temples, and blue eyes. His brown jacket barely covers his belly but it fits him somehow.

We shake the broken glass from our coats and hair, ever so careful so as not to get cut.

"Are we all okay?" Joe asks.

"Where is the driver?" I shake off my snow covered coat. It must have came in through the broken windows as we made our tumble.

"I think he's dead." The stranger glares over toward a body that is about twenty meters from the car. He must have been thrown out.

Running over to look at him, I squat down to check for breathing. Nothing. I have to do something, but what? I'm unsure of what to do next.

"We must get you out of here," I hear the stranger whisper to Joe. "We must put your things in my truck now, and leave before others arrive."

Without saying anymore the men walk over to the car, they take our three bags from it. Putting them in the back of the truck, they signal to me that it's time to leave.

Joe marches over to me, and seizes my shoulders.

"We have to go".

"But -- "

"He's dead." Joe leans down, and pulls the body toward us. In the back of his head is a small hole. "We must go now."

Almost knocking him down, I leap to my feet and run toward the truck and Elijah. I'm stunned and petrified now. I feel like a sitting duck on the water. The snow tries to knock me back down, but I can't let it. I must be on the truck.

Joe and Elijah almost throw me into the back of the truck

before they themselves crawl inside. The stranger tightens up the flaps. It's dark instantly.

"Come this way," Joe whispers to us, as we make our way to the front.

Turning on a little lantern, we can see many large, overstuffed cushions all over the floorboard. We can rest upon them.

"Is this the danger you spoke of?" I ask.

"I had hoped we would be out of Europe before it began, but yes, this is what I feared."

Not knowing what to say, I feel terrified for us. For Elijah. For Joe. For the dead driver we left by the side of the road.

I take in a deep breath and exhale slowly. A prayer comes to my lips, and I whisper it softly.

"Are we all okay?" Joe holds the lantern up, and everyone including Joe is inspected for injuries.

It's a miracle, we're all uninjured.

"Here we come Casablanca," Joe laughs, as he pulls Elijah and me toward him in a warm hug.

Barcelona and the Boat

Everything seems so real with no turning back. A man is dead. My brothers-in-law are in a German jail or German hell? Many others are dead. My whole world is turning upside down like the car. East Prussia, Mama and Papa, the Baltic Sea and all of my little students, seem like a distant memory somehow.

I'm beyond fear. Joe keeps my hands in his to warm them. The back of the truck is very cold. I wish I had the three dresses on that I was wearing when I started out from home in.

No one talks. We're all so deep into our own thoughts. We huddle together for the warmth, and the light of the little lantern.

The truck ride isn't as smooth as the car ride. Every bump and jerk jostles us around like a mama dog, angry at her pups.

I still see the look of the man's face as he helped us. He resembles my brother like a twin. Terror grips my heart, and I think of my family once more. *Can they truly be all right? What will Hannah do without Josef? Samuel is a good provider, but Esther keeps animals and grows vegetables and such. She can take care of herself and her little family.*

For the first time since I saw the Rebbe sitting in the living room, I experience intense terror.

"It's almost too quiet," Joe says.

I nod, unsure if anyone can see my face.

"We'll be in Barcelona in a few hours." Joe speaks loud enough to hear without yelling.

It's so noisy, one can barely hear the other person speak.

"Do you still have the papers?" I find my tongue wanting to ask many questions, but I know I should only ask a few. I must save my strength.

"Yes, our bags are over here." He reaches behind us.

They are there, three different colored carpetbags. The coloring and wear is a little different on each, so we can tell them apart. They are ours.

'Do you know this man?' I want to ask but don't. Barcelona seems out of the way for where we're going.

"I'm sleepy," Elijah says, after about thirty minutes of being bounced around.

"Go ahead and lie down," Joe encourages him. Leaning over

to the other side of the truck, Joe brings out several blankets, and hands one to Elijah. He wraps the other one around us, huddling us together.

"I'm sorry about the honeymoon," Joe whispers, once we hear Elijah's slight snore.

I giggle softly. "This isn't it?"

"You're the silly one now." Joe touches my nose with his index finger. "Boop."

I chuckle again, and flutter my eyelashes.

"I can do this," and with this, he kisses me longingly on the lips. I taste the sweetness of his mouth. His arms wrap tightly around me and mine, him.

Lying back against the pillows, we kiss long, slow kisses. His hot breath is on my cheek and neck, as he peppers little kisses along a trail.

It feels like feathers brushing against me, and I don't want him to stop. But I'm afraid we will awaken Elijah.

"It'll be okay. I only want to hold and kiss you. Maybe you should get some rest." Joe kisses my forehead.

I reach up, and stroke his cheek ever so gently. "Okay," I

answer.

Joe whispers "I love you."

"I love you."

He holds me so close it feels, as if I will disappear inside of his arms. It's the warmest place I have been since I was a small child. I feel safe and before I know it I feel sleepy.

###

"Wake up." Elijah pulls at our shoulders.

The truck comes to a halt. It starts moving, and prattles on for a few more meters. It stops, and the engine is off. A door opens and shuts.

"We're here." Joe jumps up, and gathers our bags beside us.

Suddenly the stranger pops his head into the canvas opening. "We're here. You must get out quickly."

Pulling our bags and ourselves to the edge of the truck, we are silent.

The stranger helps Elijah out, and gives him his bag, as well as Joe's. Elijah shifts his bag to the other hand before accepting Joe's. Joe leaps out of the truck, and twists around to help me out. Taking my bag, he hands it to Elijah. Placing his hands on my waist, he lifts me out and sets me down beside Elijah.

I gaze over at the stranger who is trying to hide his face underneath his beret. It's my brother! I recognize the scarf Mama made for him for Chanukah three years ago. Surely there aren't two scarves alike?

"Thank you so much for the ride," Joe begins.

"You're welcome. You'll be able to catch a boat from here." He keeps his face away from me, as he lifts his hand up to adjust his hat, I see nothing.

I know I must say nothing, but I'm thankful it's him. I pray he will let Mama and Papa know that we're safe. I smile and nod his way. It's all I can do to keep from running over to him, and giving him a big hug. I know that it might get us both killed. My thoughts race back to the dead man on the side of the road, and I shudder involuntarily.

We look to see we're at a Marina.

The stranger slips something into Joe's hands before he takes off.

"Help me." Joe begins to smooth out the area where the tire tracks left impressions in the snow.

We all begin to kick at the ruts, filling in the depressions.

Soon the area appears as smooth as a fresh snow. I feel funny,

but not the laughing funny. For once in my life, I don't chuckle

or giggle because I'm petrified.

"Okay." He turns to look at the different boats in the slips. He

takes our bags, and heads toward them.

The slips are numbered along the pier, and each slip nestles a

vessel inside. Not one is empty. Small boats take up the front,

and larger ones are on the far end. Some look almost new with

sails tied down for bad weather. Others are old and in desperate

need of repair. All in all, it's a harbor like many others except

there is no one in sight.

"Which one are we looking for?" Elijah asks.

"I have an old friend here who will take us to where we need

to go," Joe answers.

We walk down the well worn, wooden planks, glimpsing at

the boats as we go. Fishermen and others tread a steady path

upon them.

This is the sea. I know the sea. The salty air wafts under my

nose, and almost makes me sneeze. It reminds me of home. A

thin fog blows in, and gives off an eerie appearance to the harbor.

We're almost at the end of the pier when a man pops out of the hull on the last boat on the left.

"Ahoy! There you are, Joe man." A raspy calls out before a man walks up to the edge of the boat. His face is covered in white fur that is supposed to be a beard and moustache, but actually gives the impression that he has no skin except around his eyes. He is smiling so widely that you can barely see his dark eyes. He wears a large dark blue coat, and a captain's hat. His gray pants are stained and baggy while his large feet stand firm. He looks so comical it's difficult to keep from laughing out loud.

"Ahoy there, John man," Joe calls back.

"Are you ready for an adventure?"

My eyes grow wide as I realize that we really will be on this boat and in this water. The boat is an older model with three large sails, and a crow's nest. The deck's wood looks as if it was new several hundred years ago. The sides must have been white at one time, but are now a dingy gray with barnacles hanging here and there.

Anxiety fills me till I'm almost blind with it, but I try to smile despite everything. Mustn't be afraid now. Many people are going through much worse things than I am, right now.

"I'm first." Elijah leaps across the break between the water and the boat.

"Okay." I shrug a surrender. It's difficult not to smile at this man before us as he seems so original.

If we were at home, he might be any one of the number of fishermen from the village. Just another sea lover trying to make a living.

Joe gets onboard next. Setting the bags down, he spins around to help me.

"My name is John, actually you can call me Johnny." He holds out a hand to me.

"Kfira," I take his warm hand, shaking it as best I can considering how cold it's getting.

"You'll be warm here in a minute." Johnny turns his attention to Elijah. "And who be ye?"

"Elijah." Elijah his hand out.

They shake hands and Johnny grasps Elijah's in both hands, in a manly manner.

"You all must be chilled to the bone." Johnny points to the hull. "Go down below, and get ye something warm to drink. It's mighty warm once ye get out of the wind."

Joe pushes us toward the door to the cabin.

I open the door and go inside. It's actually quite cozy inside compared to what the outside of the boat looks like. The door opens up into a small kitchen with a long table and bench on the backside. It's connected to two smaller side benches. Food and tea are set out on the stovetop.

Three other doors are in the back. Dark curtains adorn several windows. Despite several large lanterns, the room is gloomy with all the dark wood and green clothe.

"This is nice," I say unexpectedly.

Laughing, Joe gazes at me and winks. "Only the finest for my bride."

I sit down and soak up the atmosphere. It's warm in here, and I decide to take my coat off. I remove the brooch from my lapel, and place it on the right side of my dress close the shoulder.

Joe notices and winks once more.

"Is there any food there, me matie," Elijah asks, in his best pirate voice with one eye closed.

"Aye, aye matie." Joe sniggers.

"Can ye bring some to a wee landlubber?"

I start to cackle.

"Are ye sure ye be hungry? We be on wet land pretty soon," Joe spouts.

I realize we are already moving across the water. Glaring out the window, I can't see the marina anymore. We must be moving rather quickly, but Johnny is right, the wind is blowing and it's cold.

"Here ye go." Joe hands us cups of tea, and then places a plate of food before us.

It looks like stew, but I'm not sure till I take a bite. At home I have always been strictly Kosher, but it has been difficult to be observant since I left. Yes, it's stew. The flavors are a little spicy, and make my mouth water.

Elijah and I grab up our tea at the same time and drink.

"Yeah, he likes to make it a little on the spicy side. It's a trick he learned in India."

"It's very good," I remark. I really want to say 'are we safe now?' But I don't. I eat stew with my husband and son, and make an effort to feel safe.

Other questions mill about in my head, but I know this isn't the place or time to ask them. Maybe some day when all of this is said and done, it will be time.

###

When we finish eating, Joe puts the plates into a small sink. It's good to have our bellies full and our bladders empty. We have all made the trips to the necessary room by now. It's the middle door.

"Now, I must take my bride to the honeymoon suite." Joe winks at Elijah. "Are you feeling secure?"

Elijah nods and grabs his bag. "I have something to read, and if nothing else -- " He pulls open the cabinet door we accidentally opened earlier, and points to the dozen or more books inside.

"Please yell if you need anything." I squeeze his hand.

"Don't worry about me. I'll be all right. HaShem will keep me safe."

Yes, HaShem will keep him so.

We stroll into the little room, and close the door behind us. A small lamp not too far from a bed along the wall lights it. A hammock takes up space on the other. It's easy to observe a masculine touch to it.

Joe puts our bags down and turns to me.

"I don't want you to be afraid." He runs his fingers through my hair, taking out the pins I have holding it in place. It falls out of the bun, and topples about my shoulders. "I love you." He kisses me smoothly on the mouth, and I feel warm and tingly inside.

I don't want him to stop. He kisses my eyes and cheeks, and then my mouth. His arms hold me so closely, I know I will stop breathing. I'm melting into him. His lips are on my neck, kissing the pulsating spots that say I'm alive.

I hold my breath, as I feel him remove one arm so he can take off his jacket and tie. He flips them over to the hammock. He kisses me, and his hands reach up to the front of the dress and feel my breasts, heaving against him.

I'm so scared, but I want to make love to my husband.

Feeling around the back of the dress, he pulls the zipper down and helps me shrug off the dress. He places it over on the hammock with his clothing.

The kisses begin again. And again more clothing is removed until he is standing naked before me and I, him. At first I'm shy. No man has seen me completely naked ever. I shake my head and giggle in fear.

"Are you okay?"

"I'm a little scared." I cover my breasts with my hands. Wetness forms in my eyes, as I tell myself it will be all right.

"Don't be. I will be gentle."

I nod.

"Put your arms around me."

I reach up, and wrap my arms around his neck. He pulls his body closer to me with his arms around my waist.

"You're so beautiful."

I feel the redness on my cheeks and neck.

He bends his head down, and suckles my nipple. My heart skips several beats before it starts beating faster I have ever felt. I yearn for him to kiss me and touch me all over.

He lifts his head up and picks me up. Carrying me over to the bed, he lays me down. He lies down beside me.

We make love. He's so gentle, taking his time so as not to frighten me. When it's over, he holds me tightly.

"I love you."

"I love you."

"I promise to keep you safe."

"I know." I also know that as wonderful as those words might sound, it's also up to me to keep us safe. I have to be aware of everything and everyone, from now on. I pray that this craziness will not last forever, but I worry it will.

"We better put our clothes on." I say without thinking. With so many surprises happening, modesty prevents me from being caught naked by anyone other than Deborah or Joe.

"Yes, you're probably right," Joe remarks, and gets up. He helps me up, and then hands me the clothing from the hammock.

It doesn't take but a few minutes to dress and sit back on the bed.

"Are you tired?" Joe asks.

"Just a little. I was just starting to get rested from the train ride when we started this honeymoon."

"It isn't so easy to sleep in a train or the back of a truck," Joe says.

"No, but it's worth it." I lean up to give him a kiss on his lips. So many times in my shtetl, I would hear the young brides complain about their wedding night. It's always the same, so painful. 'Thank HaShem, it's over rather quickly.' I'm thankful of my American husband who treats me differently.

"Why don't you rest, and I will go get you something to drink. I will see how Johnny is doing with getting us to Africa."

I nod.

He opens the door and quickly exits. He is back in what seems like two seconds with a warm cup of tea. "Elijah is reading a book."

"Oh good."

"Here you go. I will be back. Get some rest." Joe kisses me on the forehead, and then he's gone again.

I lie back down on the bed with the cup in my hands to warm them. It's unnecessary as making love has left me quite warm. I pray that we all will be safe in this journey. I finish the tea, and before I can think too much, I'm close to sleep.

###

I awaken to see the sun shining brightly in through the window. At first I don't know where I am. Looking around, I feel a little dizzy but decide to take it easy and not get up too quickly.

Easing myself out of bed, I walk over to the door and cautiously open it. I almost want to slap myself for having so much trepidation. *What if I walk out there and everyone is dead? What if ... ?*

"Are you awake?" Elijah spies me from the top of the book he is reading.

Smiling, I saunter in, and close the door behind me.

"Did you get a nice sleep?" Johnny asks from the door.

"Aye, Aye Captain," I say, with a salute that makes all of us burst out laughing.

"We thought you'd fallen into the sleep shark. Nah, ye need ye rest, ye do." Johnny walks over to the table, and sits down with his cup in hand.

Elijah bursts into more laughter.

"Nah, just a little honeymooning will put the sleep on ye.

Makes ye relaxed and easier to mind."

I can't help but to giggle now.

"Glad to see ye has a sense of humor."

"Where is Joe?" I realize he is the only one not here.

"He's driving the boat," Johnny says matter-of-factly.

"Huh?"

"Yep, taught him everything he knows about this ole boat. He can drive so I can get me some sleep. He tells me that ye need to stay below."

I must have a puzzled look on my face as Johnny shakes his head. "It's just safer, that's all. Used to be thought that women were bad luck on the open seas. I think they's men who need to be getting some women."

That brought on another bout of laughter.

"Now, if ye don't mind, I thinks I need to catch some shuteye." With this, Johnny rises, and stumbles over to the sink to place his cup inside. He makes his way over to the other door, and makes his way inside.

"Did you get any sleep?"

"Yes." Elijah answers, but I can tell from the circles around his eyes that it isn't much.

"Are you okay?"

Elijah gazes at me, and without saying a word I know he is. He is struggling as I am with the years of deceit, and the new dangers lurking at every corner.

"I'm sorry that I didn't remember everything before now."

"I know."

"I would have never given you away if ... ." I reach over, and grasp his hand tightly.

"Mama."

"Yes."

"It will be all right."

Something in the way he says this makes me know he is right. I feel it even with all the danger around us. I know we are protected.

On The Water

Looking back out of the window, I wonder what day it is in the world. When I started this adventure it was November 6th, 1938. *How many days ago has it been?*

"What are you thinking about?"

"Something silly."

Elijah's eyes widen.

"I was just wondering what day it is. I know this is silly but Chanukah is fast approaching. It shouldn't be thrown away just because our lives are in a little chaos."

"I don't think it will be much of a Chanukah this year."

"Well, think about it this way. Here you and I are, ready to defend our people. At least you are here for part of it anyway. What did the Maccabees do? They led a war against the Greeks in 168 B.C.E. They won the right to be Jews. Yes, everyone focuses on the miracle of the oil burning for eight days instead of one. We should really focus on the religious freedom we received. It's so important to be allowed to believe as you desire, and not forced to accept as true what someone else does."

He looks pensive for a second. "So this means I won't be getting any presents?"

Punching him lightly in the arm, I giggle. "What sort of present are you hoping for?"

"I want to see the Statue of Liberty."

I frown, the Statue of Liberty is so far away from ... . I want to say here, but I don't know where here is much less if I would rather be one place or another. "That is a tall order."

"I know, but Joe is an American. Maybe when this is all over, we can go to New York City to see her."

It dawns on me that this is true. I'm guessing this is how we were able to get new papers that don't give away our whole identity. The people think we are Americans instead of just Jews.

A knock on the door shakes me awake from my thoughts.

"Who would be knocking?"

"Why don't you look," Elijah answers.

I get up slowly, and amble over to the door. *Johnny is asleep in one of the bedrooms. Joe is driving the boat. Who?*

Another rap, rat-a-tat-tat.

"Come in." I huddle closer to Elijah, ready to leap in front of him to protect him.

Walking in, Aaron and my brother Isaac race over to me.

Without saying a word, I run from one to the other, giving them big hugs.

Isaac chuckles loudly. "You would think you hadn't seen me since 1936, you crazy girl!"

"Isaac!"

Isaac is the one with the sense of humor in the boys. He is the youngest boy, and he was born before Hannah, who was born before me. He is a few inches taller than me and well built. His hair is a light brown with hazel eyes. He sports a full beard and moustache. His clothing mismatches him, he wears faded blue pants and a striped shirt under his large coat. Something is not quite right, he isn't wearing a yarmulka!

I don't think I have ever seen any of my brothers without the little black circles sitting lazily on their heads, but here he is, without. Never have I seen so many men without yarmulkas, it's only a reminder to me that I'm not in the shtetl.

"Aaron." I turn toward the dark man. I recollect meeting him long ago, when I was so young. I thought him quite handsome, and he hasn't changed a bit.

###

"Aren't you going to introduce me to your friend?" Aaron asks, as he and Joe stroll into Jean-Pierre's parlor.

I'm sitting on the floor with the baby on a large blanket. The baby is lying on his stomach looking, as if he might start to crawl despite his being too young. He isn't making much progress when the two walk in.

"This is Kfira," Joe answers.

"Nice to meet you Kfira. Is this your nephew?"

"This is my son".

"He sure is a beautiful baby." Aaron and Joe go upstairs.

###

If my memories keep coming back I might be astounded at how brave I have been all these years without even knowing it.

I look at my big brother, and I can't stop grinning.

"So you are a married lady now? I knew it would happen sooner or later."

Scrunching up my face, I can't stop the words from tumbling from my mouth. "Are Mama and Papa okay?"

Aaron sits down beside Elijah, and glances over at the book he is reading.

Isaac sits me down. Pulling up beside me, and his puts arms around me.

"What is it?" I choke back the tears I fear will tumble out and leave me restless. The air is getting thinner, and I can hardly breathe. My eyes grow dim. *What can I do if something has happened? Nothing. I'm on the other side of the world as far as they are concerned.*

"Papa," Isaac swallows loudly "is dead."

"What?"

"I can't tell you all the details but I can tell you this much."

"I need to -- "

"No, you don't need to know. Nothing you can do to change it. I can tell you that everyone else is safe."

I don't understand. How can this be? Does this have anything to do with Josef and Samuel being detained? Or was it just his inability and unwillingness to change with the world around him? I hope to know, some day.

Isaac pulls me closer, and buries my face in his chest.

218

Noiseless tears streak down my cheeks and onto my hands. Somehow I have them folded in front of me face, I go numb. I can't really say my life has been any less dangerous since leaving home, but it has been different.

"I am so sorry," Aaron says.

"My Papa."

"Papa."

"What is the world coming to?" I throw up my hands to the heavens. I wipe away the tears just as Joe comes in.

"I would have been here sooner, but I had to help Moshe with the boat."

With this Isaac gives me one big squeeze, and then stands up so that Joe can take his place.

Joe pulls my face toward his, and kisses my wet cheek. "I'm so sorry." He wraps his arms around me so tightly I almost can't breathe.

"I love my Papa."

"I know."

"I want him to be alive."

"I know."

We all sit there for what seems like eternity, but is probably only a few minutes.

"I want to show you something." Joe pulls back slightly.

"What?" I wipe away at the tears once more.

"Africa."

I had almost forgotten all about going to Casablanca. All I can feel is grief for my Papa, and Joe brings reality back to light. At first I want to be angry with him, and the diversion. I remind myself I can't let my Papa's death be in vain.

Joe pulls away the curtain, and sure enough there is land. Trees can be seen in the distance, outlining the shoreline.

"When will we land?" I ask.

"WOW!" Elijah plasters his face to the small porthole almost smashing his nose flat as he does so.

Looking over at him, I snicker, and push lightly on his shoulder.

"We can't land until we at least get to Tangiers. We might try to go all the way to Casablanca on this cruiser," Joe answers.

I can't believe it's Africa.

"They say large communities of Jews are building up there,"

Isaac says nonchalantly.

"Really?" Elijah asks.

"Things are getting pretty heated up in Europe for them."

And us, I add to myself, but don't say out loud. We all know it's dangerous times. We also feel that heat. Even when I have my head in the clouds, I know this truth.

"Then you must know," I say turning to Isaac and Aaron who are now sitting side by side.

"Know what?" Aaron asks.

"What day it is?"

Everyone cracks up laughing as if I have told a great joke.

"It is November 17th."

Did I really start this ordeal only ten days ago? Oy Vey! Someone give me some tea!

"I will get you some tea," Joe says, almost as if he can read my mind.

I beam at him and watch as he gets up. Looking back at Aaron and Isaac, I feel a little safer now.

The men start to talk about the weather, and the conditions of the ocean. I snuggle up to Joe, feeling warm inside despite this new information. I pray Mama is safe. Perhaps she is with Hannah or Esther. *Maybe they are all together so that it will be easier for them. Who is there to sit Shiva for Papa? Or say Kaddish?* In my mind I say the words I have heard so many times. Yitgadal V'yit Kadash sh'mei raba ... .

###

Aaron and Isaac retreat into the bedroom to catch some sleep when Johnny comes out. We finally talk Elijah into leaving the porthole long enough to go into the other bedroom to catch a little sleep. Joe looks tired as well but nothing seems to take the smile on his face.

"Joe."

"Yes my love."

"What is it like in the United States?"

"Pretty much like Europe, without the German soldiers. Although there are some forced false imprisonments there as well. Governments are governments. Sometimes they make mistakes. Why do you ask?"

"Well, we're married now. I have no idea where we're going to live after all of this ... ."

Chuckling and lightly touching my hair, he leans closer to me "Wherever HaShem wants us to live. I do need to take care of some business soon, but then, who knows."

"I can't go home."

"I know."

"Will it ever be safe again?" I finally said it aloud. It's like a dark cloud lifts from my shoulders just like when the German soldiers marked the papers with Juden. The secret fear is out.

"Yes, I think it will happen for a short time after the chaos and madness. Man is always creating war somewhere."

I try to think about the things that have happened. From the newspapers I read in France, I perceive where the synagogues had been destroyed. People's lives have already been destroyed, and still it goes on. Even though there is little tension in France, tells me that it won't be able to stay this way forever.

Papa often talked about the Great War, and the changes before, as well after it. This all seems "Great" as well.

###

Everyone is awake and sitting in the galley now except Aaron and Elijah. Aaron is teaching Elijah how to steer the boat.

I'm peeling potatoes for another stew, and the men are talking about crops. Just a typical day on the farm, but we aren't on the farm. We're on a boat off the coast of Africa waiting for fate to play a hand in our lives.

Elijah runs in, out of breath. Without thinking, he turns to shut the door noiselessly before saying anything.

"What is it boy?" Johnny asks.

"There is a ship flagging us down," Elijah finally says after taking two big gulps of air.

"Do you know what kind?" Johnny jumps up, and heads for the door without even waiting for the answer.

"It looks like a pirate ship!"

"A pirate ship?" Moshe chortles.

"Yep, they be pirates on these waters, matey." Johnny turns to wink at Elijah, and he is gone out of the door.

I peel the potatoes faster, clutching the knife until it nearly cuts into me. *What now?*

Moshe gets up and races to the door, as if he's in a trance.

I watch breathlessly, wanting him to stop and come back.

Elijah and Joe open the portals and listen intently. Putting a finger to his lips, Joe makes a hush motion toward me.

I wrinkle my nose at him, but remain motionless nonetheless. We can barely hear the other people on the other boat talking to Johnny.

"We are looking for the Jade Tiger," one voice says.

"You have found it."

"We have something for you."

"I kindly thank yee," Johnny says.

Some loud thuds and motions are heard from the other side of the wall, but I can see nothing. Joe and Elijah are covering the portholes with their bodies.

"You should have a safe trip all the way to Casablanca."

"Thank ye matey."

And then nothing.

Moshe comes back in and pulls Joe aside. They whisper so low that even I can't hear them.

I start peeling the potatoes once more.

"Thank you so much." Joe grins and pats Moshe on the back.

"What is going on?" Elijah and I ask, simultaneously.

"It seems some of our 'friends' gave us early Chanukah

presents. Anyway, one of the presents is a roasted leg of lamb and vegetables and such. They will be bringing it down in a few minutes."

I smile and sigh. I want to ask what the other presents are, but decide it's best not to rock the boat so to speak.

Just as soon as Joe says all of this, Aaron and Moshe show up with the goodies. It's still warm, and ready to eat.

We all jump up to help them bring the bags in. We clear off the table, and make room for the food. I get the plates and silverware out, so that everyone can eat and enjoy the bounty.

It's hard to believe such a wonderful bounty.

"It almost looks too good to eat."

"Not that good," Moshe chuckles, as he fixes two plates. "I will take one upstairs to our captain."

Elijah opens the door for Moshe.

I'm so thankful for all the food but, I can't help feeling that something is amiss.

Everyone is laughing and joking about how the sea air gives a person an appetite. Sometimes takes it away just as quickly.

I can only think of Papa.

###

At night, as I lay in Joe's arms, and Elijah sleeps in the hammock, I dream of the day when things will be better. I pray it's soon.

Casablanca

It's a smooth ride. The coastline is a constant sight from the port side of the ship. At night it's lit up like a hundred Chanukah menorahs, all lit up at once on the eighth day.

Johnny assures us that we should only have one more night before we reach Casablanca. The bounty from the pirates will last till we reach our destination.

The men take turns at the helm with Elijah at their side most of the time. I'm still forbidden to step outside of the cabin. I anxiously await the time when I can be taken to shore.

I find myself writing poetry in my journal, or reading from the many books Johnny owns. I always have my Siddur. It feels like a short lull in the danger, so I take the time to reflect, but only for a moment.

###

Papa and Mama had been married as per arrangement by the Rebbe over forty years ago. Both were quite young, barely twenty at the time. They lived with Mama's family the first year until Papa's family gave him a small piece of land to farm.

He farmed the land till 1918 when the Germans took over. Although we still have animals, and a garden for our personal use, Papa was no longer allowed to farm. He was forced to go to work at the bakery.

He worked harder at the bakery than he did at farming, at first. In the past five years, he's been selling breads and goods made at the bakery only to the people in the shtetl. He loved this part of the work, as he loved our community. He loved being a yenta, and learning of others' business before Mama.

Sometimes they would sit after dinner, and review the latest news. Who is getting married? Any new children? Any new jobs, and on and on.

Papa loved all his children and grandchildren alike. He often brought me little sweets home, to help round me out, he would say.

And now he's gone. *What will I do without my Papa.*

###

CRASH! BANG! POP!

Leaping up from the bed, I see Joe is gone. He'd been lying with me when I fell asleep. I'm alone with my heart beating, so loud I swear there is another person in the room with me.

Then I see them, almost glowing in the dark, are a pair of blue eyes. They glare at me from the corner, beckoning me to them.

I hear myself scream, as another crash of thunder hits the air, blocking the sound of my voice. A flash of lightning slips through the open, uncovered porthole for a few seconds, illuminating the entire room. I peek over to the corner where I thought I saw the eyes, and see there is nothing.

Another crash, bang, pop and then what sounds like an explosion, somewhere inside.

I can hardly hear anything above the whoosh of my blood in my ears, as it races through the veins in my head. I touch my forehead to make sure it's still there.

RAT-TAT-TAT .... RAT-A-TAT .... RAT-A-TAT

Is that gunfire? What is going on up there? The lightning strikes once more, again lighting the way. I run to the hole in the wall to peer out into the night. Not more than seven meters from our boat is another boat and it's on fire!

Did the lightening strike it? We must do something to help them. I charge out of the room to find Elijah standing at the door to the deck, peeking out.

"We have to help the people on the other boat." I run over to him.

He shakes his head no.

"What do you mean no?"

"You can't go out there."

"I have to help."

"No." Elijah is shaking his head so hard it looks as if he will shake his brains loose. "Joe, told me to not let you out no matter what."

"Why?"

He is silent.

"I have to help those people."

By now we can hear their screams piercing the night air. Their bodies hit the water with hard thuds, and then the echo dies away.

"I don't understand."

"They aren't the people to help."

Suddenly Joe pulls the door open and rushes in.

"Joe." I reach out for him, but can't touch his blur of a body.

"Get your things together now." The stern look upon his face makes me run to the other room and gather our bags. Normally, I would stop and ask questions.

Elijah is beside me getting his and our coats.

We return to find Joe, who is pacing the floor.

"I want you to strap these on you now." He hands me a satchel and forces it around my waist. "Whatever happens, don't look back. Please don't look back. Go get that Torah scroll." He hugs and kisses me, but it seems like only seconds before he roughly opens the door. We stumble out into the night air.

Aaron grabs our bags and leads the way. A smaller boat is parked beside ours. It's parallel to the ship that is on fire. Aaron lowers the bags into the boat, then Elijah and me. He's the last to board.

I look up to see Joe is already gone. The boat's engine begins to move us away. Away from Joe, my love.

All at once the ship that was on fire explodes, and some of the burning timber lands on the boat we just left. It catches on fire. Joe and Moshe run to put it out. Johnny and a few other men, I have never seen, are carrying guns. They gun down the men who are attacking us. They fall off the burning boat. As they emerge from the water, Johnny and his men shoot at them.

RAT-A-TAT ... RAT-A-TAT .... RAT-A-TAT ....

Placing my hands over my face, I can't believe what I'm seeing. People are dying before my eyes, and I don't even know why.

Aaron grabs at my sleeve, and pulls me back from the edge. I turn and run to a dark corner inside the little boat to huddle up. Elijah brings our coats and bags over. He wraps himself around me, as if to shield me from the insanity.

"Are you all right?" Aaron asks, as he reaches us minutes later.

"I ... ." I don't know what to say. I'm petrified now. I don't even know where I am. My husband is on a ship that is now on fire. This isn't the honeymoon I envisioned as a child.

"Those men were sent to kill us," Aaron says so softly, I

almost have to lay my ear against his lips to hear him.

I pull back and look away. I move so that no one is touching me, but no one outside the boat can see me. I watch two figures being shot on our boat, and fall off.

"No!" I try to leap to my feet, but Aaron catches me. He pulls me down against him.

"I can't let you do that Kfira. It would be suicide. Please don't look."

I turn away once more, and crawl into a heap on the floor. I can feel someone lying over me, protecting me without smothering me. I lie there and cry silent tears, hoping and praying that it wasn't Joe I just saw falling to his death.

We travel for what seems like hours, but is probably only minutes. The little boat plows through the water even with its small engine. No noises are heard except the night noises. Singing and dancing are occasionally heard from the coastline.

The waves hit the sides of the boat in a lulling, rocking motion and it's all I can do to keep from falling asleep.

I pray over and over again for the safety of my family and husband.

###

"Wake up Mama." Elijah pulls at my shoulders.

I try to move, but find I'm stiff. I slept hunched over in a little ball. Who knows for how long. I try to straighten out, but shooting pains in my back prevent me from moving too quickly.

The sun is shining now and warming my back. I turn and see Aaron and another man talking softly a few meters from me. I see that we are on a small fishing boat.

"Oh good, you are awake." Aaron walks over to me.

I look around, and can't believe my eyes. A part of me wants to believe it was a nightmare, but now I know it's a nightmare with me awake! There actually was a gun battle with people really dying in front of me. I scan the boat, and see Elijah asleep beside me. He uses our bags for pillows. I must have dreamed he was waking me, as I see he is out.

"Where are we?"

"We are getting close to Rabat. We will dock there and drive into Casablanca. It should be safer. They will think we died in the boat. Our arrival will go unnoticed by any enemies."

I nod.

"Are you hungry?"

I shake my head.

"Thirsty?"

I nod.

Aaron brings me a bottle of dark liquid, and hands it to me.

I drink and almost choke as bubbles tickle my nose. My hand moves to my nose, and I rake it across it trying to stop the funny feeling. I can't stop the giggling.

Aaron starts laughing.

"What's so funny?" I playfully make a face at him.

"Have you never had Coca-Cola before?"

Chuckling lightly, I shake my head.

"Well, welcome to it. A bottle of Coca-Cola is in your hands."

I take another sip, and taste the sticky sweetness, as it slides down my throat. It does taste good.

The stranger says something to Aaron, and he walks back over to him.

Aaron returns just as I take another big gulp.

"Wake up Elijah. We will be docking in ten minutes."

Turning to Elijah, I see that he is sound asleep. I hate to wake him but I must.

"Elijah," I say softly into his ear.

He bolts upright, as if shot out of a cannon. Searching around the boat, he tries to stand up, and loses his balance. He tumbles back into the bags, and lands flat on his back. He sits upright once more.

"We're here."

"Oh." He attempts to focus his eyes, and then smiles over at me until it dawns on him that we are missing something. A ship. A Joe.

"Are you okay?"

"Yes, Mama, are you?"

I smile and touch his cheek with my hand. I don't want to lie, and say everything will be great, but saying nothing seems wrong too. "We'll be docking in a few minutes. We'll have to ride the rest of the way to Casablanca by land. Here, drink this." I hand him the Coca-Cola.

He nods.

We gather our three bags and my handbag together.

"I will be right back," I find a secluded area of the boat where

I pull off the pouch Joe strapped onto me last night. The bag is thin enough that I can slip it under my dress. Wrapping it around my body, I maintain my modesty and avoid prying eyes who might want to know what I have. It fits snuggly around me, and I know I won't need anything from it for a little while. When I finish I return to the others.

"Let's go!"

I watch as the boat pulls into a marina not unlike the marina we started from, and edges toward a slip close to the shore.

Quickly, Aaron, Elijah and I make our exit. No one says a word to the stranger, as we walk down the short pier to the grassy knoll alongside the marina. A small parking area in front of us is full with people everywhere. A few cars are parked here and there.

Aaron motions us toward a dark blue, four-door car. A green ribbon hangs haphazardly from the back window.

We hike over, and Aaron opens the door, motioning for us to get it. I sit in the backseat while Aaron and Elijah sit in the front.

"Is it always this warm here in November?" I roll down the window to catch a breeze.

"You aren't near the Baltic Sea anymore," Aaron says, with a chuckle.

Aaron and Elijah give each other quick grins and nods.

I glance around the car, and see that it's a fairly nice car, not that I have been in many cars in my lifetime. Self-consciously, I stare down at the front of my dress to make sure that the jade tiger brooch is still visible.

I try to concentrate on the countryside around us, and I'm surprised that there are so many trees on this road. It isn't much of a street by others standards as it is just an old dirt path.

"It's a good thing we came now, as they say it will rain soon. No one wants to be on these roads when it rains."

I nod. We seem to be the only ones driving down this road. I feel like a sitting duck. I find myself praying over and over the Shema.

"We'll get something to eat in Casablanca."

"Is that where the community is?" Elijah asks.

"Yes, yes it is," Aaron answers.

Who had said something about a Jewish community in Casablanca? Was it Aaron or Isaac? I can't recall right now. I feel like everything is so confusing. I'm supposed to be on my way to Casablanca with my husband for a honeymoon. And now I travel with my son and Aaron.

People are dead, and maybe even dying. Here I am being treated to a ride in the country. I can't cry. I can't feel. I am numb. But I know that whatever is going on right now, I can't feel my emotions too strongly when we get to Casablanca, or risk drawing attention to myself.

###

The drive is rather smooth, and we soon pull into a small section of town. Finally, we start to see a few more cars on the road. Then we're at a main section of town, but Aaron avoids it. He opts for another dusty side road.

It gets so thick that I have to close the window for fear of choking on the dust.

I begin to cough uncontrollably, and Aaron takes a small silver flask from his coat pocket. Handing it to me, he looks back at Elijah.

"Thank you." I take the flask. I open it, and take a long drink letting the coolness of the water clear my throat. I stare at the flask, and realize that it's just like the one Joe carries. The only difference is the initials on one side.

"Joe and I had those done when we graduated from school together." Aaron watches me from the front.

"I -- "

Aaron puts up his hand, as if to shush me. "We're almost there."

Then we turn down another road with large houses made of plaster, two and three stories tall. We stop in front of a light, brownish red one.

No one speaks as Aaron gets out of the car. He shuts his door and comes around to me, opening my door, he helps me out.

Elijah is already out, and at the other door, grabbing the bags.

I step out, and look into the bright sunshine. It's warm and gorgeous and for a moment I'm blinded by all the beauty I see. Beautiful stucco sided houses line both sides of the streets. Thick vegetation and trees adorn each yard making it truly warm weather.

"Come." Aaron takes my bag and my arm, leading me to the door.

I give him a frown, but let him lead the way.

Opening the door, I step inside and a familiar smell permeates the walls to greet me. It smells like home!

"Mama! Mama! Where are you?"

"Oh my goodness," I hear in Yiddish in the distance.

Bursting into the room, Mama is with Hannah and Esther. Several children also run into the room, and wrap themselves around my legs.

"Aunt 'fira!" They call out over and over again.

Tears streak down my face, and onto Mama, as we hug around the children. They refuse to budge from me.

"Mama. Esther. Hannah."

"It's so good to see you," Esther says, as Mama moves away to allow me to get a hug from Esther.

Then it's Hannah's turn.

"I don't understand." I turn to face Aaron.

"We had to get them out of the country as quickly as possible after Kristallnacht."

"Oy! We have such a story to tell you of our journey," Mama says, as she rubs her face in her hands.

"Papa?" I ask, even though I already know the answer.

Mama looks at Aaron, and Aaron nods to her.

"I'm so sorry, darling," Mama says. "It was his heart. Everything was too much for him."

"I'm so sorry, Mama. I should have been there."

Mama shook her head, almost violently. "No, you're where you need to be. If it weren't for you, we would still be there. Who knows what would be happening to us."

Esther and Hannah nod in agreement.

"We will eat something, and then we have to go to the hotel," Aaron says.

"Why? We should stay here." I look at him, as if he has lost his mind.

"If they suspect that you're alive, it would be better if you acted as if everything is normal. We'll come back tomorrow for a short visit."

"He is right," Mama says, in agreement.

But how can I leave them? Then I realize that they're probably in more danger with me being here than if they are alone. *But why would anyone care if I went to Bangkok, and picked up a Torah scroll to take to Israel?* I don't know. I don't

dare ask. I'm still uncertain of who is the enemy. I had thought it

was the Germans, but my suspicions leave me believing they

aren't the only ones to fear.

"Come, you must be starving." Esther pulls my arm toward

the dining area.

A large table laden with all sorts of foods sits off in the dining

area. Challah, tsimmis, borsht, fruit and many other things

enhance it. I'm thankful that I'm with my family once more.

###

The conversation is good and everyone talks about

everything, but the imprisonments and deaths. Before we began

to eat we have a moment of silence, and a small prayer for those

who aren't here sharing it with us. We pray for everyone's safety

and future.

We eat and talk for several hours.

"Kfira." Aaron glimpses at his watch.

I glare sharply at him, and eye the clock on the wall. Yes, I

know we must go. But I'm so happy that my family is here or at

least some of them.

"We will talk more later," Mama says, watching me closely.

"Where is everyone else?"

"Some will be here soon and some ... " she says, and looks away.

"Okay." I get to my feet. I understand more than I want to. We'll talk of this when it's safer. Of course, there are small children in the room, and I wouldn't want them to hear such nonsense talk about death and prisons and such. I'm sure they have been frightened enough with their fathers being taken away, and Papa's death. I find myself looking forward to the day when it will be safe for us to talk about this moment in hell.

"Elijah is staying here," Esther says, as she and the rest stand.

I knew his time with me was short, but I didn't realize how much. Running over to him, I throw my arms around him, and kiss his cheek. "I love you."

"I love you, too."

"Okay, quick hugs, and then we must go."

I squeeze everyone at least twice, but we barely say a word. Tears are in everyone's eyes except the children. They run off to play now that they have full tummies, and have said their piece.

"We'll see you tomorrow."

Aaron opens the front passenger door for me and I slide inside. Closing it quickly, he races around to the other side to get in. We drive off in the same direction we came in. The streets are still deserted, and I wonder when people come out.

"How are we going to do this?"

"What do you mean?"

"I'm supposed to be with my husband on my honeymoon."

"Meet Joe Dexter, your husband," Aaron says, with a nervous laugh.

Shaking my head and smiling, I snicker uneasily myself. "Okay." *What can I say? What does this mean? My husband may be dead off the coast of Africa, and already I'm with another man. We're claiming he is my husband. Never in a million years would I dream of something like this. More importantly, can I pull this one off? Or did the Rebbe pick the wrong one?*

"Just call me darling or sweetheart or something in case you might accidentally call me Aaron."

I nod, making a joke. "So this was in your plan all along ... mister I fell in love with you first."

Aaron grins at me, and I wink back. Inside, the tears flow for my dead husband even though on the outside there are none.

"Aren't we a sly one." Aaron reaches over to pinch my cheek.

I glance out of the windshield to see we are back to the main streets. In a matter of minutes we see several hotels in the distance.

Aaron parks the car in a large lot, and then helps me out. He gathers our bags, and we walk toward the lobby. I don't recall our bags being put back in the car, but Aaron is carrying them.

Someone yells go!

Aaron flips one of the bags to the other hand, and grabs my arm. He yanks me aside, just as two men dressed in long white robe and turbans on their heads, sprint past us. One is waving a gun at the other one, yelling something I can't understand at the other one.

Aaron pulls me into a little niche between a large pillar and the building.

The other man yells something back.

The first man is very angry, and takes several steps backward as if to go.

The other man yells again, and produces a gun from behind his back.

Now both men brandish guns, and they look each other squarely in the eyes. Both utter words that sound like gibberish. Then they aim their guns at each other.

I find myself trying to dissolve into the whiteness of the building. Aaron shields me from them with his body. I'm barely be able to see the two on the street between his body and arm, but I can hear them.

They begin to shoot, and I hear a thwack as someone is hit, and screaming. It takes a few seconds to realize it's me screaming, but I'm not alone. Shrieks are also coming from two other women who apparently were with the one whom is lying on the ground, dead.

Silently, Aaron almost lifts me up, and carries me into the hotel lobby. I'm not screaming anymore, as I had stopped before the other women. But I'm shaking so hard my teeth chatter. My heart pulsates rapidly through my chest. I feel dizzy.

"Are you all right?" The man runs from around the desk to grab my other arm, and help Aaron take me to a small sofa positioned across from the front desk.

"She just had a little fright is all." Aaron pulls a handkerchief from his pocket, and wipes at my sweat covered face.

"I'm so sorry. We caught those three stealing from the other hotel guests. We tried telling the police, but sometimes you have to take matters into your own hands. I hope it didn't startle you too much."

Blinking several times, I peek around the room. Everything fades to black.

###

When I awaken I find I'm lying on a bed. I glance around, and see Aaron sitting at a table listening to a radio. Soft music emits from the box.

"Joe."

"Kfira, are you all right?" Aaron runs over, and sits on the bed beside me. Reaching over, he feels my forehead with his the back of his hand. It feels cool against my skin.

"Where am I?"

"We're in our hotel room in Casablanca. We're on our honeymoon. I guess the excitement in the lobby was a little too much for you. I have something cool for you to drink." He gets up, and walks over to a small table where a water carafe sits on a small tray. Pouring me a glass, he brings it back ever so careful not to spill.

I grasp the glass with both shaking hands, and let his hands guide it to my mouth. I take a big drink of cold and refreshing water. I feel my senses come back to me. "Some way to have a honeymoon," I say jokingly.

"Nothing like keeping a girl on her toes, or am I whisking her off her feet? I never know what I'm supposed to be doing." He sniggers.

"Well, don't look at me. I was just fine in Paris." I wink.

"Ah, Paris."

I take two more large gulps, and realize that I really need the necessary room.

Before I can say a word Aaron is pointing to a door.

I try to stand, but the room starts to spin again. Aaron comes up from behind me, and helps me to the door.

"I know I shouldn't ask, and I wouldn't but you seem rather wobbly. Can I help you? I'm not trying to be forward. I just don't want you to fall, and get hurt. I'll close my eyes, or whatever you would want so as not to make you feel funny."

"I think that if I can feel something like the wall or fixtures I will be okay," I say, as we reach the sink.

"Okay, but please tell me if you need help." Aaron's sincere voice and face almost make me giggle like a school girl. In the other world I would have never let a man I wasn't legally married to help me to the necessary room, but these aren't ordinary times. I'll need help on this trip. I'd better get used to asking.

I think I have it. I maneuver myself around easily. When I'm done, I lean against the sink to wash my face and hands. I'm ever mindful not to look into the mirror more than I have to, after all I'm sitting Shiva for Papa, and maybe my husband.

Aaron

"I think I'll need help getting back to the bedroom," I say, as I finish and walk to the door.

Aaron opens the door, and grasps me around the waist. "I can help you."

"I don't understand it. I thought you were supposed to be sick when you first get on the sea, not the other way around."

"Well, maybe you just need a little rest. Would you like a nice hot bath and maybe some food?"

"The bath sounds great. I couldn't eat a bite, as I'm still stuffed from Mama's."

"I can run the bath water while you rest and then ... I might have to help you. I promise not to try anything funny. I know you're a married woman."

Aaron helps me to the bed.

I sit down, and elevate my legs up onto the bed.

Aaron goes back into the necessary room, and I hear water running.

I have to admit I'm feeling very shmootsy right now. I tried to clean myself up while we were on the boat, but no matter what I did I could still smell the salt.

I lug my bag around, and search through it for a clean dress. I know this will help as well. I sigh, as I feel my Siddur in the bottom of the bag. *What am I to do? I feel so afraid and yet, somehow I'm not. I feel alone and yet, I'm not. I can't seem to make much sense of everything that is going on around me.*

Our watching the man get shot on the streets of Casablanca because he was a thief makes me feel vulnerable.

"It's ready," Aaron says, as he steps back out. He walks back over to me, and places one arm around my waist. The other he uses to hoist me up, and guide me to the door. Leaning me against the sink, he helps me to stand.

"Thank you," I say, almost out of breath.

"Would you like me to bring you the bag and dress?"

"Yes."

"Okay, two seconds." It seems like he is gone exactly two seconds. He places the bag and dress on a table that sits between the bathtub and sink. Several towels are on a small shelf under the tabletop.

"Thank you."

"If you need any help, please don't hesitate to call me. I don't want to come in here, and find you dead because you fell."

I smile and push him toward the door. I leave a small crack in the door, and turn back to the tub. Quickly, with modesty thrown aside, I undress and slide into the warm water.

"You know you nearly scared the life out of the concierge."

I chuckle.

"Really, when you fainted he almost passed out right next to you. Luckily, I was still holding on to you so I held you up, and placed you on the sofa. He almost gave us the room for free." More laughter.

My head starts to clear, as I wash off the scum from the trip, and begin to see flesh once more.

"Would you like to see anything while we're here?"

"What is there to see?"

"I'm not really sure. I've been here a couple of times, but usually it was for yacht racing. I can't say I saw much more than the marina."

"I think it would be nice to see something. Of course, I want to see Mama again."

"Tomorrow, I promise."

Unless someone tries to kill us here as well, I want to add but don't. I really don't know much about Casablanca except people die here.

"Are you feeling better?"

"Much better." I pull my head into the water, and get my hair wet. I scrub it as well. After all, I'm supposed to be a typical American on her honeymoon. I should at least look clean, even if the accent is going to give me away.

"We could go see El Hank."

"What is that?"

"That's a lighthouse that stands forty-five meters tall. It's by the marina, of course."

"That would be nice."

"We could go to a club, and get something to eat afterward."

"Yes, I may be hungry by then."

I rinse off my body, and delicately stand to get out. I feel much better. I rapidly dry off. I wrap the towel around my hair and get dressed. Yes, it does feel better to be clean, and wear a new dress.

I grab my bag, and step out of the bathroom. I'll unplug the drain in a few minutes. The room is rather steamy, and I can hardly see. Pulling the door open, I feel Aaron grab the bag from my hand. He pulls me toward the bed.

At first I want to fight, as I fear he's trying to take advantage.

I realize he's just trying to help.

"I promise, no funny stuff." He says this over, and over again as if to reassure me that his heart is pure.

"Okay," I giggle. "I'm fine. I need to fix my hair."

"Do you mind if I go get a newspaper?"

I stare at the door, and take a deep breath. Now that I'm really in here I almost dread going back out. I have to believe that nothing will happen to Aaron once he walks out the door. He will come back.

"If you're too afraid, I can get it when we go out?"

"No, it will give me a chance to fix my hair in peace and put on makeup." Something I still don't feel comfortable with, but makes others feel good. I realize I'll have to use a mirror to do so. I feel the pains of guilt for not being kosher while sitting Shiva for my Papa.

"Okay." He takes a key. "Don't open to anyone."

I nod.

Then he is gone.

It's hard to fight back the tears and anger I feel. I'm supposed to be here with my husband, and not his best friend. I want to go see Mama, but I don't want to hurt her or the family. I hate all of this pain I feel. I try to cry, but nothing comes out. So I turn to the comb and brush, and work on my hair.

###

"Are you ready to go?" Aaron asks, as he steps inside.

"Yes." My hair is done, and I have makeup on. I drink the last of the tea, and I'm ready to see Casablanca.

"You look beautiful."

Blushing, I avert my eyes from his. "Thank you."

"You are welcome."

"Do you think our bags are safe?"

"They're a lot safer here than if we take them with us. Be sure to take anything of value with you."

"Done." I even have my small Siddur in my handbag. Only clothing and such are in the luggage we leave behind.

"Let's go." He holds out his arm to me with an almost pleading look in his eyes that say I understand.

We're supposed to be a honeymooning couple. If I don't take his arm then it might look suspicious, and put us in danger.

"Let's see how many more can be killed today." I say under

my breath, and to no one in particular. As before, I make sure the jade tiger is visible to anyone who might need to see it.

"It's good to see you are well, Madam," the concierge says, as he almost runs to our side.

"Yes, I guess it's just the new climate."

"But of course. Where you come from it must be cold this time of year."

I smile and nod.

"We're going to see the sights, and get something to eat."

"Very good, may I recommend seeing El Hank?"

"Yes, it's our first stop."

"The open market is also good. You will pass it coming back from El Hank. Many lovely cafes along the market have good food. I hope you will stop at one while you are there."

"Thank you. We will," I say, as Aaron maneuvers me to the outside.

As I stroll out into the bright sunshine, I peek over to the spot where a body lay only three or four hours ago. Not even a bloody spot is left of the man.

We get in the car and drive. Aaron talks about how it might

get chilly tonight, but I should be dressed warm enough.

It doesn't take long to get to El Hank. The lights are off, as it is daytime. A flock of seagulls gather on the balcony around the glass lights, as if searching for the perfect spot to fish from this height. Their sing song voices call out to others who are staying closer to the marina.

The body of El Hank is a dull gray white in need of a wash and paint. The roof and balcony are red, and although I have seen several lighthouses in my day, never have I seen one so large.

"Isn't it magnificent?"

"Yes, it is."

People are everywhere, taking pictures of it, and talking amongst themselves. They're all laughing and having a good time. I wish I could be having a good time as well.

"Kfira."

"Yes."

"I'm so sorry about everything."

I beam at him. I take his hand in mine, and give it a good squeeze. I know he wants desperately to understand.

"Let's go see the market place," he says after ten minutes. He waits for me to scoot closer to him before we walk back to the car.

The open-air market isn't very far from the marina. It's huge compared to the markets at home. We almost can't find a place to park. People from all over, are milling about, selling and buying wares. Clothes and food as well as live animals are displayed everywhere. Anything is yours if you but ask.

"This is open, like the open markets at home." Only in those it's mostly food and a few goats or sheep, depending on the season. Although, at times I have seen some live chickens.

Today several little boys with dark skin and almost no clothing, are chasing four or five chickens around the yard. "You want to buy a chicken?" one of them asks in broken English.

I snicker, and shake my head.

Suddenly one of the chickens flies up, and sits on Aaron's shoulder as he bends down to look at some fruit.

I crack up laughing, as the bird doesn't seem to want to leave no matter how many times he tosses him down.

"He likes you."

"True, but I think the hotel will frown on our bringing our

dinner back while it's alive."

Chuckling, and grabbing a few grapes, I try to coax the chicken down with them. Finally, the chicken flies down, and goes back to the little boy.

"Thank you." The little boy grabs up the chicken and runs off.

I'm still giggling, as Aaron tries to be dignified while cleaning the feathers off his jacket. He sneers at those laughing at his misfortune, until he too, begins to laugh. We must look funny, cackling like a couple of chickens.

"Let's go get some fruit for the road." Aaron picks up some orange and green fruits, and takes them to the owner to pay for them.

We stroll along, and watch the people milling from stand to stand, trying to decide what to buy.

The sky starts to darken as it gets later.

"Let's find something to eat."

"That's a very good idea."

Before us is a long row of cafes. Even more variety is displayed in the different cafes than in Paris.

"Let's stop here at Marrakesh." It's a small indoor/outdoor

cafe. Large rugs hang from the ceilings like walls, and one section is open for easy entrance.

We amble inside, and see its elegance. Tables are placed strategically around the room. Throw pillows placed on the floor are sat instead of chairs.

"Two?"

"Yes."

The short, dark man with the turban on his head leads us to a place not far from the door. He lights the candles on the table, so as to illuminate our area. "You sit, I bring bread, water." And he disappears.

I sit down on one of the red and gold pillows, and let my eyes adjust to the new lighting. Aaron sits on one next to me. We face the door, so we can watch the people. We do this without even thinking.

My eyes begin to focus after several minutes of almost blinding darkness despite the candles. I realize there are many people eating here. People from many different countries are here, chatting and eating. They are enjoying themselves.

The little man with the turban returns with a large basket of flat, round bread, and two large glasses of water. Setting them in front of us, his face is clearly visible to me. He's an older man of fifty who walks with a slight forward hunch. He wears a white blousy shirt with sleeves that billow and a red vest. After every sentence he bows slightly.

"You have such a beautiful brooch," he says, almost reaching out to touch it. "A jade tiger, they are very rare, very rare in deed."

Aaron beams. "Yes, yes they are. I bet I have the only one for ... ." He puts his arm around me, and squeezes my shoulder.

"Thank you." I feel my face turn crimson under the light red blush. I divert my eyes, and sense a moment of intense heat.

"I know what you want. I'll get for you the roast lamb k-bob, vegetables and couscous." He disappears once more.

I glance over at Aaron, as he pulls his arm away. He picks up one of the flat, puffed breads and sits it before him. Tearing it apart, he eats a nice size hunk. I follow his example. It's still warm, and tastes wonderful.

"Tell me about yourself," I say.

"What is there to tell?"

"Where are you from?"

"Nice, France."

"Do you have any brothers or sisters?"

"I had two sisters and one brother, but they died in the Great War. My parents were also killed. Jean-Pierre took me in after it happened. My parents were quite wealthy, and they left me a sizeable inheritance. She actually managed to make my money grow, and treated me like family. I'm truly blessed by knowing her."

"I'm so sorry for your loss."

"It has been twenty years. I'm okay."

"I can't imagine what you might have felt back then."

"I think you know."

The little man appears with our food. He brings huge platters of meats, vegetables and of course couscous. We eat. The food is spicy and sweet all at the same time.

"What is this?" I point to a huge platter of something that looks like mushed potatoes with vegetables imbedded in it.

"This is couscous. Eat well." With this he takes some bread and scoops up a big hunk of couscous, and puts it in his mouth.

I giggle, as he makes faces as if it's divine.

I try it. It is good.

The music starts, and people around the room begin to clap.

Aaron and I both peep to the back of the restaurant to see what is happening. A couple of women wearing veils that cover their long hair and faces come out of a little curtained off area. One is dressed in a light peach, and the other blue. The veils and dresses are sheer and their makeup is heavy, accentuating their dark eyes. One can see their bellies jiggle and vibrate in time to the music. Their short, tight tops with flowing sleeves and billowy pants billow in time to the music, as they move about the room. Little bells on the bottom of their pants jingle with each step. Clappers in their hands make time with the music as they dance all around us.

Before long I stare, as if I have no manners, at their seductive dance. I feel my cheeks redden as they dance around Aaron and me. Their veils tickle my hair.

"Is this fun?"

"Yes," I answer.

The singing and dancing seem to go on for hours. We eat till we are full. Never are our teacups empty.

Finally, Aaron glances at his watch. "It is getting late. We should head back."

I nod.

He calls out to the waiter, and tells him that we would like our bill.

I can't hear everything they say, but I gather that the meal is free. Aaron slips some money into the man's hand anyway, and returns to me.

"Let's go."

"Okay." I get up, and grab my handbag.

We saunter along the path back to the car, and notice how dark and quiet it has become. Where people stood earlier, selling their wares is now emptiness. The vacant stalls look as if they have been deserted for years. Around the area where the desolate chicken booths were once full, only a few feathers float about to show any signs of recent life.

Fear grips my heart, but I say nothing. I know he will protect me. He puts his arm around me, protecting from the wind that has came up. It's silent except for the low whistling the wind makes against a few rugs hanging from poles above the street. We quickly dash to the car, both feeling the paranoia of being watched.

Aaron lets me in before getting in himself. We try to act as if we have done this many times, and it's natural. The tension is thick until we are back on the road.

It only takes fifteen minutes to get to the hotel, and another dark parking area. I shudder several times, as I step out of the car, anxious to be in the room even if it's with Aaron. It's just as it was at the market. No one is in sight.

We walk up the stairs, and find the lobby is empty. Isn't anyone here to man the front desk? Of course, the worker is probably in the little room behind the desk having his tea. It doesn't stop me from getting the feeling that we are alone and vulnerable.

"Probably asleep in the back."

We take the next set of stairs to the room. Aaron unlocks the door and opens it. Aaron turns on the light, and I almost scream.

Chills run up and down my spine at what I see. I want to cry, but I can't. The tears just won't come.

The whole room is torn apart. Our clothes are thrown here and there. The mattress is on the floor with the chairs upturned.

"It's okay." Aaron pushes me into the room, and shuts the door.

Looking around, we find that nothing is missing.

I would like to say what can they be looking for, but I don't. I just begin to help Aaron clean up the mess, and remake the bed. Soon the bed is in place, and our things are in our bags.

Something pokes me inside the bra cup. Ouch! It's really digging in. I peep to make sure the jade tiger is still in place, and it is. I reach inside my bra cup to find a tiny piece of white paper. *How did they manage this*? I pull it out, and hand it to him.

"I don't know how this got in here."

Opening it up, he translates.

"What is it?" I pull his hand with the note toward me.

"You must catch a plane tomorrow to the Middle East. It has the flight number on it."

"You will be with me, won't you?"

"Yes, two plane tickets are waiting for us at the airport."

I sigh. So, we leave tomorrow. I sit down on the bed and

glance around.

"I think you should get some sleep. It's rather late."

"And you?"

Aaron points to a small sofa over by the window. "I will rest there. I will take the extra blanket."

I know he won't get much sleep tonight, and neither will I. An airplane. I have never been on an airplane. I get up, and go use the necessary room and then come back to the bed. I don't want to change so I take my shoes off, and lie on the bed, covering myself with the blanket. I find myself wondering if the people who ransacked the room earlier will return. I pray they don't.

Aaron puts all but one light out. We both cuddle up with our bags. It's going to be another long night. I tell myself over and over again that everything will be all right and to have faith. The next thing I know I can barely open my eyelids.

Aaron, Airplanes and America

I must have fallen asleep, as I open my eyes I hear the sound of water running in the necessary room. I gaze to see if Aaron is still lying on the sofa, but he's gone. Thank HaShem, it must be Aaron running the water.

I try to get up. I try to sit up too quickly, and find myself burying my head in my hands. I'm getting dizzy a lot lately, and I don't understand why. The room spins like a dreidel. Oy! My head and my hands have to stop meeting like this, I think as I massage my temples.

"Good morning, sunshine." Aaron opens the door and walks out.

"Hello." I beam at his smiling face. I try to return it but end up wincing.

He dries his hands on a bath towel. He appears to be on top of the world now. "You slept well, I trust."

"I did." I actually did sleep well. Every time I find myself on a bed on this adventure, I can't stop myself from sleeping if I tried. Laughing to myself, I figure I'll probably die in my sleep as I won't hear the intruders.

"I slept pretty good myself. I bet you are pretty excited about riding on an airplane today."

Oh no! I almost forgot about the airplane. I know Aaron has

ridden many planes, but for me they are a novelty. A feeling of apprehension floods over me. *Can a person really get into something so heavy and soar across the sky?* Seems ridiculous as Papa would have said.

"You will love it." Aaron brushes his hair.

I shake my head, as if my grin will leap off if I shake it too hard. I'm excited about riding a plane. I can't deny it. I just wish the circumstances were better. I glance toward the necessary room. "I can be ready to leave in fifteen minutes." I move my legs so that my feet dangle to the floor.

Aaron squats before me, sincerity deep in his brown eyes. "It won't be so bad, I promise."

I touch his face and almost cry. He looks so sweetly at me. I pull my hand away, and look at the necessary room door.

"I'd better let you take care of yourself," he says with a light chuckle and, rises to go over to the small desk. "Whenever you are ready we can go."

"All right." I walk into the other room, and stare into the mirror. I don't look bad. Unlike most nights where I toss and turn till my hair screams at me the next day, today it appears as if I just combed it. Quickly taking care of business, I go out to see Aaron drinking a cup of tea.

I pick up my cup, and down it in one gulp.

"Easy, girl, you must be thirsty." Aaron pours me another cup.

I down it as well, and decide if I drink more I'll be sick.

"Would you like more?"

"No." I move away from the desk before I change my mind. I sit back down, and peer around the room over once more. It really isn't a bad little room. Isn't much in the way of decor, but it's a hotel room and not home.

"Are you sure?"

"Yes, I think I'm ready to go." I grab up my bag and handbag, and head for the door. I'm ready to see Mama once more before I take the most dangerous ride of my life.

"Okay." Aaron jumps up from the chair. He picks up his bag and takes mine from me. He carries them in one hand, as he leads me out of the door.

"Thank you."

We stroll down the stairs. The concierge from yesterday is working again today.

"I hope your stay was pleasant," he says to Aaron. "Are you sure you wouldn't like to stay one more day?"

"No, I'm afraid I have a family emergency. I spoke with a friend yesterday who got the call. We have to leave Casablanca immediately."

"Where will you be going?"

"Back to New York City. We hope to come back, and visit Casablanca again soon."

"You must! It's a wonderful city." The man waves his arms around appearing as if he might fly off himself.

I stifle my funny bone, and gaze into the lobby. He really does look comical.

Aaron reaches out for my arm with his free hand, and we head to the garage. Getting into the car, we see people once more strolling along, taking care of the daily business of living.

"He really wants us to stay?"

"Maybe, but better to be safe and leave."

It doesn't take long before we're back to the old part of the city.

"We can't stay long, maybe an hour, and then we must go. I'm sorry."

"It's all right. I understand. So many things need to be done."

When we get to the house, no one runs outside to greet us. I worry that something has happened to them. I try not to race to the doorstep, and break down the door. Aaron helps me out of the car, and then we stroll over to the door. Aaron knocks lightly, and Isaac opens the door.

I try to contain my relief and excitement, as I see his face. Once we're inside and the door is closed, I wrap my arms around him, as tears of joy burst from my eyes.

"You scared me," I whisper.

"I'm sorry."

"And Joe? Is he here?" I pull away, and begin to search around. They gather in the living room, arriving from all directions.

"I'm so sorry."

I crumble to the ground. *Already I'm a widow? Is that what Isaac is saying?*

"Be brave bubala." Mama cradles me in her arms. Tears flood my eyes, and I can barely make out anyone else in the room. My shoulders heave with heavy sobs. My Papa and now my husband are dead, and there is nothing I can do to make them come back. I want to stay in the warm comfort of Mama's arms, but I know I can't.

"I don't understand."

"It's not for us to understand, but only HaShem."

I can see that Minka is here, as well as her children, but not her husband. My brother Isaac is next to my brother David and Ezra but no Shlomo. I want to ask. I know with only an hour, there isn't enough time to hear about everything that has happened to them since I last saw them.

I run from sister to brother to sister to Mama, giving away my hugs. We barely speak, as there is too little time to say all the things I would want to say. All of us have tears running down our cheeks, as if we are sitting under the rain. Sobbing from the pain, our hearts are imbedded with it.

"I love all of you."

"We love you," Mama says.

"This thing you do, it's great." Ezra jostles my hair.

At one time I would have cried, and pushed him away for

touching my hair, but today I'm warmed by his touch.

Ezra, David and Minka are all tall with gray eyes, light brown hair and similar facial features. For our family they look out of place. People often think they're triplets, as they are so close in looks. All of a sudden, I realize that their wives and husband are not here.

"Where ... ?"

"We have German wives. They chose to stay."

"But they are Jews."

Ezra shrugs and looks away.

David takes my hand, and buries his face in my shirt. "She is dead."

"I'm so sorry." I stroke his face, and stare at the others.

Minka comes over, and takes David by the shoulders, pulling him away. "My husband is dead also. He was shot in front of our house. You go do this thing you need to do so we can be safe."

I nod.

"We really need to go now." Aaron glares at the clock on the wall.

Already it has been an hour, although it feels like I just got

275

here. I realize that most of that time had been spent holding Mama, as I felt everyone's sadness. I take in my family's faces, as they huddle together before me. I memorize the way the look, and I wonder who will be left when I get back. I pray it's all of them.

"We're not going to say good-bye. We're going to let you walk out without hugs and goodbyes so you will come back to us." Mama stands before the others.

I turn, and march toward the door. It's all I can do to keep from turning around and racing back to them. I twist around for one second to see them one last time. I love you I say under my breath. I pivot back, and walk out of the door.

Aaron helps me into the car. I want to say thank you, but it doesn't come out.

"We'll get checked in at the airport, then we can make a breakfast out of the fruit we picked up at the market yesterday."

I nod.

"We have three hours before the plane takes off so we'll be there in plenty of time."

Joe is dead.

"I hope you like the fruit. You've probably never eaten this kind unless it was at Jean-Pierre's."

Papa is dead.

"We will be flying on one of the safest airplanes made. I think they have French pilots."

I feel numb.

"Kfira."

Finally, I turn to look at Aaron as we drive.

"I'm sorry."

"I know."

I sigh and stare back out of the window. I hope and pray my family will be here when I'm done.

We get to the airport a few minutes later. Aaron parks the car in the lot, and we stroll to the airport. From the outside it looks something like a train station except that instead of railroad tracks beside it, there is a large expanse of flattened land. People are running about, as if their hair is on fire. They search for water to put it out.

The long building has many sets of stairs leading down to the airplanes. A few airplanes are on the ground; some are taking off or flying.

We walk in, and Aaron finds the right counter for us to check in. The man looks a lot like many of the other men in this town. He is taller than the waiter and concierge, but older and constantly bowing. He speaks with a heavy French accent, and Aaron converses with him in French.

"He says that we are to take flight 118, and its right down the hallway, on the left-hand side. We'll be going to Amman. Then if everything works out well, we will eventually get to your final destination." We walk as he talks.

I listen.

The number hanging from a post by another desk indicates that this is the right place. Three men are working on something on the counter.

We stop and glance around at the seats. They're everywhere.

Aaron steps over to converse with the men and check in. I had given the papers Joe gave me to Aaron when we were at the hotel. He gives them to the men who look them over, and stamp visas on them. No questions asked.

"Let's eat fruit." Aaron sits down with me and our bags in one of the many hard seats clustered here and there around the room. He produces a small knife from his pocket. He peels the fruit into a small wastebasket he found in a corner.

"All right." I find myself watching every person who walks past us, eyeing them as if they might attack us at any second.

"Kfira."

"Yes." I turn back to Aaron.

"Here, taste this," he says, as he forces a piece of orange colored flesh into my mouth.

It's sweet and juicy, and I find myself laughing as the juices begin to slide down my chin.

"Here." He pulls out a towel from his bag. "Compliments of the Ali Baba Hotel and Killing Spot." He holds it up to me.

Giggling, I take the towel, and wipe my face. I'm laughing so hard I'm sure someone will see me, but suddenly I don't care. I need this, this moment of juice and insanity.

"I have some more for you." He hands me a few more slices, and once more I find myself dabbing the juices off my chin, and chortling like an old woman.

He takes a few slices for himself before giving me a few more bites. We carry on this way till all three fruits are eaten, and we're satisfied. It quenches our thirst and hunger.

Once we clean the mess up, we sit back down to once again watch the people.

###

"Sir." A man marches over to us.

I must have fallen asleep, as I open my eyes to see one of the three men from the counter standing before Aaron.

"Yes." Aaron sits up, and looks patiently around the room.

Other people continue to wander about the room. Some are sitting, and some are standing. Their dress is that of foreigners from many countries.

"I think we have you on the wrong plane," he says, in a low whisper.

Aaron pulls out the tickets and looks them over. He hands them to the man. The man shakes his head, and swears in Arabic. "No, no sir. You need to go to number seven. That's the plane all jade tigers ride. I'll take you there myself."

I listen intently to the pair

"Okay," Aaron says, as he stands up.

He helps me up before grabbing our bags, and following the man. We stroll down the long hallway until the chairs we sat at are nothing but a blur. The man is very quick for his size. We stop at another station. It's just like the other one, except one less person is behind the counter. A number seven is painted on the desk.

The two men are happy to see us.

Our guide gives them our tickets, and they check them over. They hand them back to Aaron.

"You have a very safe trip to America," one of them says, as the other one ushers us to a door leading to the outside.

Now my heart is beating in my throat, and it goes dry instantly. I'm sure that we are done for. *Why else are all these people pushing us to get on this other plane? To the United States no less? Aren't we supposed to be going to Amman?*

Our guide turns to us just as we saunter out the door and says, "May the jade tiger keep you well." He disappears.

The new man opens the door and helps us down the stairs. From a distance we can see the airplane that we are supposed to be on. Many people are boarding.

He leads us to the plane, and we watch others climb another set of steps up to the plane. I feel dizzy, but manage to amble along with the help of the railing.

Aaron ducks his head down to enter the plane. It's cramped compared to riding on the train. All of the seats are jammed together. A man as tall as Aaron shows us to our seats.

"Would you like to sit by the window?"

"I ... " I'm unsure.

"Go ahead. It'll be a treat."

I take the seat next to the window and glance outside. Our guide is standing at the top of the steps of the building, waving. *What did he say about the jade tiger, as we were boarding the plane?* I wave back without thinking. I turn to view the other planes, one of them is the one we should be on.

Their door is shut, and people are moving away from it. Our plane's door is also shut. Everyone takes their seats, and Aaron demonstrates to me how to put on a safety catch. The plane engines start up, and I can see the propellers begin to turn faster and faster. I turn away, as I find their spinning makes me nauseated.

When I look back they're moving so fast I can't see their motion anymore.

Someone is saying something very loud over the engines, but my mind is racing so fast I can't understand the words.

I stare back out at the other plane, and just as we start to move away. I notice a spark then a flash. Sounds like a loud whoosh! .... Wham! As if something slams against the side of the plane. Rumbling, like thunder fills the sky and echoes in the little plane. Something lights up the sky, making it too bright to see anything. The ground shakes for what seems like an eternity, but it's only a few minutes. The vibration jiggles my stomach so much that I know I will vomit if it doesn't stop soon.

The other airplane explodes. What parts aren't flying in all direction is on fire. Metal hits the ground and anything close to it, as well as the building. Several pieces imbed themselves into the walls of the airport. People watch in horror as a few of the workers dodge the falling debris.

Part of the bottom of the plane is still visible.

Our plane begins to move faster, making the engine whine, as if it's trying to pick up speed too quickly. Our plane maneuvers to get away from the other plane.

Flames shoot in every direction.

Someone screams on the plane, and I know it isn't me. People are gasping and shrieking, just as they had when the train went through Kristallnacht. People sitting in the window seats smash their faces against them, as if this might get them a closer view. Others from the aisle seats lay on top of the window seat people, pushing them unmercifully into the wall.

People scamper out of the building, and then race back in, as they try to dodge the flying debris. Metal flies toward us, but falls short by a mere meter. We advance farther, and farther from the fireball that once was a plane. A place we were supposed to be on that plane.

I heed someone's voice, the man who showed us our seats? He is yelling something in Arabic to the men who are in the cockpit.

I listen to the people in the back screaming "GO! GO! GO!" until it becomes a mantra or prayer.

"I ...." I try to say something, but the nausea is choking my voice. I cough several times, as the realization of how close I came to kissing death becomes my reality.

Aaron grabs something from the seat in front of us, and places it over my nose and mouth. It's a small paper bag.

All of the fruit that was so sweet and juicy going down is bitter as it comes back up. I don't want anyone to hear me, but no there's no place to hide. I'm not used to vomiting in front of a group of people. My belly aches but only for a few minutes, and then it stops.

"Is she all right?" a man asks, as he races over to help.

"She will be. She always was a little nervous about flying. I keep telling her it's safer than boats." He laughs nervously.

No one mentions the plane that just blew up, or the boat that was gunned down off the coast of Africa.

He goes back behind the first row of seats, and brings me back a towel to wipe my face. "I'll get you some tea once we get into the air." He returns to the front.

Everyone is settling in, and talking amongst themselves. It's as if a few minutes ago an airplane wasn't on fire, and it was all a dream.

Aaron wipes my face with the towel he used on it earlier. I let him. He lays it on the arm of the chair. He takes the little flask from his pocket, and hands it to me.

I'm so glad to see it. The water tastes refreshing as it slides down my sore throat. I cough several more times before I take another sip.

"The tea will taste better I'm sure."

I glare back at the chaos that seems to slip away in the background. I can still see the fire, but we are starting to ascend into the heavens. My stomach starts talking again, as well as the cotton building up in my ears.

I vomit once more, and then I'm done. Grabbing up the towel, I wipe myself off with the towel. I take another drink. My heart is still in my throat, and every blood vessel in my body feels alive. I try to close my eyes, but my eyelids won't cooperate. I struggle to blink, but this is impossible as well. The air feels thin. I find it difficult to breathe.

Like in the mountains, I feel as if someone is sticking sheep into my ears. A soft ringing in my ears turn into large bells.

"Just take slow, easy breaths." Aaron takes my hands in his, as we rise to the clouds.

Up, up, up ... until finally we level off. My ears feel just as they did when we were in the mountains. I try to get the cotton out of them, but they itch. I shake my head like an old sheep dog, nothing.

Aaron is grinning and making breathing sounds.

Finally, I give up and begin to take deep breaths with him. My stomach calms, and my ears return to normal. I sigh.

Our man in the red shirt returns with a cup of tea.

"Thank you." I accept it from him, and take a sip. My stomach thanks me. The tension in my fingers begins to fade, and I start to relax. I still can't get the image of the plane on fire out of my mind. *Did I see someone falling out? Did I see people on fire?* It all seems like a blur to me now.

"Are you all right?"

"Yes, thank you." He returns to his station, and I notice that he is wearing a white vest over his red shirt and black pants. His black hair is long and thick, pulled back into a ponytail.

"Are you sure?"

"The plane ..." I start to say something but nothing comes out.

"I know," Aaron whispers, and squeezes my knee.

I finish the tea, and sit back in the seat. *It's almost as comfortable as the train seats.* I gaze back out of the window to see clouds passing us by. I watch them intently, searching for HaShem.

###

"Wake up! Wake up," Aaron says, in his best high whisper.

Opening my eyes, I turn to catch a glimpse of what Aaron is doing.

The excitement in his voice moves me to sit up. I glance around, and see that I'm in the airplane. It's not a dream. *We left a plane on fire back in Casablanca. We left my family.*

"Don't you want to see the Statue of Liberty?"

"What?"

"Look."

Just as I turn to look, I see her. She looks like a shadow at first, but she's definitely a tall statue of a French woman. We don't get close enough to see her details, but I know now I'm in America. Thank you HaShem.

"We should be landing soon. I don't know if we'll get any time to sight see, but if not, we will the next time we're here.

We're off to San Francisco." Aaron sounds so cheerful.

I smile and wish I had some of that lovely fruit we had earlier.

As if reading my mind, Aaron pulls bread from his pocket, and hands it to me. "You slept through the food so I saved you something. I have another if you want."

I beam, as I take his arm, and snuggle my head against his shoulder. I should be ashamed, but I'm not. I'm hungry. I take the bread, and give him a smile.

"Thank you."

New York City

"I can't believe we might get to see the Statue of Liberty." I think about Elijah wanting to visit it for Chanukah. I had no idea at the time of that conversation that I would see her myself only a day later. Or is it two days? Time is flying past me as if on the wings of a dove.

"We'll land at the Newark Liberty International Airport, and I'll see if we have time to sightsee in New York City," Aaron says.

The man strolls by, and notices I'm awake. "Can I get you anything?"

"Something to drink?"

"Yes, right away." He flashes a smile full of bright, white teeth. He is gone maybe a minute, as he returns with a large teacup in his hands. "It's still very warm so be careful"

"Thank you." I take it from him, and hope it won't put me to sleep. I'm starting to get a little paranoid of tea. Every time someone gives me a cup I fall asleep. Laughing to myself, I realize how meshuggah that sounds even to me. Deborah mentioned something about it when I was first in Paris, but I never really asked her more about it.

"And?"

"It tastes wonderful."

"Good. We'll be able to get you something to eat when we land, unless you would like the other bread now."

"Please," I say with my biggest smile, and hold out my hands.

Pulling it from his pocket, he stares over the weird shape it has become after sitting in his pocket. "It doesn't look edible."

"It looks just fine to me." I grab it from his hands.

Chuckling, he winks at me.

The bread is warm from his pocket, but tastes just as good as the first piece. My stomach thinks my throat has been cut. I hear it growl over the sound of the man's voice in the front telling to us about landing. The wind hits against the wings and engines, vibrating the plane.

I peek out of the window, and see land below us. The same ear cotton is back, but it leaves much quicker than when we rose into the air. I finish off the tea and bread.

"We'll be landing in New Jersey in about ten minutes." Aaron takes my cup.

The man comes by, and picks up our cups, as well as others. He returns to the front of the seats and disappears.

I sense the plane move closer and closer to the ground. My fingers begin to dig into the armrests. Even though I try to take deep breaths, in and out, it seems impossible to breathe properly.

"Breathe slowly," Aaron says as he does the same.

Finally, I'm breathing in the same rhythm as he is, slow and steady.

The wheels hit the ground with a thud. The plane heads to a

door, and set of stairs just like the ones we used to board the plane.

Aaron gathers our bags under his legs.

"We'll let the others get off first, so we don't get separated," Aaron says softly.

The engines are almost too loud for me to hear over them, and I can barely understand Aaron, but they are turned off once we glide into the right space.

The man says something in several languages about thank you for your business, and have a nice day. People file in a single line out of the plane. I can't help but notice that I'm one of three women on board. At least thirty men are passengers. They shuffle by, talking about their plans. Some are going to New York City, and some have destinations elsewhere. All in all, they seem to be happy to be back on solid land again. I wonder if they will ever think about the plane we saw blown up, as we were departing Casablanca. I know I will.

"Okay." Aaron watches as the last person heads for the door. He stands and grabs the bags up with one hand. He leans over to help me stand.

My legs are wobbly, almost as if they are made of rubber.

They tremble beneath my dress as a toddler's legs when trying to

take the first steps. I frown. A sharp pain of pins and needles

attacks my left foot, and I giggle as I realize my foot went to

sleep.

"Are you all right?"

"My foot went to sleep."

Aaron smirks.

I drag the sleeping foot a little behind me, all the while

mentally challenging it to wake itself and work right. I try to flex

it and nothing happens. I feel silly as the three men at the front

watch with pained looks upon their faces, as I make my descent

to the door. Two of the men are wearing dark blue suits. They are

both tall with thick, curly black hair and dark eyes just like the

first man. Two days growth of stubble shows on both of their

faces. They have toothy smiles as well.

Aaron says something to them in French, and they smile and

say "Aaahhh!"

"What did you say?"

"I told them that you had a sleepy foot who thought we were

still in Casablanca."

I snicker. Finally, the foot begins to get the blood rushing back through it, and I can walk like a normal person.

We walk down the staircase to exit, and back up the staircase to enter the building. My legs are alive with feeling by the time we reach the top of the second set of steps.

"We have to go to customs," Aaron says.

"What is customs?"

"It's where they ask you questions about where you are going and such."

I shrug. So I tell them what I think. But from the look on Aaron's face, I realize this is another one of those, do as I do moments. So I smile and wink. After all, isn't a new wife supposed to wink at her husband? I know Aaron isn't my husband. We both know this is a part of the assignment. I can't help but to find myself feeling very affectionate toward him. It scares me.

Finally, we stop at a long table where two American men are sitting.

"Your passports?"

Aaron hands them to him.

The man with the blue eyes and short, slicked back blonde hair glimpses through them over. He has no facial hair that only proves to make him look younger than he really is. His blue shirt almost matches his eyes, and I notice that neither of the men are wearing the same colored shirts.

The other man is dealing with a man we traveled with. The customs man is making the passenger open his suitcase, while he rifles through the passenger's belongings. The passenger looks around anxiously as the other touches the clothing inside. Apparently there is nothing to find, and soon the customs man closes the suitcase. He sends him on.

"Do you have anything to declare?"

"It's good to be home. Go Yankees!" I say without thinking, and try to disguise my accent. Where had I learned of Yankees. I'm not really sure what the Yankees are to this man. Of course, we Europeans call all people from the United States, Americans Yankees. I realize the customs man may not know this one.

The man smiles, and sends us on our way.

"Let's go see when our next plane leaves." Aaron scans the

room looking for the desk, and the people who take the tickets.

"Can I help you?" a young woman asks, as she saunters up beside us. Her light brown hair is short, and curls about her face. Her green and white uniform is tight about her figure and she stands tall in her high heels.

"We are going to San Francisco, and I need to know when this flight leaves?" Aaron shows her our tickets.

I survey the people around the room. Some run to greet their loved ones for hugs and kisses. People sit in chairs strategically scattered about the room just like the airport in Casablanca. Others walk around, looking disoriented as if they are just drifting.

Many more people are here than any of the train station, marinas and Casablanca airport that I have been in. People must travel more here in the United States. The people are all ages, from babies in their mothers' arms to a few elders, sitting with the children. Most are dressed in gay traveling clothes of many colors. What a contrast to the dark suits or mismatched clothing of their European counterparts. They all seem happy to be here.

"The flight won't be leaving until noon tomorrow," the lady

answers.

"Will we have time to get to New York City, and do a little sightseeing?"

"Why of course. I was off duty five minutes ago. I was on my way out when I noticed your wife's beautiful jade tiger broach. I don't think I have seen anything so exquisite and brave."

"Thank you." I try to hide my face behind my purse, as I grin at her.

"I can take you there now. I share an apartment with three others on the island of Manhattan. They're all off on assignment now, so I have the apartment to myself."

Aaron nods approval. "That would be great as long as you are sure it isn't any trouble for you."

My eyes shine and my lips turn up in a huge grin. I hope we will be safe during this trip.

"No, having you two with me will be no trouble at all." She winks at me. "You must need the bathroom. It's right over there, I will take you to it."

The necessary room sounds great to me right now, as I realize I'm unsure of when I used it last. All three of us walk over as the men's and women's are right next to each other.

"Do you mind? I need to freshen up myself," she says, as I walk toward the door.

"All right with me." I suddenly realize I need my bag and purse. Turning back, I grasp the handle of my bag, and pull it out from under Aaron's arm.

"It must be nice to be married to such a gentleman," she says.

"Yes, it is," I answer, as I watch Aaron's face. He readily relinquishes the small bag.

"By the way, my name in Katya but everyone just calls me Kat."

"I'm Kfira, and he is Joe," I say without sputtering, and still trying to smooth out my very thick accent.

"Good to meet you," Kat says.

"I'll meet you right here." Aaron turns to go to the men's room, and I enter the women's with Kat in tow.

The bathroom is huge with walls dividing the smaller areas where the toilets are located. A small door is attached to each two walls allowing for privacy. It's truly an outhouse inside the house!

"It's so wonderful to come to New York City," Kat says, as I take care of business.

I come out of the little toilet room, and go over to the sink to wash my face and hands.

Kat tells me about moving here from Idaho several years ago when she learned of the airport needing workers.

"I don't miss it at all."

We are done.

I grin and start walking toward the door. My hunger is starting to eat at my nerves. I want to be friendly, but it's impossible, as all I can think of is food.

"We are ready," I say to Aaron, as he takes my bag as well as my arm.

"Let's go."

Kat shows us the way out of the airport. Taxicab drivers linger outside to take people wherever they need to go. We grab the first available one.

A short, stalky man with a thick Irish accent opens the doors for us, and we get in. He is a little taller than me with thick red hair and dark green eyes. He wears a red plaid cap atop his head.

His heavy green coat barely conceals his bulky frame.

Kat gives the directions to the driver, and we pull away from the airport. Kat continues to talk non-stop to us, but I only half listen. I look at all the cars there are, as well as people. They are everywhere.

"Maybe we can go to Battery Park, and see the Statue of Liberty after we get something to eat," Kat suggests.

"The Statue of Liberty?" I perk up, and turn toward Kat to hear her speak.

"We should definitely see it. We can get something to eat close to where I live. The park isn't far from there. We can walk over. They have a boat that takes people over on tours."

"Sounds great," says Aaron.

Soon we are riding to New York City. Aaron is smiling and listening, and I watch the traffic.

###

It has been an hour since we got into this car, and my eyes are starting to burn and water. I feel so hungry that I know I will throw up again if I don't eat something soon. But I know this isn't possible, as we seem to be on a bridge going over the ocean to nowhere. Fear reaches into my chest, and tries to pluck out my heart once more. I pray the bridge won't fall. I pray we will reach food soon.

"Mind my manners." Kat looks me over. "I have something for you." She reaches into her pocket, and pulls out a candy bar. She hands it to me, and winks. "I should have given you this when we left the airport. I bet you are starved."

Without thinking or looking at the wrapper, I grab it up and tear it open. I take several big bites, and my stomach stops yelling. I look down to see something ...shey. Well, whatever it is, I know I like it.

"It's good, yes?"

"Yes."

During the time it takes me to eat the candy bar, we reach solid land once more. Another fifteen minutes, and the taxi driver pulls over and we get out. Kat pays the man, and Aaron shuts the door.

"Shlomo's Deli is about a block from here. They have the best chicken soup I have ever tasted."

"Shlomo's it is," Aaron answers for us.

Soon we are sitting in a little booth watching the people. The dark blue seats are made of soft material. The tables are all covered with crisp white tablecloths. It's a nice atmosphere, and I can't help but notice not one, but two Stars of David on the window, as we came in. Are Americans forced to mark their buildings as well? Several nice gentlemen wearing aprons and yarmulkas stand behind a long counter. For a second I feel as if I'm home.

They're both in their fifties. One is a little heavy, and the other is thin. They both have full beards and moustaches.

"What would you like?" Kat asks me.

Looking at the menu the thin man handed us when we came in, I see it's written in Russian, Yiddish and English. "I will have the corned beef sandwich with chicken soup."

"Are you sure? They are pretty good-sized meals."

"My Kfira can put away all kinds of food. Can't you, honey?

"Yes." I smirk, as my cheeks turn a dark shade of crimson.

The waiter comes over, and takes our orders. I drink water and eat from the relish tray he sits before us. The pickles are sweet and yummy.

Aaron and Kat are still talking, as I observe the atmosphere. It's the kind of place even Mama would like. The pictures on the wall are of different artifacts such as Torah scrolls, mezuzahs and great Jewish leaders.

The food comes, and even Aaron and Kat are now silent, as we enjoy our meal. She's right, the portions are huge. I pull a handkerchief from my handbag. I place my other sandwich half in the middle, wrapping the sides around it. No one says a word.

When we are done the waiter brings the check. "I want to tell you what a beautiful brooch you wear," he says, in Yiddish to me. "It is a jade tiger, yes?"

"Yes," I answer.

"Very beautiful indeed." He grins and walks over to the counter. He says something to the other man, and the other disappears behind the door. He returns to give something to the thin man.

I watch as Aaron walks over to the counter. The man takes the piece of paper, and hands Aaron a cloth bag full of something.

"Let's go." Kat grabs our bags.

We get up and meet Aaron at the front door, who then takes

the bags from Kat. She picks up the cloth bag from the counter.

"Shalom."

"Shalom."

We make a stop at Kat's apartment to drop off the extra food and our bags. Kat tells us it would be too conspicuous for us to carry them around.

Our first step is Battery Park. It's huge with more trees than I would have dreamed of in a large city. In fact it's one of the largest cities in the world. The buildings are so tall that they look as if they are kissing the sky. Even from the park they can be seen. The statues are strategically placed throughout the park, as well as park benches. The pigeons have a home with them, guarding them and sometimes covering them up. People gather around them to feed the birds.

Even on this very cold day, there are mothers watching their children play in the distance. The children laugh and run around carefree. A few dogs are even barking in the distance.

We hike for what seems to be an hour, but is only about thirty minutes. Then, we see it again, the Statue of Liberty.

"Wow!" I run to the rail, and Aaron chases after me. He

grabs the back of my coat, as if he is afraid I might plunge into the murky water below.

We laugh, as he hugs me. We look around to see Kat quickly on our tucas'.

"I really want to see inside."

"Then your wish is my command." Aaron points to a boat not too far from us.

We stroll over to the boat, and see about ten others waiting in line. It's cold here, and I am glad I have on my warm coat. The wind blows lightly from the salt water, and I smell it again. Salt. Just like home.

Kat goes over to the ticket person, and pays for the tickets.

I notice there are men and women in line. They're all dressed quite warmly with large coats and hats. They all look as if they are laughing and having a great time. It's hard for me to conceal my emotions. The excitement courses through my veins with my blood. A permanent grin is on my face.

Soon we are on the little boat, and they're taking us to see her. Someone's announcing something into a large megaphone. They're giving the history of the statue, and how the French gave her to the US. I try to catch some of it, but I'm too excited to pay attention. History I can read in a book, but seeing it and feeling it! OY! I wish Elijah was here and I think ... next time. I can't believe that I actually feel like there will be a next time. I pray.

It feels as if we are moving at a snails pace to reach her skirt and platform, but it takes only a short thirty minutes to get there. We all walk in a single line, as if we were at Ellis Island instead of the Statue of Liberty.

Aaron is right behind me with his hands on my shoulders almost guiding me along the way. I observe everyone, and scrutinize everything around me. I try to take it all in.

Then we start the long ascent up the winding stairway to the top. Some travel faster than others, and I fear I'll have a nose bleed before we get to the top. Aaron keeps a hold of me nonetheless. I listen to some of the others huffing and puffing around us. A few people even cough, but only for a few seconds. Then they seem all right. No one wants to stop, not when they're this close.

The metal is cold, but with all of the bodies around us, it's warm. I try to grasp the rail, but it feels like ice. So I hold onto

Aaron instead. He doesn't seem to mind, as he gladly holds me up. Kat give the impression that she is fine on her own. At times she even helps others who seem to be struggling.

Finally, when my knees can't stop shaking, and feel as if they will fall off if I walk another step up, we reach the platform. We stroll into the face of Lady Liberty herself. Actually the crown, as her face is a wall. We can see New York City through her eyes, so to speak, and what a glorious sight it is to behold.

The skyscrapers are so tall they really do seem to scrape the sky. I push myself closer to Aaron, as I feel the silent tears run down my face. *Is this what freedom looks like?* I look out to the Atlantic Ocean, and see boats and ships heading toward the harbor. I know I'm a long, long way from home. I pray.

San Francisco and China Clippers

By the time we return to Kat's apartment, and I'm starving. We made a long trek through the park twice. I'm gushing. I can't stop talking about the view from the crown of Lady Liberty.

Laughing, Aaron slides his arm about my shoulder and

smiles.

"We're so glad you had a good time," Kat says, as we get closer to her apartment.

"I'm hungry." I start to pull my purse around to see if I have any little candies that I picked up from Kat's place. They insisted I leave the sandwich for fear of attracting the attention of the dogs in the park, as well as other animals. I knew I would be hungry at some point while we were out.

"We're almost there," Kat chuckles.

Walking up the stairs five flights seem like a breeze compared to the ones we took inside the statue. I find my knees giving me second thoughts on it.

"Are you all right?"

"I feel a little lightheaded."

"Here, lean on both of us, and we can help you up."

Aaron gets on one side while Kat gets on the other. Their shoulders go under my armpits, almost lifting me up into the air. My arms instinctively go around their necks. Aaron carries my handbag in his free hand. Very carefully, we begin up the last three floors.

They travel along with me so gracefully, neither getting out of breath. Finally, we reach the top and they let me go.

I stand and wiggle my shoulders for a few seconds, my hands almost went to sleep in that position. "Thank you so much."

"Don't worry about it." Kat turns to open the door.

We saunter in, and she turns on the lights. I finally get a chance to take a peek at her place. It's a very beautiful, yet simply decorated apartment. Three doors are visible with two leading to bedrooms, and the other to the necessary room. I try to say bathroom, but it just won't come out. The kitchen is in an open corner of the main living area. A large wooden table with eight chairs sits off to the side of the kitchen. No shlepping hot dishes too far here.

Several sofas and chairs are placed around the room, giving it a homey, comfortable look. They are mismatched colors and fabrics that may not work in other places, but here they give a homey look. When they close the front door, I notice a mezuzah on the doorpost. I'll have to remember to touch it before I leave tomorrow.

"I'll get the food ready," Kat says, from the kitchen.

"It all smells so nice." I walk around the room, looking at everything. In one corner by the windows, an overstuffed chair rests beside a tall floor lamp. On the little table, next to the chair, is a book copy of Torah. I caress the smooth leather cover, touching it with my fingertip, as if it's the cheek of a baby. This is what it's all about I remind myself. This is why I'm in New York City.

"It's ready." Aaron walks over to me.

I take a quick look over at him and beam. I'll have a chance to look at this later I say to myself. "I'm so hungry."

Aaron takes my hand, and heads me back to the table.

We all grab a chair and sit down. The food looks wonderful. Not only is there my sandwich half, but a plate full of other sandwich halves. Latkes, blintzes, kugel and rugalach are on other serving plates. Everything looks and smells delicious and I find my mouth watering uncontrollably.

"We want you to say a prayer," Kat says.

"Ha-motzi lechem m'in ha'oretz we give thanks to HaShem for bread. Our voices rise in song together, as our joyful prayer is said. Baruch atah Adonai elohenu melech ha'olam ha-motzi lechem m'in ha'oretz ... amen."

"Amen," Kat and Aaron say together.

"I'm so famished." I take my sandwich half, and a few of everything else.

"I'm so glad to see you eat. I don't know that we've had much to eat since our feasts in Casablanca."

I think of Mama's cooking, as well as the restaurant. They bring a smile to my face.

"This is good," Kat agrees. "I saw you looking at the Torah book in the study, thinking about reading some?"

"Probably after dinner," I answer.

"I'm so glad you were looking at it. Makes me know that we made the right choice."

Aaron nods as his mouth is full of blintz.

"Chosen?"

"Yes, you were chosen to do, you know? To go to Bangkok and get the Torah scroll."

"Actually she doesn't know much. We've only been able to explain a little at a time. We've been followed and shot at, as well as had our room ransacked. There just seemed to be no place where we could talk openly about this deal," Aaron says to Kat.

She nods in understanding. "It's time to tell."

"Actually, why don't we wait until everyone is full, and then we won't be letting this good food not get the attention it deserves," Aaron responds.

I chew as fast as I can in order to answer this request. Swallowing, I grin. "I agree."

"Then after dinner we talk."

Everyone takes another bite.

Dinner conversation is pleasant, and everyone enjoys the wonderful meal. Once it's over, we all help carry the dishes over to the kitchen. Kat prepares warm tea, and she and Aaron have another glass of wine. We sit down to talk.

"What do you know?" Kat asks.

"I know that I'm to go to Bangkok to get an ancient Torah scroll then I'm to take it to Palestine/Israel. I knew it was better not to ask questions after Elijah came to be with Joe and me. I didn't want to risk hurting him. I saw a dead man. I'm no dummy. I'm not naive. I understand that Jews aren't safe in

Europe. I feel like there are so many other things I don't understand. Like, why me?"

"Rebbe says you're one of the bravest people he has ever known. He compares you with Miriam and Deborah."

I frown. One is the sister of Moshe, and the other is a great warrior. And I'm like them? Someone in authority must be meshuggah. I take a deep breath in, and let it out slowly. As I take a sip of tea, I think of all of the things that were obvious to others but not to me. The Rebbe asked me to make this trip, and I must do it. No questions asked. That's the fate of a young Orthodox Jewish girl for all times.

"From what I know and what Aaron tells me, you are brave. Your Papa is dead, and still you go on. You know how he was killed?" Kat asks.

Aaron shakes his head no just as I stare into Kat's eyes.

"No, of course you don't know. He was killed outside the bakery. Two Gestapo men detained him, wanting to know of your whereabouts. One of them was your son's father. When he refused to give them any information, they shot him. I'm so sorry."

"Papa was killed because of me? He was defending me?"

"Yes, but you know in your heart he would have died for you or any of his family before he'd give in," Aaron says softly.

Tears stream down my cheeks. Yes, I know Papa. He would have done anything for his family, even send me away so that I might live.

"They've been watching you, as well as the Resistance. The driver in France was an informer to the Germans. We almost found out too late. He was sent to take you to a secluded spot right over the Spanish border and kill you."

"That was why he had to be the first to die?" I ask.

"Yes."

I take another sip. I still feel the tears running down my cheeks, but the fear, anxiety or sad emotions are fuzzy. I try to digest all of this new information, and still maintain the sadness for Papa and Joe's deaths.

"Joe did love you." Aaron he reaches for my hand.

I let him take it.

"He gave his life for you, and for a new Israel," Kat says, reassuringly.

314

"So he really did die?" I guess there has been a part of me who has always believed that at any point he would show up and say surprise. He wouldn't be dead, and he would have an adventure tale of how he washed ashore in Africa. An African tribe took him in and healed him until he was able to come home.

"Yes, I'm afraid he did. I don't know all the details, but he and Moshe died that tragic night. I'm so sorry, a widow when you were barely a bride."

I glare at the heavens and cry out. Our one night of love will be forever a memory too lovely to recall. I try to cry, but the tears just won't come, not now. I cried with Mama and the others. I will weep when this is done, and I can feel once more.

"I thought it was safe at the hotel in Casablanca. I was going to give you more information after the sightseeing, but when we got back the room was ransacked. I knew it might be bugged. I didn't want to take a chance."

"And the tea?" I ask suddenly. I want to know if the tea is really sleepy medicine, but I don't say it.

"There were a couple of times when something was in it, but not all of the time. Your body is tired. Look at all of the things you've been through since November 7th. It's amazing that you are still walking and talking, making any sense," Kat says, with a chuckle.

"Jean-Pierre?"

"She is one of the leaders of the resistance. She did take you in for two years, but I know that will come back to you, as soon as this mission is over."

I take another sip. I have to remember everything I'm going through right now. I can't let it slip away from me like before.

"Mama and the others?" I ask, after I swallow.

"They will be safe for a while. We hope to move them to Israel soon. We have to plan it just right as the British aren't allowing many Jews to enter. If they knew the significance, they would do all they could to keep them and us out. They will be safe on a Kibbutz. Others will be there to protect them. They will be with people who have been in the country for a long time." Aaron reaches for his wine glass and another taste.

"How many are there?"

"Zionists or British?" Kat asks.

"Both."

"Enough."

"So, I'm still going to go to Bangkok and get the scroll, and take it to Israel. Will I be alone?"

"I will take you to Bangkok, but you will have to travel to the Buddhist retreat alone. They'll give you what you need to take care of you. I don't know what sort of deal was worked out, but I know from what Rebbe says they are honorable men." Kat picks up her wineglass and stares into the red liquid.

"So what do we do?"

"We'll get a good night's sleep. We'll catch the plane to San Francisco. From there we will catch a plane to take us to Asia. We'll have to catch another from there to reach Bangkok. You'll get the scroll. We have to keep heading west from there. We aren't sure about all of the details but it will work out. Hopefully we'll go through India and Saudi Arabia to Safed. That is your final destination."

I listen intently. If I hadn't already been to so many places, I would swear what he proposes is impossible. I take another drink. This is good tea.

"Do you understand?" Kat asks.

317

I smile. "Yes, I understand."

"Of course we hope there are no glitches, but you and I already know that plans sometimes have to change," Kat says.

Aaron squeezes my hand.

"You'll still have to pretend that Aaron is your husband. Are you okay with this?"

"Yes." I push my hand into his.

"Any other questions that might need clarifying?"

"What happened in Prague during Kristallnacht?"

"Well let's just say a some of the resistance didn't take well to the Synagogues being destroyed and retaliated, wherever they were."

"I'm okay," I say at last. I know if I think of something later I can ask as long as it is before we leave for San Francisco.

"I have one more thing to say before we all clean up ... thank you so much for doing this wonderful mission." Kat reaches over, and squeezes my shoulder.

I feel my cheeks burn red, as I stare at the table. I'm lucky to be here, and I do it all for Papa, Joe and Moshe.

###

I take a nice warm bath. A luxury I may not have for a while.

We go to sleep early. When I awaken, I feel refreshed.

"How are you doing today?" Kat asks.

"I'm good." I think for a minute and look at her solemnly "What day is it?"

"It's November 22nd," Kat answers.

I'm satisfied. I know it seems like such a little thing to want to know what day it is but somehow it is important. It means that I have been dealing with this mission for fifteen days.

We eat more leftovers, and they're still delicious. Then we head for the airport. We want to make sure that we get there early. Kat has placed some food in the bag from the deli to take with us. She fears I will go hungry again, if the food is questionable. She also smuggles three Hershey bars into my bag.

When we get to the airport it's the same as before. In fact I think the same driver takes us back that brought us into New York. We go in, and Kat helps us find the right gate as she calls them.

I feel better. I'm still watchful of my surroundings, but starting to feel a little more informed. I sense there are other

319

things I still don't know, but maybe they don't have the information either. Kat and Aaron seem confident that because we are in the United States we must be safe. I experience no such security.

"I can't go with you two." Kat hugs Aaron and then me. "You take care of yourself," she whispers.

"We'll see you later," Aaron says, as we stand at our gate.

A young woman about my age takes our tickets. Everything is perfect about this lady, with tightly pulled back hair, and makeup. Even her clothes are pristine, I laugh to myself. I guess I'll never be mistaken for an airport worker.

Aaron turns around to survey the area. A large crowd is gathered compared to all of our other times. It would be easy to get lost in the crowd. Finally, Aaron finds us seats.

###

Soon they are calling our flight. We rise, and stroll over to the door that will take us to all the steps.

"Can't they make it easier then the up and down stairs business?" I ask Aaron jokingly.

"Wouldn't it be great if they had ramps that took us directly to the plane?"

"Yes, yes it would," a young woman in a uniform says, as she helps us down the stairs.

"Now when they start the plane, and it starts moving, remember to take deep breaths so that your ears won't get clogged," Aaron instructs, as we walk down the aisle to our seats.

I giggle. *Where was this information yesterday or whatever day it was when I first got on a plane? It would have definitely helped then.*

"Sorry, I should have told you sooner, but I didn't think you would understand. Plus you were sick the last time."

Now I really let out a loud chuckle.

"Well, thank you for telling me now." I scoot over to my seat by the window.

"You're welcome."

We strap in, as a lady in a blue and yellow uniform helps the others with their seats. She looks a lot like Kat, except not as pretty. Her yellow blouse is taunt against her skin. She tries to smile but occasionally frowns, as passengers become needy.

"If everyone is strapped in the pilot can start us rolling," she says loudly.

Everyone is strapped in but her, and another woman I've only caught a glimpse of.

I turn around to gaze out of the window. No planes are parked on this side, ready to blow up. I'm thankful. I realize I forgot to ask about plane during our talk. I'll have to save it for later. My guess that won't be until we reach Safed.

"Will we be in San Francisco long?"

"We actually have to catch a China Clipper about an hour after we get there. It will take us over the water again."

Looking back over at the terminal, I pray that we will be back.

###

The plane ride is uneventful. The uniformed woman gives us food bags of sandwiches. I peek inside, and see they are ham. I hand it back. I get the pinched up nose face from the woman that tells me she is irritated with me. A large man behind me volunteers to take it off her hands. She reluctantly

"What is it?"

"Pork."

"Oy."

"Are you hungry?"

"No, I will nibble on a candy bar." I accept several cups of tea. I know if I get too hungry I can pull something from the bag. I find the rocking of the plane, and staring out into the clouds makes me sleepy.

###

"Wake up sleepy head." Aaron kisses me on the cheek.

I stare up into his shining eyes, and smile. I'm starting to get used to seeing his face every time I wake up.

"We're almost there. We'll be landing in ten minutes."

"No customs?"

Laughing softly, "No customs. We're still in the same country."

I stretch, and shake my head lightly against the back of the chair. I hope this doesn't mess up my hair too badly, as I contemplate what he is saying. Where I come from there have been many times when I was made to carry identity papers, and been checked. I assumed all countries did this.

"You look beautiful," Aaron says.

"Thanks."

"We are making our descent," the woman says into a microphone.

I glance at the land below us, and for a second I fear that we will crash into it, but we don't. I'm thankful.

Once we're off the plane, we go to the desk so Aaron can ask for information about where to catch the China Clippers.

The lady laughs, but then draws him a map on a small piece of paper.

"Ma'am?"

The voice behind me startles me. "Yes?"

"Are you the lady with the jade tiger?"

"Yes."

Aaron overhears, and says thanks to the lady at the desk. He walks back over to me.

"I'm here to take you to the China Clipper."

I take a deep breath in and out. Thank HaShem.

He's a tall man with sinewy arms and legs wearing a black suit and tie. His hair is almost all gone from his head but not his face.

"My name is Conrad."

"My name is ... "

"Kfira and Joe."

"Yes." Aaron puts out his hand.

Conrad takes it gladly. "Our ride is close by."

We follow behind Conrad, as he leads us to a waiting car. It's a black sedan. I can't put my finger on it, but there's something about Conrad that makes me feel uneasy.

Aaron must be feeling it as well as he hasn't taken his arm from around my shoulder since we got in the car.

Glancing around the car, I notice nothing in particular to get me upset. Seats and a floorboard. I look around several times, and then I look at the doors. No door handles. It's too late, as we're both in our seats when we realize it. Aaron grasps my hands in his, as we wait to see what will happen next.

Watching out of the window, I can't help but to panic as the airport leaves my view. I stick close to Aaron. The hairs on the back of my neck stand at attention. My heart skips several beats. I just can't believe I feel this scared.

After about fifteen or twenty minutes, Conrad pulls into a large tin building. "How are y'all doing back there?"

"We are okay." Aaron eyes the man in the mirror.

"That's good, real good. I just have to make a stop here, and we can be on our way."

I want to ask why we're stopping, but don't as I see Conrad roll up a glass window between us and the front seat. I hear laughter, as he gets out of the car.

Aaron pulls me closer, and glares at Conrad. He stands next to the car, smiling at us. Pulling something out from behind his back, he places it over his face. It covers his nose and mouth. It's a gas mask!

A funny smell begins to fill the backseat, as well as the front.

I know 'follow my lead' is in place.

Looking around the car, there is nothing to break the window with but our bags. Aaron begins to kick as hard as he can against the glass petition between the front and back seat. I turn to a window, and try to kick it. I keep landing on my tucas in the floorboard. I feel adrenaline coursing through my body making me feel strong enough to lift a house. I see the same adrenaline flowing through Aaron's veins.

I cough and my eyes begin to burn. Aaron is also coughing,

choking on his own spit. It's hard to see where he is or anything else for a few moments.

Smoke infiltrates the car and our lungs. We hold our noses, and try to breathe through our mouths. But we still find ourselves becoming a slave to the slowly leaking gas, filling the car.

Aaron yells something, but I can't understand him. My mind is starting to feel a little fuzzy. I don't want to pass out. I'm still slamming my body against the window and door now. I can't die here, not now. I've got to get to Bangkok.

Aaron shatters the window, and pushes me through the crawl space before following me. Aaron grabs the bags before he helps me open the car door open. He pulls us to the ground. He pulls himself up, and slams the door shut as hard as he can. It caves into the side of the car just enough that it won't open.

We choke and gasp at the air, coughing out the poisons that tried to fry our brains and lungs seconds ago. I claw at my neck trying to catch my breath, but Aaron pulls my hands away. Finally, I let the oxygen fill my lungs. I wipe away the tears on my cheeks.

"Come on." He crawls along the floor to the front then

thinking better of it he starts pulling us back to the backside. To the wall.

We both need more air, and Aaron starts to breathe easier before I do. It feels as if we are in a tunnel and all I can see is a little stream of light. Aaron is pulling me, and I don't know if I'm walking, crawling or laying still.

Fear fills me once the adrenaline of the fight with the door leaves. I feel better as I breathe in the oxygen. I stop coughing and wheezing. I wipe my eyes and no fresh tears take their place. My nose opens up. My head starts to clear and I can see and think again.

Aaron points to a door in the back, and rises to his feet. I do the same, and follow right behind him. No one is around. I guess no one wanted to stay for the show.

We get to the back door, and hear screaming and shooting in the front. A tall black haired man with large muscles has Conrad by the neck. He is squeezing him, as he drags Conrad kicking and screaming back to the car. Conrad no longer has his gas mask on. Instead, the dark haired man sports it over his face.

Aaron and I stare, motionless as the scene plays out before us.

"Open it!"

"No, please," Conrad says over and over.

"Open it!"

"No, please."

The big man compresses tighter until Conrad is choking, and his face becomes almost purple. Then he opens the car door, and tosses him inside.

Instantly Conrad begins to beat on the door but, it doesn't budge, as the big man leans against it. He crawls up to the front seat, but one door is jammed. The other has the big man leaning against it. He races between the front and back, screaming with all his might.

This plays out for what seems like eternity, but it's only fifteen minutes. Finally, Conrad presses his face against the window. His eyes and nose smear red with blood and he slumps down into the back seat, dying. Only a bloody handprint marks his exit from this world.

I realize that we have no place to hide. I swallow hard, and gaze to the door. *Where can we go?*

The big man pivots around to see Aaron and I standing there.

"Aaron! Kfira! Come give Jeremiah a hug!"

Aaron races toward the big man, half dragging me and the bags to this stranger. Running up to the big man, Aaron lets go of me and the bags. He embraces Jeremiah. Aaron is only a few millimeters shorter than the big man. They look alike in the face. Aaron isn't as muscular, but they look almost like twins.

"We're cousins," Jeremiah says, before I have a chance to ask. "We've got to go. The clipper is waiting."

"Thank God you got here," Aaron says, as we hike back through the open front door.

What lies beyond the door almost makes me want to run back inside. Two more dead bodies lay on the ground beside a large green truck.

"We tried to catch you before you left the airport. That little snot somehow got info about you two. He and his clan buddies dreamed this up. He was trying to help Hitler."

Jeremiah opens the truck door, and we get inside. Jeremiah gets in the driver's side, and soon we're back on the road to the real China Clipper.

"I'm so sorry that it got this close. Our people went after the others from his group."

It doesn't take us long to get to the water and the China Clipper. It sits majestically on the water. The wings and propellers go across the top of the body instead of on the side. This one is white with a black nose, and sits delicately on the water.

"They don't normally take passengers, but the pilot is a good friend of Abraham," Jeremiah says.

I will learn later that it's a term meaning the person is Jewish.

"He wants a homeland too."

We get out, and stroll over to the plane. It looks larger close up than far away. Two men stand outside, waiting for us. On the side of the plane written in English is the name Jade Tiger.

I feel instant relief.

One man is tall and about thirty while the other is short and about twenty-five. They're both wearing gray jumpers.

"Are you two okay?" the tall one asks.

"Yes," Aaron answers.

"Let me help you," the other one suggests, as we step inside the aircraft.

With every step I feel and say a prayer under my breath. I know in my heart that these two are all right, but I can't shake the three dead bodies or gassed car off so quickly.

"I'm Isaac," the short one says.

"I'm Jonah," the tall one says.

"And you know who we are."

"Yes, let's get you in your seats so we can take off. We don't normally take passengers, but we have set up accommodations just for you."

We amble through to the back of the plane. A small lounge is arranged here with two seats and two cots. The necessary room, and kitchen are right next to it.

"Sometimes we're in the air for three days, and one of us needs a nap. We'll be making stops, but basically we're on the go for three days, sometimes six."

"Thank you," I say.

"Don't worry about it. Get buckled up, as we will take off in ten minutes," Jonah says, and they head back to the front.

We really are going. I find I must go to the necessary room before the plane takes off. I can't say good bye to San Francisco.

Asia and Jade Tigers

Coming out of the necessary room, I see Aaron holding a cup of tea for me. He's sitting in his chair. He seems so darling, as he tries to juggle two large cups.

"After our little ordeal Jonah thought we might need something to drink."

"Yes." I sit down, and strap myself in. I take the cup from his shaking hand. I had thought about asking Aaron for his flask when we were in the car, but couldn't get the words out of my mouth. The warm liquid soothes my burnt throat. I wish there was a way to ease my eyes. I washed my face in the necessary room, but still don't feel quite right until the tea.

"Are you sure you are all right? I heard you coughing in the bathroom."

"Yeah, I guess there's still a little poison in my system, but I'm okay now."

I take a sip of tea, and it feels warm and comforting.

I notice that I'm sitting next to a small window, and without really looking too hard I can see outside. Jeremiah is undoing ropes that have the Clipper tied to the dock. I notice I won't be able to see the propellers from here. I won't know when we're starting. I realize that I won't really need to see it, as much as I will be able to feel it. The vibrations and motion start to quicken, I hear the whine of the engines just as with the other airplanes. I'm amazed at how far I have come from a little shtetl in East Prussia to San Francisco.

"Are you sure you are okay? You look tired?"

"Me?" I laugh. "I hope you slept well last night because I know I did. I slept better than I have since the night before the wedding." *It dawns on me as I'm saying this that it doesn't make sense. I really want to say I'm okay, but the words aren't coming out.*

The wedding. I was once a bride. I was so beautiful too. Was that a dream? No, if Aaron is reminding me then I know it isn't a dream. I take another sip of tea.

"I'm so sorry for your loss."

"So am I."

"We can only hope that things will get better after the Torah is back in Safed."

I nod. I glance out of the window, just as the engines whine, and the plane bounces against the water. We are move forward. I suddenly realize that although there were two clippers docked, this was the only one preparing for a flight. I'm thankful.

"Do you know these men?" I'm bold.

"They are friends of my cousin."

I nod.

Soon I feel the ascent of the plane, as it drifts upward to the sky. Peeking over at Aaron, my heart skips a beat as he touches my arm. He breathes with me. No one says a word, as we exercise our ability to take clean air in and let bad air out. This goes on for what seems like an eternity, but is only fifteen minutes. The plane levels back off again. Funny, my ears hurt much less. I'm thankful.

"Aaron."

"Yes."

"Are we really going to be on this plane for three days?"

"Pretty much, I think it's actually less than that, but we have to stop and refuel at Honolulu, Wake Island and Guam."

Those places sound so exotic to me now.

"We won't be able to get off and see anything, but maybe after all of this is over we will come back."

I snicker.

"We've been saying that a lot, haven't we?" Aaron chuckles at the irony of it all.

I nod.

"I would like to show you these places afterward, if you will let me."

"That would be nice." I glance back out of the window. "What is that?"

"What is it?"

"It's a large bridge."

"Oh that." Aaron peers over to the window. "That's the Golden Gate Bridge."

"It's huge."

It looks like a merry-go-round except instead of the poles in a circle, they are in a straight line. The ropes cross, and then up and down, make for a very interesting pattern in the air. It almost looks like an old wooden bridge not far from the old house. No one knows why it was built, as there's no water under it. But as a child, I played on it with the other children. We played tag, and hide and seek. It was great fun.

The floor on this bridge has tiny mice that I know are cars, going across it. No one is playing tag here. Underneath the bridge are kilometers and kilometers of water. Blue water.

"It's the largest. They just completed it last year."

"I can't believe people use it. I would be afraid that it would break."

"Nah, it's solid."

Hmmm ... it doesn't appear very solid to me. It gives the impression of being able to sway.

"Pretty soon we'll be passing close to Alcatraz the prison. It's supposed to have some of the worst convicts in the country there."

"What are convicts?"

"You must be kidding?"

"Are they people who have done something against the government?"

"They have done something against the government, you and

me, and anyone they can. They have rob and kill people for a living. Prisons in other parts of the country didn't know how to handle them so they developed Alcatraz."

I shake my head. I don't think they're as mean as the people in my country, or Europe, but one never knows. For them killing is done if you are the wrong religion, or because it's Monday.

"I forget, we came from hell didn't we?"

Watching closely, I see it. It looks small in the air, but it's easy to distinguish the towers and to know there are guns in them. It looks like a large square with the sides being larger than the middle. Away from the prison are houses, and I wonder who might have to live there. I'm guessing that the workers may live there. It's probably too difficult to get people to ride over the water every day, and what about bad weather. No, too risky. Better to stay and leave seldom. Makes me think that maybe the workers are in a sort of prison of their own.

"Are you hungry?"

"A little."

"Let's have a snack." We ate some of the food on the airplane when I found everything was treif. I'm thankful that we did, as I look in the bag, I realize that some of the poison gas may be on the food.

"Don't worry about that food." Aaron unbuckles and stands up. He eases over to an icebox, and opens it up. "We're in luck. They have sandwiches in here. Corned beef." He takes several out, as well as bottles of Coca-Cola.

Bringing them back, he hands me the sandwiches and opens the Coca Colas before sitting down. Putting them between his legs, he is able to maneuver the safety harness back on.

We exchange a sandwich for a Coca-Cola.

I giggle, as I take a sip of the drink.

"Still tickles your nose? What about champagne?"

I frown. "I don't think champagne has nearly as many bubbles as this does."

"You're probably right."

The food and drink hit the spot. Apprehension leaves immediately, and I start to settle into the fact that this is my new home.

I begin to glance around, and see compartments all around. I guess they're for carrying packages. Maybe they're even for carrying important messages, but then if they're very important then they would be wired or telephoned. I wonder if I'm an important message.

I take out my journal, and begin to write about the Golden Gate Bridge and Alcatraz.

###

I shut my eyes, but I'm not really asleep. The vibrations from the plane lull me into a serenity that's unusual for me. I feel safe despite the fact we're crossing a large body of water. For as far as the eyes can see there is only water.

"Everything okay?" Jonah walks up.

"We're doing great," Aaron answers.

"I know this isn't the most exciting trip with sitting back here, and everything but it's a ride."

"Are you kidding? She's seen the Statue of Liberty and the Atlantic Ocean. She was able to see the Golden Gate Bridge and Alcatraz. I'd say she's been one busy woman."

I almost laugh out loud, but I really don't want them to know I'm awake. I want to hear what they have to say. Yes, I'm being a yenta!

"The weather is clear all the way to Honolulu. We'll stop and refuel, and then be right back on schedule. I just thought I would come back and let you know everything is going well up front."

I hear the icebox door open, and two bottles clink together. I know that he is getting some nosh. I heed the footfalls, as he walks away.

"So how long have you been awake?"

"Huh?" I flutter my eyelashes coyly at him and he smiles. *A part of me tells I'm an Orthodox woman, and shouldn't be so shameless about this flirting. After all I'm a recent widow. I'm far away from home, but the other part of me says that I'm a woman. I'm not used to such attention from a man. Yes, my husband died, but I'll be a widow longer than I was a bride. Oy! Such a life!*

###

I must have fallen asleep as when I wake up I can see a few specks on the water.

"Are those islands?" I ask, without glancing around to see who else is with me.

"Yes, they are."

Immediately, I turn to see Isaac sitting in Aaron's seat.

"He went to talk to Jonah about the flight plans."

"Oh, okay." I stare back out the window. Yes, the little specks are getting clearer, and it's possible to see they're islands.

"I can't get you anything special while we are here, but are there any foods I can get for you?"

I think for a minute, not sure of what is in Honolulu. Finally, I think of only one thing. "Do they have fruit here?"

Cackling like a rooster, Isaac's body shakes with laughter. He slaps at his knee and misses, plunging him nearly to the floor. "Yes, ma'am. They have fruit. I will get you some fruit."

"Thank you." I almost laugh with him, but I smile instead. I wonder what I said that was so funny.

"I'd better get back to the front. I can tell this is going to be a heckofa ride." He pulls himself up by the arm of the seat, and heads back up front.

A few minutes later Aaron is back.

"We will be in Honolulu in about an hour."

I nod. I lean back, and close my eyes. I pray that I can sleep again.

The plane ride goes smoothly, and I don't even hear us land. When I wake I find Aaron pacing.

"Are you all right?"

"Yes, don't worry about me. I was just trying to get my legs some exercise. Don't want them to fall asleep too long, or I'll have a hard time walking once we get to Guam."

"I have a silly question. I know we're going to Guam, but how will we get to Bangkok from there?"

"We should be able to catch a plane to Manila, and then to Bangkok. Manila isn't very stable as Japan is trying to take over all of Asia."

"How?"

"We'll find a way."

True, we always do find a way, but I was hoping it might be a little easier than ... I don't know. I was just hoping it would be a little easier.

Jonah pops his head around the corner. The big grin on his face tells a story, and I want to hear it. "I have a special delivery for a Kfira."

"What is it?"

"Fruit!" He hands me a bag of orange fruits, green fruits, bananas and others. Never have I seen so many fruits in one place, and I'm thrilled beyond belief.

"Thank you so much." I grab up one, and then the other, inspecting each one. It all looks so good to me.

"We'll be leaving in ten minutes so take care of business, and get strapped in."

I know this is my signal to use the necessary room. I have fresh fruit to eat, and I can't wait. I don't know the names of them, I just know they taste good. Aaron shows me how to eat them.

###

I stare out the window until I lose focus. I eat. I sleep. I talk with the others. I pray. I hike around the area so that my legs don't go to eternal sleep. I feel fairly calm, although there is a little piece of me that has an anxious moment or two.

I'm thankful that Aaron is here when the fear overwhelms me. He gets me a cup of tea, and breathes with me. He's so patient. I find myself falling in love with him, and I don't know how to stop it.

###

The ride to Midway is shorter than the one to Honolulu. I ask Aaron why. He says that Midway is closer to Honolulu than Honolulu is to San Francisco. Technically, we could probably go to Midway directly from San Francisco, but they had a delivery. They will make it on the trip going out.

Again we stop for nearly an hour while the plane gets fuel and Isaac gets supplies.

It's hard to tell that day is turning into night, as I fall asleep so easily on the plane. I always wake up feeling stiff. Jonah tells me to lie on the cot, but I feel very insecure doing this with strange men around. I know it sounds silly after everything I've been through, but a woman has to have some dignity.

###

The ride to Wake Island is also short. Every time I stare out of the window all I can see is ocean. The water looks clear even from up here, and I hear that sometimes we fly low to avoid something. I don't understand what they are talking about, so I usually stop listening once they say radar. I hope to see an ocean creature, but I'm sure it would scare me to death if I did see one.

Again, we arrive and Isaac goes for supplies. I have eaten several large orange fruits, and they have eased my tummy. I don't understand it. Sometimes I'm so hungry, and sometimes I couldn't look at food if I was forced to. I pray I'm not coming down with something. I have too much to do.

###

Now we're headed for our final destination, Guam.

"How long have we been traveling?" I ask.

"Long enough."

"Seriously." I push him lightly on the shoulder.

"Over two days."

"Did I see you reading a newspaper earlier?"

"Yes, but it's old, and in English. You wouldn't want to read it." Aaron nonchalantly picks up his book.

"I will ask Isaac or Jonah for it." I feel the old spitfire coming back. I grin, and make a face. I want to tell him I can read English, but I don't. I can read some English.

Aaron chuckles lightly. "Okay, you're probably going to find out soon anyway." He hands me the paper.

I glare at the front page, nothing too great on it. Then I turn to the second page, and a large headline catches my eye.

In bold letters is Das Schwarze Korps ... it explains the question, "Jews: What next?" It states that the only solution for Jews is extermination. Death. They want to kill all of us! How? Why? What did we ever do to these men?

I feel the blood drain from my face, and I turn to gape out of the window. I feel like a woman without a home.

###

Finally, after almost sixty hours of flying and landing, Jonah steps to the back once more. "We'll be landing in thirty minutes. We want you two to make sure to take some sandwiches for the road. You might be able to get something to drink, but you won't get food."

I nod.

"Thanks," Aaron says scratching his ear.

I haven't spoken since I read the newspaper.

"Did you know?"

"Did I know what?"

"That this was going to happen?"

"We had an idea. That's why it was important to get you out when we did."

I sigh, and stare out of the window. I know I'd better go use the necessary room and freshen up. It may be a long time before I get to see one.

I gaze over to see Aaron putting food in our fruit bag. He even tucks away a roll of toilet paper.

I have to laugh when I see him do this, as he puts a finger to his lips in a sh motion. I know that Isaac and Jonah do not care. They have a box of it in the necessary room.

"We're going to be all right." Aaron pulls me over and hugs me. "My turn in the little room," he says after a minute, and pulls me away, still holding my arms. At first I think he will kiss me, and then he winks. "Be right back."

I sit in my seat and wait. Soon Aaron is back. Very shortly I see land on the horizon. It's still daylight and I'm thankful.

After we land, Aaron and Isaac come back to our den.

"Thank you for flying with us," Isaac says.

"Thank you," I say. I run over and give them each a huge hug and kiss on their cheeks.

They blush and stammer about.

"We can't take you to where you should go, but a young man named Sampson will be picking you up." Isaac holds up a black and white photograph of a young man of about twenty-two. He has light brown hair and thick glasses.

"Thank you so much." Aaron hugs them, but doesn't kiss them.

"Take care," Aaron and Isaac say simultaneously.

We amble to the door of the plane. We must wade through a little water. It feels like the walk up the Statue of Liberty all over again. My legs fill like the ground is swallowing them up. Aaron has our bags, and I tote the food and my handbag. He touches dry land first, and helps me cross the small space of water. I look down and almost lose my footing. I gaze to Aaron to see where he is, and leap across.

We hike up the pier about twenty meters when the man from the picture, Sampson strolls over to us. He is carrying something.

"Hello, I'm Sampson." He hands me a stuffed animal. It's a large, stuffed jade tiger!

"Hello, I'm ..." Aaron starts to say something, but is

interrupted.

"I know, you're Kfira and Aaron. I know I am supposed to call you Joe, and after now I will. I want you to know we do have safe passage for you two to Bangkok." With this he leads us over to a car.

Aaron can see the anxiety in my eyes, and with his own he tries to reassure me. I start to feel protected.

Asia and Sampson

Sampson opens the car door, and allows me to maneuver inside the car with the food bag, the tiger, the handbag and me. He shuts the door, as Aaron opens his own, and sits in the passenger side of the front seat.

I know we're both a little shaken from our San Francisco experience. Neither of us too trusting.

I immediately stare down the door to see if there are door handles, as well as window cranks to roll down the windows. Everything is intact. I thank HaShem. I hear a similar sound from Aaron in the front.

"You two look a little spooked." Sampson gets into the car and starts it.

"We had a little misunderstanding with the driver of a car in San Francisco."

Aaron turns around to see if I'm comfortable.

I smile and wave.

"That must have been scary," Sampson says, in a sympathetic tone. "I don't think it will happen here, at least not by me. I work for Mr. Rothschild's family. They have been taking care of Jews for a very long time."

"So what is the plan?" Aaron asks.

"We will fly you from Manila to Bangkok."

"So how do we get to Manila?"

"That we will find out very shortly."

I start to feel uneasy. So far everything has gone relatively smoothly, except for the shootings and near gassing. I know they have another plan. I'm waiting to hear it.

"I wanted to put you on my boat, and take you that way but Mr. Rothschild insists that he talk with you before the matter is settled."

"He's in Guam because ... ?" Aaron asks.

"He has some investments to check on here. We'll be there soon," Sampson says, as we drive along a dirt road.

The road forks to the right, and then back again to the left. We move along the road for a good hour before we see it.

As we ride, I turn my attention to the beautiful jade tiger on my lap. It's a little over a meter long with golden eyes. The stripes alternate between green and black. White fur ruffles about the face, and the pads of the paws. A menacing look upon the cat's face warns all. I find myself snuggling against the warmth of the fur.

I glimpse down, as I have many times on this trip to make sure that my own jade tiger pin is still attached to my dress. It's still securely fastened, and I'm thankful.

"Here we are," Sampson says, as he pulls up to the huge, white house that seems to suddenly pop out of nowhere.

It's two stories tall with four large pillars holding up the porch roof. People are sitting on a second-floor balcony, watching to see who is here. I can't tell if it's anyone I might have seen before, or even if there is a mix of men and women.

Upon parking the car and turning off the key, Sampson leaps

out of the car and opens my door. I allow him to take my hand

and help me out. I bend back down to snatch up my things. He

shuts the door, and once more grasps my arm, as if I'm an old

woman.

"This way, shall we?"

Aaron and I can do nothing but follow. Inside the house, I feel

as if I've stepped back into Jean-Pierre's home. Elegance is

everywhere. I feel overwhelmed by the magnitude of it all.

"They are upstairs." Sampson shows us the way to the grand

staircase. By now, he has loosened his grip on my arm, and I

start to relax.

"They?"

"Well, there is family of course."

Aaron and I exchange a glance with question marks in our

eyes.

"I promise, you will understand everything as soon as we get

upstairs," Sampson tries to reassure us.

The steps are made of sky blue marble, and the clip clop from

our shoes sound like the hoof beats of horses on cobblestone roads. The gold plated railing is thick with bars attached to each step, magnifying its true beauty.

As we reach the top of the stairs, an older man steps out of the first room on the right. He's tall like Aaron. An air of distinction is about him like a halo. His silver hair is combed back, but not greasy in any way. He has a silver moustache, but no beard. His moustache seems to meet the top of his earlobes. He wears a dark blue suit with a vest and tie that likens to the color of his eyes.

"Hello! Hello!" He steps forward to greet us.

"Hello," we say simultaneously, as we peek shyly at one another.

"Come in! Come in!" He leads the way into the drawing room. Turning to look at us once more, he stretches out his hand to Aaron and then me.

"Hello." Aaron takes the man's hand warmly.

"Hello." I shake hands with this stranger.

"My name is Abel Rothschild. My grandfather built the empire you see and I'm enjoying its fruits. Come in and have a seat." He points to several large sofas of light peach color.

Several chairs and tables are placed strategically around the room with just enough space for the patrons and wait staff to get by. The tables are covered with heavy white cloths and then large embroidered dollies top them. Each table has a different pastel color. The chairs are cloth bound. Each table has six chairs.

I can't help but notice that the others that are sitting on the balcony, make no move to come inside or acknowledge us. It's as if we are invisible. I'm thankful.

"Would you like something to drink?"

"Yes, please," I say, as a young woman with olive skin and dark hair walks into the room.

She is beautifully small in stature, with thick black hair pulled back. Her dress is colorfully dotted with different flowers scattered about on it, and she is smiling. She wears no shoes.

"Bring us some tea, please," Abel says, to the woman.

The woman turns and leaves.

"I know you are probably wondering why you are here in this house. I trust that you know why you are here in Guam."

I nod.

"Well, I always like to meet the people who are helping me

and vice versa. I, along with several other backers who wish to remain nameless, am financing this little excursion. We find it's in the best interest to ourselves, and others to keep the others anonymous."

The young woman returns with three tall glasses of tea. She starts with the men first, allowing them to choose from the glasses. Then it's my turn, and I take the only one left.

"Thank you." I take the glass. Although I wish to learn more of what Mr. Rothschild is saying, I can't help but to find myself fascinated with the green leaf floating in my glass of tea. Until reaching America, I had only heard of cold tea. This is my first experience, and I'm not sure what to do with it. I decide to drink around it.

"The leaf is mint. You can leave it in the glass," the woman whispers to me.

"Thank you," I say, and nod at the same time in affirmation. I'm afraid with both of our accents that there might be a miscommunication.

She grins and leaves the room once more.

"If you're helping us, then who is trying to kill us?" I ask, and then bite my tongue for speaking out of turn. I glare down at the mint leaf, as I feel my face begin to burn with its redness.

"Don't be shy. You're the one in danger here. You should know who is after you. The Gestapo would like to stop you, and I suspect sympathizers have helped them such as with the attack in San Francisco. The young man was an American German who believed Hitler's philosophies. He was a part of a growing group of Nazis in the United States. Of course, I don't see it going very far, but you never know."

This news sends a shiver up and down my spine. *Germans want all Jews to die. They would never want a renewal of a homeland. What will they do to keep me from performing my task?*

"This is why it's so important to get the Torah scroll to Palestine/Israel as fast as we can. Of course, the Resistance fighters and Zionists have been on your side. Trust me, I'm sure there has been nothing you have done for even the last six months that someone from either group hasn't known about. They've been watching you."

"ME?" I can't stop myself from laughing at this idea. "That's so silly. Until the day Rebbe came to ask me to do this, my life has been boring."

"Believe me, you have made up for it in the last three weeks. I don't think your life has ever been boring if you think about it." Aaron chuckles.

"So what's next?" It's the burning question that everyone wants to know the answer to.

"We'll fly you to Manila, and then to Bangkok. When you get to Bangkok, Aaron won't be with you. Aaron will take another route. He'll catch up with you once you get to Delhi, India. He'll help you along the rest of the route, as it'll be too dangerous for a single woman to travel alone in the Middle East. But, don't be fooled. You're never alone."

I sigh.

Aaron opens his mouth to protest, but stops when I put up my hand up. I can see the urgency in his demeanor that makes him want to protect me, but I know this can't be. He must let me go.

"We'll make sure you have all the right things with you. I assure you the Monks will be very helpful."

"How will I know the monks?" I take a sip of my tea.

Chuckling loudly, Mr. Rothschild points to the pin on my dress."They will be wearing pins like the one you have. Oh, and you must take the stuffed animal with you everywhere you go."

I frown, hugging the tiger close to me. I sigh, and look at Aaron and Mr. Rothschild. I pray I can do this task that is set before me.

"You are almost done, young lady. You have done much better than anyone suspected you capable of. It's your turn to fly solo. We believe in you." With this, Mr. Rothschild takes a long drink from his glass.

"Is there anything else you can tell me?"

"There is probably more I should tell you, but I won't until you're on your way to the airport. I will tell you this, these monks shave their heads except for the long braids down their back but. They'll have no facial hair."

This is good information to know. Now, how to get there carrying my bag, purse, and the tiger without being noticed. I realize, there's no way.

"Would you like to freshen up?"

"No, thank you, I freshened up on the plane." I begin to notice all the paintings of elderly people on the walls. They're dressed in the costumes of their era appropriately.

"They're dearly departed family members."

I smile at Mr. Rothschild.

"When do I get to leave?"

"Anytime you're ready. Sampson will be your pilot. Thank you, Kfira, and I'll see you when you get to Safed."

I feel like I'm being dismissed, but no one says anything more.

Sampson walks in, and looks for me. "Are you ready?"

"I'm ready." I stand. Aaron and Mr. Rothschild rise. Aaron strolls over, and gives me a hug that feels so tight I'm afraid he might melt into me.

Mr. Rothschild shakes my hand warmly. "Someone will contact you once you are back in Bangkok with the scroll to give you further instructions."

I wish I could scream, I want to know everything. But I don't. I know that even if I did, something would happen to spoil the plan. No, this time I will have to think for myself. I take a deep breath in and out, and pray I'm ready. I hand my empty glass to

Aaron.

Sampson picks up my bag, and hands me the tiger. We head back out the way we came in. I know I'm not alone, but I feel so lonely. A part of me wants to run back to Aaron, and beg him to stop this nonsense, but I can't. Rebbe asked me to do this favor, and I can only fulfill it to the best of my ability. Saying no isn't an option.

Just like the first time, Sampson helps me into the car.

"I bet you are really excited about this trip." He checks to see that I have everything I need before he shuts the door. He gets into the driver seat, and starts the car.

I grin. Right now, my heart is breaking for I'm by myself with a jade tiger on the way to Bangkok with no loved ones in sight. Only HaShem to light the way. I'm thankful for that light.

Sampson babbles about something all the way to the airport. I think he's talking about how he would do the mission if he had been assigned to it. All I can think is you don't know.

###

We reach the airport within an hour. The road is dusty and there are a few people walking both ways. They carry their belongings in bags, and try to move off the road when they see automobiles. Trees are lined up along the sides of the road, as if they are protecting it from the rest of the world.

Sampson says something about the island being controlled by the Americans, and that's why there are so many here. But so far, all I have seen are natives except Mr. Rothschild, his family or friends and Sampson.

We get to the airport, and there are planes parked around the field. The place is deserted.

"I'm going to drop you off at the plane, and my partner will help you. She's a great gal, her name is Sarah. She can help you get settled in. I'll walk up here, and we'll be on our way."

The plane he drops me off at is a small plane compared to the others I have been on. It's even smaller than the Clipper. It's painted white with red stripes on the side.

As we park and get out, Sampson begins to call out Sarah.

Sarah pops her head out of the passenger compartment. She smiles and waves at us, before stepping down the few steps to the ground. She races across to greet us.

"My name is Sarah." She stretches out her hand to me.

I take it warmly in my own, "Kfira."

"Yes, I know. I'm very excited to be meeting you. Let's get you inside." She takes my bag, and leaves the tiger and purse with me. "Take very good care of this one." She pats the tiger's head, as if it's a child.

I giggle. "I will."

We march up the steps, and into the passenger section. Sarah familiarizes me with everything that is on board. Six seats in the back leave me plenty of room to stretch out. A small necessary room and kitchen round it off will all the necessities.

"I want to show you something." She takes me to my seat. Pulling out what looks like a heavy bag from under the seat next to mine, she plops it in the seat above its resting spot. "This is a parachute in case something happens to the plane."

Now I panic, as I look at this meshuggah woman standing before me in her gray jumper, thick, curly red hair and freckles. Her blue eyes sparkle with her full smile beaming, but it doesn't help alleviate my worst fears. I will have to jump out of the plane.

"What do I do with it?"

"You strap it on like this and then this." She puts the two large

363

straps across her shoulders. Sarah demonstrates clicking the harness about my middle and even how I can place the tiger between me and the belt. Then, she shows me a cord with a metal circle attached to the left side. "You pull this when you're clear of the plane. Don't worry, if you don't open it for whatever reason then it'll automatically open once you reach a certain height."

"Will I have to do this?" I'm not sure I can.

"I'm sure you won't need to today, but it's always good to know. We haven't had any trouble yet, but I thought it best to tell you now, as Sampson doesn't like to talk about it."

"Are we ready to go?" Sampson boards the plane. He too, is now wearing a gray jumper. He closes the door before we can answer. "We'll be leaving in ten minutes so get ready.

He and Sarah go up to the front.

I lean back in my chair, and try to get comfortable. I try to recall the breathing that Aaron has taught me, and suddenly I feel lonely. This is going to be a long trip without him. I knew I would be alone for part of this trip, and now it's time.

I recline back against the cushions, and try to get comfortable, as I watch the propellers start to turn. The engines begin to vibrate the plane, and I commence to pray. Soon, we are moving along the dirt path.

I find myself eyeing the other planes, and the fact we're still the only people in sight frightens me. Soon, I see trees, trees, and more trees. I try to watch, and do the breathing that I did with Aaron. Soon I find myself relaxing despite everything.

###

People are shooting and screaming. I try to run behind the building, but I can't seem to get there. The faster I move, the farther away it gets. I struggle with wheat shafts that keep slapping against my face. I hear myself scream over and over again.

I awaken suddenly to hear gunshots being fired at the plane. I attempt to look out of the window to see where they are coming from, but I see nothing.

"Wake up! Wake up!"

I jump up in the seat, and nearly choke myself on the safety straps, as they catch my shoulders and neck. I glance around, and for a second I'm unsure of where I am. The lights are out in the back of the plane, and it's dark. The engines are making a strange sound. I smell smoke. I suddenly see the tucas of the other plane, leaving as quickly as it came.

"Kfira! Wake up!" It's Sarah's voice from the pilot's room. She stumbles out, and grasps the seat as she comes out. She is having trouble moving her legs at first, and then she sprints over to me.

"What happened?" I struggle to pull off the safety harness, and run to help her. I pull her over to the seat by my stuff. She feels very heavy as she has the parachute strapped to her back.

"You have to get yourself out of the plane. We've been shot down. We're about five kilometers south of Bangkok. I don't think we're going to make it. You need to put on your parachute."

I watch blood ooze from the corner of Sarah's mouth, and a gash in her forehead where more blood drips into her eyes. She tries to stand, and help me put the parachute on. Leaning against the back of a seat. She hands me, my handbag and tiger. We manage to strap the two onto the parachute so that they can't be separated from me.

"There's no way to carry your bag. Is there anything in there that you need?"

"No, all of my valuables are in my handbag." The engines begin to make a whining that sounds like a million wolves howling in the night. I try to control the fear that has me wanting to run. The blood coursing through my body is on fire, and I fight the urge to scream.

"Where is Sampson?" I stare back over to the door she just emerged from, half expecting Sampson to pop his head out. Nothing.

"He's dead. We've to go." We feel the airplane taking a dive downwards. Suddenly, the plane begins to spin.

Sarah pulls the door release and it pops open. "Take my hand," she says above the engines and the wind. "If we get separated, go to Bangkok. Do your job. You'll see me later." With this Sarah jerks us both out of the airplane so hard that I will have bruises on my arms for weeks afterwards.

At first it feels as if I am falling from the hayloft in Mr. Meyerson's barn, and I feel exhilarated. The wind whips my face and hair, and tries to rip the tiger from my arms. He sits beneath my harness, as well as my handbag.

Sarah tries to keep a hold of my hand, but it's of no use. The wind pulls us from apart. I stare at her just in time to see her pointing to the cord that she showed me earlier. She pulls hers and suddenly, a huge white pillow pops out of the pack. It pulls her upward.

I wrap loose straps around the tiger for extra security, cinching it tightly. I pull my cord as well. I feel the parachute open up, and at first pulls me upward. I look back over to the plane to see it getting closer to the ground. The wind tugs on me, and pulls me northward, while the plane travels southward.

Suddenly, the plane makes an impact with the ground. Several minutes later, a loud thud and pop echoes through the night, as it explodes into a ball of flames. A layer of billowing, black smoke encircles it. The ground trembles beneath it, and sounds as if the world is caving in. I say a prayer for all of us, even Sampson. I watch as the people scrambling down on the ground try to figure out where I will land. It's hard to see them very clearly, as they look so far away. I can't keep from closing my eyes. My stomach is in my throat, and I know this is no place to be ill.

Even though the smoke looks so far away, I begin to feel the familiar tickle in the back of my throat and eyes. Itching, I'm thankful my hands can't reach my eyes, as I would scratch them out.

My stomach is in my throat, and I need to vomit. I don't think it's a good idea. I search for something to focus on. Finally I see a dirt road, and a group of people sitting on some kind of car.

I discover myself going right in their direction. I'm scared to land. When I was young and jumped from the hayloft, I broke my leg. I don't know what I will do if that happens now. The wind floats me about as if I'm an angel on a cloud. Maybe I'm dead, I think. But then I realize that it isn't true; as I stare over at the fireball that holds Sampson's lifeless body. I know, he is the one who's heaven bound.

It seems like forever before my legs hit the grass and dirt. It isn't nearly as scary as the hayloft. I try to stand but, I fall, all wobbly and out of breath.

Two men come running up to me from behind and touch my shoulder. I nearly scream in their faces. Instead, I yelp and clutch my belongings. Everything I own is in my handbag and stuffed tiger.

"It's okay," the tall red haired man with a strange uniform says to me in English.

"Are you," I say with a gulp "Americans?"

"Yes, we saw your plane get shot down. We came to help you," the blonde says. He's almost as tall as the red haired man, and also wearing the same uniform.

"I need to get to Bangkok." I glance around to see if I can see Sarah, or even catch a glimpse of her.

The airplane is a ball of fire and smoke. Every once in a while sparks fly from it, but only shoot a half a meter or so before they die out. People are racing over to it, attempting to put it out.

"Let's get this parachute off you." Tom shows me how to unhook the latches, and pull the weighted burden off my back.

It feels as if he has taken a hundred kilograms from my back. I make sure to keep a tight grip on both the tiger and my handbag. I don't care what they do with the parachute, but they can't ruin my mission.

"I'm Joe, Joe Meyers and this is my buddy Tom O'Malley,"

2 Joes?

2 Toms?

Americans?

the man with the yellow hair says to me.

"I'm Kfira, and I need to get to Bangkok. Another girl was with me, but we were separated when we jumped out." I gaze around once more.

"One of the other soldiers probably found her. Let's get you to Bangkok." Tom helps me into the back of the topless vehicle.

Fear embraces my heart. I find myself clutching the tiger very tightly, as we head down the dirt road to Bangkok. A part of me says be afraid, but I can't let it speak. I have to be brave. I know these men are strangers, but I have to trust them. I just wish my heart would stop beating so fast.

Bangkok

"You must have floated down a couple of thousand feet," Tom says, as he twists around to talk to me. He seems friendly enough.

"I ... ." *I must look confused because he is laughing at me*, as the young man chuckles.

"Where are you from?" he asks.

371

"East Prussia." I'm not sure why I said this as I'm certain I should have said New York City. The bile from my belly, is in my throat, and still hasn't gone back down. The bumpy ride of the metal car is making me feel uneasy. I want to ask about Sarah. I want to demand that they turn this vehicle around, and help me look for her. Pains in my stomach say otherwise. *How could I have lost her?*

"Are you okay?"

I shake my head no, I'm afraid if I speak my stomach will erupt through my mouth. I want Sarah to be all right even if Sampson isn't. I want to stop the nausea, but nothing helps.

"Joe." He taps the driver's shoulder. "I think she's going to be sick, man."

Joe quickly pulls over to the side of the dirt road.

Without thinking, I leap over the side of the door, and nearly knock myself out when I hit the ground. My calves struck the door, and I know there will be some nasty bruises from it. I position the tiger and handbag behind me so that I don't spray them. Then, as fast as I can, I lean against the cool green metal. My stomach comes out through my mouth.

I wretch for what seems like eternity, but is more likely ten minutes. Not a lot is coming up, as I haven't eaten in a while. It doesn't stop my stomach from talking to me. Now my ankles are also screaming. I know they'll be all right in a couple of minutes. My stomach, I'm not sure.

I listen to someone else in the background also retching.

"Hey man, are you all right?" Tom asks Joe.

He mumbles something in return.

I pull a handkerchief from my bag, and wipe my face off. I check for spots on my clothes and stuff. Luckily, there are none.

"Here, let me help you." Tom opens the door, and holds out his hand to help me get back inside.

I toss the tiger and handbag in the back first. I allow Tom to take my hand and help me up. "Thank you."

"Yeah, freefalling can do that to a person." He laughs, but it's a sincere.

"Huh?"

"Make them sick."

I take a seat, and several long, deep breaths.

Tom gets in and opens a bottle of Coca-Cola. He hands it to

me.

It burns my raw throat, but my stomach begins to feel better almost instantly.

"Hey, ole buddy, come get your Coca-Cola," he says to Joe, who is now wiping his mouth with a white cloth.

"Joe has a weak stomach."

I understand.

"Do you speak English?"

"Yes. Can we go back, and look for my friend?"

Joe gets back into the vehicle and takes the Coca-Cola from Tom. "You sorry asshole," he mutters under his breath.

I feel my face redden, as I cower my eyes. I have only heard such language from the Germans.

Tom turns back to his buddy once Joe starts us rolling back down the road.

"Can we go back, and find my friend?"

Tom frowns. "I'm pretty sure our friends picked her up. Is she a red head wearing a gray jumper?"

"Yes."

"Don't worry about her. They took her to the hospital on the base. We'll see her in a little while." Joe stares back through the rearview mirror, and tries to say more, but thinks against it.

I heave a sigh. I'll have to check up on her after I get the Torah scroll. I know that Sarah would want it that way. So many things are going through my mind. Sarah going to the hospital and Sampson dead. Two men wearing green American uniforms, and I feel nothing bad toward them. *But why were they there? Shouldn't I fear them. Did I sleep through our stop in Manila? We were supposed to stop in Manila so I could catch a boat. It was going to take longer, but thought to be less suspicious. I don't understand, I hadn't slept through any of the other stops. I hope and pray someone will have answers to these questions some day.*

It doesn't take long to get to Bangkok. On the outskirts of town are little shacks for homes, and the closer we get to the center, the better the buildings become. People are everywhere, taking care of the daily chores of living.

Most of them are on the short side. They all have the trademark dark skin, dark hair and eyes. Their clothing is very colorful, and I can't help but to gaze at them. I wish I had one of their outfits, especially now that mine are in ashes. They wear pants under their long tunics, which are split from a little below the knee to mid thigh for easy mobility. I've never worn pants. I can only imagine the freedom of not having to worry about someone lifting up one's dress.

"We'll be at the main market soon." Tom glances back at me.

I've drank down the drink, and now I'm wishing I had food. I realize that this is probably not the place to be kosher. I've eaten all of the little candies that I picked up at Kat's. I was going to get something to eat in Manila.

"Are you hungry?" Joe asks.

"Yes, I am."

"Good, we were just about to go for chow," Tom says, as we pull over to the side. A few other vehicles are parked along the way but, not many.

— We're at the main market place. In a way it's just like the open market at home and in Casablanca. People are friendly, as they call out the names of the things they're trying to sell.

Several women are wearing fancy, silk dresses. Their skirts are slit up the side with no pants, and their tops are too tight.

They try to stop Joe and Tom by making kissing noises and winking at them, as we walk past. Both men say something in Siamese, and wave them away with their hands.

I'm now clutching the tiger.

We stop in at a little cafe, and take a seat at a round table with three chairs.

The metal shows through the white paint. The chairs are hard, but at least they aren't falling out of the sky.

A tall, bald man wearing a light peach colored robe comes over to us. He's wearing a jade tiger pin just like me! He stands before me, as if he doesn't see the other two.

"Can I help you?" His accent is so thick I can barely understand him.

"Can we get something to eat?"

"For you, you can have anything." He pivots around, and dashes back inside. We hear them jabbering in their own language about something.

"What's that all about?" Joe asks gruffly. He frowns, and taps his fingers nervously on the table. It echoes against the sidewalk. He shakes his head, and coughs several times.

Suddenly, the man returns with a large tray. He sets it on the empty table next to us. He hands the men fresh bottles of Coca-Cola, and for me, a cup of tea. He lays out plates before each of us. Because there's barely enough room on the table to add the silverware and the different dishes of food, he uses two tables.

"You eat." He bows in my direction, as he walks away.

"Thank you."

"Wow! We need to bring you with us more often."

Tom and Joe both begin to fill their plates with some of the different delicacies of the region.

"It all looks so good."

Joe and Tom agree, as they stuff food into their mouths. All three of us eat, as if this is our last meal. The food is spicy and pleasing at the same time. Rice, meats and vegetables make up the main staples. Some dishes are scary. I dare not ask what it is, but eat it anyway. I'm sure HaShem will understand. I find myself hungrier than ever.

I can't remember when I ate a meal last.

Every once in a while the waiter comes back out to refill my cup, take away empty dishes or bring fresh Coca-Colas. We eat until we're ready to burst our britches.

"That was good." Joe scoots back his chair.

I agree.

The man with the baldhead and peach robe clears everything off, but the drinks. Another man strolls outside.

He is taller than the first man with a long, black braid down his back. The sides and front of his head are shaved. He wears jade tigers on both shoulders of his peach robe.

"Hello." He pulls a chair over to sit beside me.

"Hello, jade tiger."

He chuckles.

Joe and Tom look over at each other, confusion on their faces.

"He's the one I'm to see while I'm here." I try to say this in the best English I can speak.

The men say nothing.

"I am Chou Yan. You are Kfira."

When he says my name it sounds like Kfila, and I almost laugh at his voice. I dare not for I haven't tried to say his name. My accent will definitely destroy it.

"Yes."

"We have waited a long time to meet you."

He places his hands flat upon the table, as if contemplating them.

"Where?"

"Not far from here. I will take you, but you must come alone."

"Yes, they just brought me here. I was only with them until I found you."

"I know."

I would like to feel uneasy, but I don't. I pray that it wasn't sleepy tea I just drank, as I want to be awake in case I need to fight or run or whatever.

"Thank you so much for bringing her to us. Your meal is on the house. Please go now, and we will see you again soon." The man says this with such sincerity that it's hard to say no.

"Are you sure about this?" Joe turns toward me.

"I'm sure."

"Okay, but if you change your mind all you have to do is yell."

"Okay."

"Thanks for the meal, Papason," Tom says, as he and Joe

stand. They glance at me one more time before they take off.

"Come with me." Chou Yan rises, and helps me up.

I grab the tiger and my bag. We walk along the path to the back of the building where an empty rickshaw waits. I know it's a rickshaw as someone has made a wooden sign with the word rickshaw painted across it in illegible English. It's a little three-wheeled cart with a red padded seat and canopy.

Chou Yan helps me up and I take a seat. I notice him attach a bicycle to the front, and hop on. Before I can ask any questions, we are biking down the road.

###

We ride along the road for quite a while. Just as when we come into town it went from old to modern, it now goes vice versa. Soon we are riding on roads that are barely paths. Several times we must leave the path so that a larger car or truck or whatever may pass.

Chou Yan moves us swiftly through, and for some strange reason I feel safe. I'm thankful. I survey the thickets of trees, so dense that it feels like night under them. It would be constant darkness for those who lived inside there.

We turn off onto a smaller path. We reach a small village

about thirty minutes later. Chou Yan is quiet, and I'm thankful. I

can't believe that I'm this close to the Torah scroll. I can do

nothing more than pray.

We reach the compound next. About twenty grass huts are

placed in two circles. One circle surrounds the other. People are

everywhere. Half-naked children are chasing each other. Women

stand over the fires in front of their huts, cooking or doing

laundry. No men are in sight. I guess they are at work

somewhere.

Chou Yan waves at a few, and pinches a couple of children's

cheeks, as we wheel through very slowly. They all look at me

with huge grins, and pats on any part of me they can reach.

"They heard you were coming. They think you are good luck,

and if they touch you then they will have good luck, too."

They're so beautiful and friendly. I want to stop the cart, and

give them all hugs, but I don't. I'm anxious to get out of the cart

before I lose my lunch once more. The bumpy ride does not help

my queasy stomach.

A part of me is extremely flattered that they should hold me in such high esteem. I find myself not feeling worthy of the honor.

We leave the small village, and we're back on a small trail. The rickshaw barely fits in the small path that is meant for walking or bicycling. Before long I see a huge, red earth colored building that must be the temple. The roof is shaped like a triangle. Several buildings along the way are similar in structure, but smaller. Other monks are also out and about, working.

We stop at the main building, which is the largest building in the center of the area. Without saying a word, Chou Yan gets off the bicycle, and removes it from the rickshaw. He lifts me and the tiger out of the back in one swift motion.

"Thank you."

He turns to the door and points. I realize he may have taken a vow of silence when he is near the temple. I return his point, and go toward the doorway, tiger and handbag in hand.

"Uh huh."

I gaze over to see him pointing toward my feet. I laugh when I realize he wishes for me to take my shoes off. With one hand, I gladly pull them off. I place them on a small mat next to the entrance. I continue to stroll up the seven steps to the entrance.

Inside is a large open space with many mats of different colors placed in rows. Open window holes hold no glass while large, multicolored, multi-designed tapestries cover the walls. At the back are three steps into the inner sanctuary. Many candles adorn the holders, all are aflame. A tall man with a long braid, in a peach colored robe, sits before the candles with his back to us.

He gazes up when he sees me, and glances sideways to get a better view.

"I didn't mean to interrupt."

"Come in Kfira. I have been expecting you. You took longer than I predicted, but then you are right on time."

Cautiously, I amble in, but I feel no apprehension. It's almost as if I've been in this place before, maybe in a dream.

"I am Master Chou Len."

As I get closer to the man, I realize that he's probably much older than he appears. The skin on his face seems almost as smooth as mine. His full lips betray solid, white teeth when he smiles.

"I am glad to see that you still have the tiger. I want to show you something." He rises, turns and almost looks as if he is gliding toward me. It's as if his feet never touch the floor. He takes my hand, and shows me to a hallway that is on the right behind a large tapestry.

I feel like I'm in a trance. The walls are dark red, but they sparkle as we stroll past them. When we get to another hallway, it leads us to an open doorway. I can see sunshine through it.

We move out of the door, and instantly I witness one of the most beautiful sights I have ever seen. A dozen tigers lie here and there along the rocks, and amongst the small out buildings.

Master Chou turns to me. "You are the Jade Tiger."

A young tiger cub waddles up to me, as I clutch the jade fake tiger in my hands. I lean down, ever eyeful of the other tigers in the area, and caress the soft fur of the top of the cub's head. It purrs instantly. It's a feeling of joy for me.

I put the tiger down beside the cub, and sit down as well. Soon all three of us are bonding on this rock. I have forgotten the danger of the other animals around us. It feels like I hold the cub and talk to it forever, but it's probably only a few minutes.

Then the mother tiger saunters over. She doesn't look as if she's in any hurry. Attacking seems to be the last thing on her mind. Padding gracefully over, she nuzzles against my neck. I find myself snuggling her neck as well. Her fur is soft to the touch, I listen to the loud purring noise coming from the back of her throat. When I gaze into her eyes, I see they are the same color as mine, jade.

Finally, after maybe ten minutes, she returns to the large rock only ten meters from me. I experience a sense of protection, and she does, too.

I stare up at the sky to see the sun starting to set, and I'm sorry. In a way I wish this moment could last forever, but I know it's time. Master Chou is deep in thought, as he rests on a rock like the one I sit upon, only a few meters away.

"The cub needs to nurse."

With this the mother makes a deep wah-ooh sound that calls the baby back. She licks my hand once more before racing back to her mother.

"You were here before."

"When?"

"Thousands of years ago when the sun set from the east. You were the one to calm the tiger. But, you have been gone a long time. They missed you." He glares at the ground down, as if he too, is sad to see me leave the tigers. Looking back at me, he sighs.

I take in his words, but don't know what to say. I sense the meaning of his words. A part of me says I can tell him all about the area and the tigers. My common sense tells me I'm being meshuggah that I'm a simple peasant girl here to pick up a scroll.

"This thing you do is great not only for your people, but all people."

I scratch my cheek nervously. I'm not afraid to be here, or of him but of myself. I pray.

We sit there for how long, I don't know, but I do know I feel shalom, inner peace. It's not the peace that Rebbe often talks about on Shabbos, but neshama. The fullness of spirit that Rosh Hashanah brings. Every sense in my body is alive, as I observe the tigers.

"We must go inside." Master Chou stands, and walks over to me. Gracefully, he pulls me up, and we hike toward a small hut in the corner. He opens the door, and allows me to step inside.

The hut's furnishings are very plain. A straw mat in the corner is for sleeping. A small altar in one corner with many candles on it is for praying. Only one is lit. He lights the others to illuminate the room better.

I sit on a large pillow on the floor near a small table. Tea has been set out with a huge bowl of rice, and another of steamed vegetables. I rest patiently for my host.

Taking his place across from me, he smiles. His eyes light up the room. "You have done very well."

"Thank you."

He pours the tea, and pushes my cup toward me.

I take it graciously and drink. It quenches my thirst, and gives me a warm feeling in my stomach.

He places vegetables and rice into two bowls, and hands one to me.

I rest it before me. I watch as he picks up the chopsticks and I follow suit. I'm shocked when I find myself handling the sticks, as if I had been doing it for years. We eat the food without a single word spoken.

Finally, the food is eaten, and the tea drank. Master Chou leans back, and surveys his hut.

"I suppose you think I live a simple life."

"I think you are comfortable. I sense security in your way."

Master Chou beams.

"When my master's master lived on this earth almost two hundred years ago things were different. Things are changing, but yet they stay the same. People search for something that is already in their heart. They just don't know it. They refuse to let go of the earthly matters in order to achieve this peace."

I gaze into the candles on the altar and sigh. *Yes, they do.* The world outside of my shtetl is so ... I don't have a word for it, but I know it isn't good. People are too busy for their own good. It saddens me.

"A great rabbi came to visit my people so long ago that I could not tell you when. Jews had been forced out of Israel again. He had with him a Torah scroll. That is what he called it. He said that it was one of the first scrolls ever to be written upon with the words of Moshe. He said that at one time everything was only spoken until someone decided it should be written, to stop the misunderstandings. People have a way of forgetting the truth.

"There was a great enemy of the time who was determined to destroy all of the Jewish people. He thought he could do so by destroying these scrolls. Of course, the great leader was wrong. He and his people died off, but the Jewish peoples still live, even to this day.

"He had been picked among his tribe to make sure that it never fell into enemy hands. He was a very brave man." Master Chou sighs.

"It was a great thing for this Master to take the scroll, and care for it, as if it were a part of his own culture and heritage. No one must know who and why it was given to him. Master took it upon himself to learn the language of the scroll, and to teach it to his disciples. Then in turn, they must teach it to theirs and so on.

"The tradition continues today. As long as this scroll has survives then my people will also survive. It has been a great blessing." Master Chou peers into the bottom of his teacup, and contemplates his words very carefully.

"It is said that the one who can tame the tiger, is the one to must take the scroll home."

The tiger cub and mother, even the reactions of the other

tigers, showed a calmness inside of me that even I didn't understand. I appreciate it. They're as at ease with me, as I with them.

"I saw that tonight with you." Tears well up in his eyes. "I never dreamed I would be the one to help the chosen one take home the world. I dreamed of this day since I was a small boy in China."

Now my eyes are misting. I want to get up and hold him, but I don't. Despite everything, it feels as if we are holding each other. Hugging for dear life for the changes that are being made in our worlds at this very moment in time, despite us.

"The scroll has no dowels so it will be easy to hide." He coughs several times."Inside the tiger."

I frown, until I realize he is speaking about the jade stuffed tiger I have been carrying. I drag the tiger around, and hand it to him.

Plucking a knife out from under the table, he slits open the belly of the beast. He pulls out the stuffing, and hands me some papers that are written in English. He puts a small pouch beside my teacup.

I glimpse through the papers. It's the address of where I'm to meet up with Aaron in Delhi, as well as a hotel name and address for a night's rest in Bangkok.

Master Chou slides a large oriental rug from under the table. It's a little over a meter long and thick. As he unrolls it, I realize that it's thick because of the scroll inside. A simple red sash holds it tightly together, keeping it strong.

"This has survived ages, weather, wars, and peace. Now it must go home. You must look." He urges me to gaze at it.

My heart beats so loud, I swear someone has a drum somewhere outside. I handle the parchment, as if it's a baby with delicate skin. I can't believe I have it in my hands. Ever so gently I remove the sash, and unroll a small portion to be sure even though all my senses tell me this is it. This is the ancient Torah scroll. I can see Bereshit right away. Tears are in my eyes, as I contemplate what the Rabbi must have thought when he was forced to Asia to hide this piece of history. Did he feel alone? Did he see the tigers?

I immediately close it back up, and retie the sash. My heart is in my throat as I realize I'm actually accomplishing something.

My task is half over, and yet it's just beginning.

Without saying a word we pull enough stuffing out of the tiger, so that the scroll fits snugly into the empty space without being felt. Placing some of the stuffing back, the tiger begins to take her old shape once more.

Master Chou produces a bone needle and thread and as quick as a whip, has the tiger tightly laced back together. No one can tell that it hides a scroll, or the future of a nation inside. The delicate work is invisible to the naked eye.

He passes it to me.

I fluff the fur back out, so that it looks as it once did.

Master Chou walks around, and puts his arms around me in a very warm hug. I don't know how long we stand there before a young man knocks on the wall.

"Master, master."

"What is it?" Master asks angrily.

"There are men coming this way."

"We must get you out of here." Master Chou picks up the jade tiger and stuffs her into my arms. He grabs up a long, green sash, and binds the tiger to my body tightly, so it will be easier for me to carry.

I snatch up my handbag, and we race out of the door, and toward the temple. We rush inside, and over to the altar. Master Chou pushes a hidden button, and the altar shifts to the left. It's just large enough for a small woman and tiger to crawl through.

I duck down into the hole, and see that it's attached to a tunnel. Torches light the way. I scramble down several meters, before I lift my body into a large hole, and walk upright once more. With my bag in one arm, and the tiger attached to my belly; I start my trek.

It dead ends at the altar entrance on one side. The other side leads to a long tunnel. I decide this is where I need to go. I pull the bag over the torch handle, and start the journey through the tunnel.

I travel about a hundred meters or so when, Chou Yan appears as if from nowhere. He motions for me to follow him and I do. We travel another hundred meters until we find ourselves in the jungle next to a clearing.

I look back to Chou Yan to ask a question, but stop short as I realize that he has been shot in the arm. He has a bandage wrapped around it, but it's still seeping blood.

"You're hurt," I whisper.

"I be fine. You go now."

I stare out into the clearing, and I see nothing but field. We hike a hundred meters or so. The torch lights the way. Glancing back to ask Chou Yan a question, I see he is gone. With that, I begin to stumble across the clearing toward the lights, and what I think is town. I'm sure I should feel fear now, but I don't.

Delhi and Aaron

I make my way toward the village, wondering what I will find. I must find someone who speaks English, as I doubt anyone will speak Yiddish or Russian. I pray whomever was at the temple did not follow me. I also pray that the monks are safe for I fear for their lives more than mine. Every once in a while, I turn to peer behind me, and I see nothing.

Glimpsing down at my clothes, I notice they are caked with soot and dirt almost making me heavy. The tiger is barely touched, as if it is protected somehow. I will need to find some new clothes, as well as a bath.

I must be hiking rather quickly, as it doesn't take long for me to reach the outskirts of the village. I get rid of the torch once I get into a well-lit section. People are everywhere just as they had been during the day. In fact with all of the lights, it looks like day. No one seems to notice me, and I'm thankful.

The open market is still doing business. Unlike the Casablanca market, it's busier than ever. I wonder if I'll be running into the little cafe we stopped at earlier. I realize the chances of that happening are slim, as I don't even know where I am. I have the piece of paper with the name of the hotel in my handbag.

I turn down a corner that looks familiar, but it quickly turns into a dead end. Rubbish is piled here, and there against doorsteps. A few piles are in boxes while others lay on straw mats. Some of the buildings are several stories tall. Long, white rope lines are strung across between the buildings. Someone's laundry is still visible. The sheets glow white against several lights.

I start to turn around when suddenly something hits me hard

against the back of the head, and sends me sprawling head first into a pile of trash, landing me on top of my tiger. I'm stunned for a minute, but the stink from the can of trash next to me makes me feel ill. Quickly, I try to shake it off so that I can get up and run.

My first thought is that someone is trying to rob me, but then unexpectedly I feel rough hands rip at my skirt, almost tearing it off of me. My slim, secret belt is still well hidden around my breasts.

I feel the hands searching inside my underwear, and I start to feel angry. How dare this person touch me. I try to stand, and shake the person off of me, but the hands are more insistent.

I hear no noises coming from my attacker, but I feel his hot breath against the nape of my neck. I smell the sour sweet aroma of sauerkraut and rye bread. I'm more than angry now, as I hear my heart beating loudly in my throat. The blood flowing through my veins could set the world on fire with such heat.

Several times the hands move, and I can see enough to know that the hands of the person who attacks me are white. I see a ring on the right hand, index finger. In the dark, I swear it looks like a Gestapo insignia ring like the ones I saw on the train. I stare over the garbage to see a tall brass stick of some kind on my left. Leaning into the debris to reach it, I feel my attacker getting a grip on my upper right thigh.

I grab the heavy metal object, and whirl around so fast I knock my attacker off his feet. It connects above his right eye, and knocks him backward. The metal slices his thin skin open, and blood pours down his face, and onto his unmarked uniform.

He's tall with blonde curls, and deep blue eyes. He's wearing a German uniform, but without any insignia, no matter, he is still a German soldier. He steps forward just as I bring my metal filled hand back, and take another swing.

"What're you doing?" he yells in German. "You stupid bitch."

All of the fury from the past comes to a head inside of me now, as he sneers at me with contempt in his eyes. He's still not afraid of me even when I have just struck him. I can hear screams, and I realize they are coming from me.

He reaches for a weapon that isn't at his side. His commandant had cautioned him to leave his weapon in the room, to be caught by the soldiers might be considered an act of hostility. He has no desire to see the inside of a prison cell in Siam.

With all my might I hit his face once more from the other side. A gash matching the first one, opens up and blood gushes from it. He reaches out to touch the gash, but this only brings more ranting.

Curses in German flow from his lips, as he reaches into his pocket for a handkerchief to wipe away the blood. He still lies on the ground, almost as if he's stuck on something. He kicks his legs out in an attempt to move, but he is immobile. His arms and legs flail around, as if he is a turtle on his back. No words come from his lips but sounds of pain.

Then as hard as I can, I bring the weapon down upon his chest and stomach. He closes his eyes and gasps for air. He coughs and sputters, as blood pours from his mouth. He's still alive, but barely."You will never hurt me," I say softly in German. I can speak German! Of course, I stopped speaking German after the rape! I blocked it from my memory, and now it's back.

I want to scream at him for trying to hurt me. I need to shout at him for being a part of this meshuggah world. I want to yell at him for Papa and Joe, Sarah and Sampson; and all the others who have been hurt. I need to hurt him for the rape when I was twelve. I want to damage him for the pent up emotions that have kept me in numbness for too long. I desire to spit in his face, but I always thought it to be wrong, so I don't. I pray he doesn't die, but I pray he doesn't live.

Tossing the brass pipe down, I snatch up my handbag and stroll away. I check the tiger to make sure she is unhurt. Everything is good with her. I realize that the only clothes I have are now shredded from the waist down, and splattered in blood.

I search around to see if I can reach a sheet left out on a clothesline. About ten sheets of all sizes grace one line. They appear white in the dim light. I take one, and because of the fear of guilt of stealing, I attach a five-dollar bill to the inside corner of one of the others. I chuckle, as I realize I have no idea what five dollars means here. I hope I didn't cheat anyone.

Then I wrap the sheet around my waist making a makeshift skirt for myself, and head back towards the lights. It feels like I'm moving in slow motion, but my body tells me otherwise. My heart is still pounding loudly in my ears for fear of being caught.

I half run, and half walk away. Soon I'm back at the open market. Noticing a small booth selling clothing, I decide to stop inside.

A young woman about my age walks over to me. She is beautiful with long black hair tied in back. She is dressed modestly in a pink top and pants in the same style I have seen on the other women.

"Can I help you?" she asks, in broken English.

"I want something like what you're wearing." I try to point to her clothes and shoes. Normally, I wouldn't point, but I fear she won't understand me.

She grins knowingly.

I must look funny with a sheet wrapped around my waist, and a tiger being held like a child. All of a sudden I realize I'm barefooted as well. My shoes are at the temple.

"You come." She takes me to the back of the booth where we are away from prying eyes. She picks out two tops of light pink silk, and two dark blue pants with little blue slippers to match. She puts them into a cloth bag, and hands them to me.

"How much do I owe you?"

She shakes her head no. "Tiger."

I nod. "Can you tell me how to get to ... ?" I try to say the name of the hotel, but muttle it pretty badly. I remove the paper from my bag, and show her the name of the hotel.

She nods in acknowledgement. "You go down street. Take left and there it is."

I think that's what she's saying. Her English is so bad that I'm not really sure. I place a ten-dollar bill in her hand, and say thank you. I walk in the direction that she pointed.

In fifteen minutes, I'm at the hotel and checking in.

The Siamese man standing behind the desk is tall and thin. He wears a white shirt and brown vest. He smiles and shows many brown teeth, but his English is almost perfect. His hair is thick, and his eyes are so slanted that they look closed. He picks up his cigarette, and takes a deep drag before setting it back down to ask me what I need.

"A room please."

"You will have room 18." He removes a key from the post, and strolls around to the other side of the desk.

I trail behind him, and we amble down a long hallway to the

last door on the left. No numbers are on the doors. I start to fear I'll get lost if I leave the room, but there are other things to worry about now. I can't help but wonder what the man is thinking of his newest guest, but then I realize he has probably seen his share of strange things before.

He unlocks the door, and hands me the key. "Enjoy." He saunters back down the hall, singing.

Cautiously, I peek around the hallway. I wonder if I have made a mistake checking in here. I really need to get cleaned up, and put on fresh clothes even if I don't get sleep or food. I sigh, as I prepare myself for anything when I saunter through the door.

I turn the door handle, and swing the door open, hoping if there is anything bad inside that I can outrun it. I take a quick look inside and almost scream.

"Kfira!" Sarah dashes over to me, and grabs me up in a big hug, as she pulls me in through the doorway. She shuts the door.

My eyes try to pop out of my head, as I eye Joe and Tom sitting in chairs by the window. They wave hello. Tears trace down my cheeks, and sobs escape my throat. I'm so happy, I'm speechless.

"I know. I'm sorry I scared you. I didn't want to, but they had to think I was dead."

"Who?"

"The Gestapo, silly! They want to get you, but they haven't made any deals with the Siamese soldiers so ... here we are, safe and sound."

I think about the man I left in the alley, bleeding. I know she is right. The danger is always out there. I have to admit that I'm so used to seeing soldiers that I didn't notice that even in Siam there seems to be an abundance of soldiers walking around. Most are Siamese.

"You look ragged. Let's get you in the bathroom and cleaned up." Sarah pulls me into the bathroom.

Sitting me down on a small stool, she begins to run bath water. I stop for a minute to catch my breath. I wipe my face with the back of my grimy hand, and giggle as I realize I'm probably smearing gunk back on my face. My hands are caked with dried mud and blood.

"You look like hell." Sarah saunters over to help me with the bags. She places them on the counter top. "Of course, we will need to burn those clothes." She glares at me.

I unwrap the sheet from my body. I want to say something about the man in the alley and the attack, but I don't. I didn't notice until under the lights that there are blood splatters making a pattern on the sheet. No wonder the young woman was smiling so. I pass it to Sarah, as if it's the most repulsive thing I've seen in my life. I still can't find my tongue to speak.

She gets it to the door, and hurls it out to the guys. "I have some things for you guys to get rid of."

"You know these men?"

"One is my boyfriend."

I laugh, it's too ironic. Of course, there are people everywhere, watching. They may not always be able to help, but they're there nonetheless. Isn't that what was told to me a million years ago?

Protectively, I release the tiger from my body, and lay it very gently on a small table next to the tub and the two bags. I would give my life for the scroll inside this tiger. Maybe I already have. Either way, it's not getting far from me.

I undress and hand everything except the bra to Sarah. It goes with my handbag, tiger, new clothes and tiger sash.

"Yes, these will have to be burned as well." She then throws them to the guys.

I stare down at my legs and see bruises all over as well as a few on my back. I slide into the warm water and grab a cloth. I want to wash the sickness off my body. I'm thankful I fought off the attacker. Was I really that brave back there? Maybe it was the spirit of the tiger that helped me fight. Either way, only a few more bruises show that anything happened to me. With the contusions from the airplane crash, I'm sure no one will be the wiser.

Sarah is talking, but I can't hear a word she's saying. At first it irritates me, but then I realize I do the same thing when I'm nervous. Something is said about getting me food after I clean up. I find that I am hungry after all.

"Honey, are you okay?"

I gaze at her and smile. "I'm okay." These are the first words I have spoken.

Soon, I'm clean from my head to my toes. I dress quickly, and then retie the tiger back to my body. I take the extra clothes, and place them and the bag, into my handbag.

"Look who's clean," Sarah says, as we sashay through the door.

Sarah combs my hair and puts my makeup on me before we walk out. Both men whistle with delight. I must look much better than when they first saw me, an hour earlier.

###

The men take us to an open-air cafe. It's not the one from earlier, but it's nice place. A short man who could have passed for the younger brother of the hotel clerk takes our order.

"I don't know if the food is as good as it was earlier, but I'm sure it will be edible," Joe says, as the waiter brings our drinks.

"I'll eat." I realize that I'm very hungry.

"Here's to us." Tom holds up his Coca-Cola bottle.

Everyone, including me, clink our bottles together. We laugh, and the men begin to spout jokes nonstop until the hours and food roll by.

"Okay guys, our princess needs to get some sleep, so we need to head back to the hotel," Sarah says, as the waiter clears off our table.

"Yeah, that's a good idea." Tom winks at Sarah.

Sarah pulls him close, so she can whisper in his ear.

"Ahh," Tom says softly, before kissing her on the cheek. He nods in agreement.

"Okay. Are you ready Kfira?"

I know I'm sleepy, but I'm unsure if I will be able to slumber. I know I should be afraid, but with Sarah and these two men, I'm not. In my exhausted state a thought that Sarah, Joe and Tom may hurt me crossed my mind, but is soon overtaken with a sense of peace. I don't know where it's coming from, but sense it's the tiger and HaShem guiding me now.

"Let's go." I stand, and the others follow.

Sarah and Tom stroll ahead of Joe and me. They're arm in arm, and for a second, I envy them. For two seconds, I had that feeling. I'm a widow now, there is no one to stroll with.

"Are you all right?" Joe asks.

"Yes."

"You scared us when you got sick earlier."

I chuckle. "I don't jump from a plane much."

"You should try it more often."

We both laugh this time. We stop in front of the hotel.

"Thank you for helping me." I stop in front of him.

"You're welcome."

Our eyes meet for just a second, as I feel a sense of brotherly protection coming from them.

He turns away. "Come on Tom, get the lead out."

"Okay, okay," Tom says in protest, as he kisses Sarah several more times. They walk back over to us.

"I'll see you two later." Sarah turns to me. She wraps her arm around mine, and leads me back into the hotel.

I'm beat. I want to sleep.

"Lie down and rest. I'll get things ready for tomorrow."

"What're we going to do?" I lie down, wrapping my arms about the tiger for extra security. My purse rests under my head.

"We're going to see Aaron."

My eyelids feel heavy, as I can no longer keep them open. Everything is quiet, but the soft hum of the ceiling fan.

###

The warm sunshine on my face wakes me. I gaze around to see the room is empty of Sarah. The tiger is molded to my body with scroll inside. My purse is still under my head. I wonder if I dreamed that I saw Sarah and the guys last night.

"Hello." Sarah enters the room.

"Hello."

"Did you sleep well?"

"Yes."

"Good, I will bring breakfast in, and we'll eat." She pivots around and walks back out, leaving the door open. She returns with a tray of food and drinks.

She places it on the dresser.

I glance around the room, and realize there is furniture in here besides a bed. A small table with two chairs sit by the tall, floor to ceiling window. Against the wall is a dark, six-drawer dresser with a plain, white lamp sitting on it.

"Doesn't it smell divine?" She inhales deeply, filling up her lungs with the aroma.

I try to do the same, and suddenly the queasy feeling is back. I make a face, and hold my nose.

"Aren't you hungry?"

"Yes and no."

"Hmmm." Sarah saunters over, and feels my forehead.

"Funny, you don't feel feverish. Do you think you can make it to Delhi?"

"Yes." I almost shout this word. I look at the food. It looks too good to pass up.

"Good, cause we're going. Here," she says, as she hands me a cup of tea.

I grasp the cup in both hands, and manage to take a large sip. It begins to calm my tummy. Soon, I'm eating with Sarah, and we're chuckling about the plane wreck, but not about Sampson.

It's not the fancy food of yesterday, but it's good.

"As soon as we get done then we'll catch a ride to the airport. We'll be in Delhi post haste."

Thank HaShem.

We eat with Sarah gabbing between bites. I don't know everything she's chatting about, but she thinks she does. I wonder what she's feeling about Sampson, as she doesn't seem to show any feelings.

###

After we finish eating, we hike through the main streets of the city to catch a taxi. The driver is friendly, but keeps his back toward us all the way. Sarah is her usual bubbly self. Soon she and the man begin an engaging conversation about the meaning of life. I lean back and half listen, and half survey the scene ahead of us.

Soldiers are everywhere, and the driver is explaining how the soldiers took back the country from the royalty recently. He states there will be big changes here soon, and he hopes they're good ones. He even tells us that next year they are going to change the name back to Thailand. I'm reminded of the issues with my own home country. First it's Russia, and then it's East Prussia, who knows what it will be next.

We reach the airport after only a half-hour of traffic. Sarah pays the man, and we walk into the terminal. It's larger than the Casablanca terminal, but not as big as the ones in America. It's clean, but basically it has the same design as the others. People stream by absentmindedly, as they make their way through their travels.

We check in and find seats, but we don't have to wait long before we're on the plane and taking off. I find myself searching out of the window for planes on fire. I pray for the monks. I also hope that some day I'll get to come back and see them.

They're saying something about making a stop, but they're unsure. They'll let us know soon. I start to ask Sarah where our parachutes are now.

"You can relax."

"Huh?" I turn to Sarah.

"I know you're still tired. Maybe even a little scared. Go ahead and relax. Before you know it, we'll be there."

I really don't want to go to sleep, but as I stare out of the window I see that everything; the plane, the people outside and the people inside are acting fairly normal. I'm not afraid. I relax a little, and delight in the people and scenery. None of them seem in a rush, they're just doing their duties with a light heart. It's nice.

I find my mind drifting to Delhi and Aaron.

###

I look around, and see that Sarah's resting. A man has just announced in several languages that we'll be landing in Delhi in thirty minutes.

People begin to gather their things together, and make small talk with another. The door to the necessary rooms is busy, as someone is constantly in there for the next twenty minutes.

I struggle with if I should wake Sarah or not. Before I can, she opens her eyes.

"You look refreshed." She yawns and stretches.

"Thank you." I shake my head, trying to get the kinks out of my neck. I try to stretch but, it's difficult in the tight space with a tiger strapped to my body. I'm unsure of how many plane rides I can make after this one. I pray this is over soon. I caress the head of the tiger, and reflect on home. *Where is home now?*

"You slept well?"

"Yes."

She reaches over, and hugs me tightly. "It'll be over soon."

I beam.

The plane moves closer to the ground, and this time I know we won't smash into it. I'm happy. As we get closer to the terminal, I hope that Aaron is there to greet me. I'm sure he won't be. He's probably tucked away in a hotel somewhere, waiting.

The people begin to leave the plane just as fast as they can, once the have a nice day is announced. Sarah takes my hand, and we follow along the line. I wonder if we'll have to stop at customs, but I'm sure that's probably an American idea.

"Can I help you?" the man says, as Sarah and I get a few meters inside.

A long desk is off the door just like at the other airports. Several men sit behind it. This one talking to us wears a red turban, and is tall, taller than most. His face can barely be seen through the black facial hair.

Sarah hands him our passports.

He peeks at me and the stuffed animal, and then the jade tiger pin on my sleeve. It's almost as if he sees right through us. Nothing. Or maybe he watches women carrying large stuffed animals strapped to themselves every day. He checks the passports over again, and wordlessly, he stamps the visas. "Thank you and welcome to Delhi. Please, have a nice stay."

We rush through the crowd, and there, standing by the back wall is a familiar figure. Can it be? Yes, it's Aaron.

I see no one else but him, as I sprint over, and wrap my arms around him. He chuckles, as he attempts to get closer to me despite the huge tiger clutching my belly. Silently, I sob and clasp tightly to his arms.

I can't stop crying, even though I'm not making any sounds I don't want anyone to see. I struggle to shake off the fears, as he pulls me away from him. He wipes my cheeks delicately, and then kisses them.

"I missed you, too," he whispers.

Sarah smiles, and pulls us closer to her. "Okay lovebirds, I think we should go."

"Okay."

Sarah and Aaron begin talking about Delhi's airport. They discuss pleasant it is, as if this is an ordinary day.

I observe the people. They're all dressed in their native costume from their area of the world. It's a sea of color around us. Most of them are busy taking care of their travels. A few are sleeping in the uncomfortable chairs. Others are cleaning. No one seems out of the ordinary. No one seems to pay attention to the two women, a man and a stuffed tiger. I pray it stays this way until I reach Safed.

Crossing the Desert

Aaron leaves his arm about my shoulders, as we leave the airport. I can't help, but to watch the people as we stroll by. I'm a little wary of all strangers. Never have I seen so many brown faces than on this trip. Soldiers are here and there, but they are British soldiers and speak English. I don't feel threatened by them. I sense security.

"I'll take us to the hotel so we can all freshen up." Aaron squeezes my shoulders.

I beam up at him.

"That sounds great. I'm ready for some rest, and a good meal," Sarah says nonchalantly. She traipses a little ahead of us.

I speculate if she is thinking about Sampson. I wonder if I'll ever get the images of the dead men, and the half-dead man out of my own head. I try think about it. I'm here in India, safe for the moment.

Aaron escorts us out to a black four-door car. He and Sarah are still rambling about the weather, and places to see while in Delhi. They've both been here before.

I eye the people around us. The Indian people seem to be taking life easy, but not as easy as the Siamese. The women's colorful clothing is something like what I'm wearing now, except they show off their bellies. I giggle at the thought of me showing off more skin. It's all I could do to agree to a cinched waistband and hems sewn a few inches below the ankle. I've always worn modest, full-length skirts that billow when you twirl around.

Their clothing is beautiful. I notice that many of the women have a little red dot on their foreheads. Some of them have designs on their hands, and feet that almost make them look blue. Some men wear turbans, and some don't. The men are more simply dressed than the women. So many questions I wish I could ask about the customs and costumes of these natives. They interest me.

"Here we are," Aaron says, as we get to the car. He opens the passenger doors on the left-hand side for Sarah and me. I notice that the steering wheel is on the wrong side, but I say nothing. He waits patiently, as we get in before he makes his way around to the driver's side. He gets in. We close the doors simultaneously, and the noise is so loud that it sounds like a gun going off.

Sarah and I immediately duck down in the seats.

"Relax, girls, no one is shooting at us yet." Aaron chuckles, as he starts to pull the car out in traffic.

Two heavy sighs of relief, and we lay quietly for a few seconds. Contemplating gun shots of the past and the slamming doors of the present, before we sit back up.

"Are you all right? You look pale," he asks at a stop. He reaches over, and caresses my hand.

"Yes, I'm okay."

"Are you okay, Sarah?" He eyes her reflection in the rearview mirror.

"I'm just great. For a minute I thought I needed to look for my parachute again." She laughs nervously. She tugs gently on a red curl and looks away.

"You two are safe for now. I got us a hotel suite not too far from here."

I learn that a hotel suite is when two bedrooms are attached to one common area. Each bedroom has its own bathroom. A small balcony sits off of the common area.

It doesn't take long to get to the hotel. Aaron parks the car. He gets out and opens Sarah's door. He opens mine, taking my hand, as if I'm a princess. He assists me out.

"Thank you." I grin. His hand is warm to my touch. I don't want to let go.

"I can't wait to take a nice hot bath, and change out of these clothes," Sarah says, as we go up the steps to the suite.

The staircase almost looks like the staircase at Jean-Pierre's. I find myself lightly touching the decorative leaves adorning it. It's wide with yellow marble steps. But this time, my feet don't make any noise, as I'm wearing the slippers that I received from the Siamese woman.

"Maybe we can order room service," Sarah says.

"That sounds great," Aaron answers.

We're on the fifth floor, but this time I have no trouble walking up the steps. My legs are sore from the bruises, but I'm none the worse for it. I'm ready to be a part of civilization once more.

Aaron opens the door, and we step in. It's not a bad looking common area. Three large green sofas and two overstuffed brown chairs occupy the middle of the room. Over by the balcony is a round glass table and chairs. A string of lights along the walls, as well as various paintings, give the room definition and color. Two bedrooms, one on each side of the larger room makes the room appear circular. It allows for a bit of privacy for us as well.

I race over to the balcony doors and peer out, not daring to go outside right now. It's wonderful. I view an open market several blocks away, and I hope we can go see it before we have to leave. I twist back around to find out what the others are doing.

Aaron's on the phone, talking to room service.

"I think I'll take a bath." Sarah heads for the room on my right.

I amble over to the other bedroom, and open the door. A huge bed is sitting in the middle of the room. Strolling over to it, I lightly touch the thick green spread covering it. It has a very intricate design in red across it. It's easy to make out the fluffy pillows underneath. It's very inviting, but it's not time to rest but to eat and drink.

I go back into the living area to see what Aaron is doing.

"I've ordered the food, and it should be here about the time

Sarah's out."

"Good."

"Come, sit with me." Aaron is sitting on one of the large sofas.

I rest next to him, and stare deep into his dark eyes. They're very warm and friendly, almost sparkly.

"Did everything go well?"

I shrug.

"Would you tell me if something went wrong?"

"Yes, I'm all right for now. The important thing is to finish the mission. We can talk about what happened later." Petting the tiger's head, I feel like the past couple of days are all a dream, no a nightmare. Being in Delhi with Aaron, I know it's a wonderful vision. I find a sense of happiness that I'm not sure I deserve.

"Would you like to go out tonight?"

"No."

"Okay, because I know Sarah will probably go out."

"No."

He wraps his arms around me, and we snuggle close together, all three of us.

###

By the time the food is here, Sarah is out of her room. Sarah is beautiful even if she is just wearing a bathrobe, and a towel wrapped around her hair.

All sorts of foods are brought in, and I only recognize the bread and rice. It does smell and look good. I find that I'm famished. We set everything up on the round table, so it looks like we're having a normal meal. I say the prayer, and everyone starts dishing food onto their plates.

"So what is the plan, Stan?" Sarah asks.

"Well, tomorrow Kfira and I catch a private plane to Riyadh, Saudi Arabia. It's too unstable in Iran and Iraq to risk going through them, even though we have sympathizers there. Since they discovered oil in Saudi, and some of the other Middle Eastern countries, many non Middle Eastern people travel around the countries without fear. We won't be sticking out like the sore thumbs that we are."

"Hmmm," Sarah says.

"You, my dear, get three days of rest and relaxation, on the house for your part in helping Kfira make it here."

"How will we get to Safed from Riyadh?" I wrinkle my forehead, as I bite into something very spicy. It burns my tongue, and makes my eyes water, but I can't seem to put it down.

"Ever ride a camel?" Aaron begins to chuckle.

I almost choke on my food. I've seen pictures of camels, but never seen one up close and personal. "No."

"Well, you get to now. We'll have to get some clothes for you to wear, but you and I will ride ships of the desert to Safed." His voice sounds so dramatic as he rolls his eyes upward. He sways his hips to and fro. One hand forward pretends to hold imaginary reins. The other grasps the back of a 'saddle'.

We snigger at his outlandish behavior.

Oy Vey! This is definitely going to be a meshuggah ride for me! How will I ever make it through I wonder.

"It'll be fun." Sarah reassures me when she finally stops hooting.

"I don't know."

"It'll probably take a few days, but I'm confident we can do it."

I pet the tiger head with my chin. I know he's right. I

wouldn't have came this far if I wasn't going to complete my mission.

"Okay. It'll be fun."

"Good."

Sarah tells us of the plans she is making for tonight, but I only hear half of her words. I imagine myself sitting atop a camel. I never would have dreamed about doing these things at one time in my old life. I feel good about it. I hope I won't be too bored when I have to go back to a normal life.

###

After the food is eaten, the waiter comes back, and takes away the empty plates and dishes.

Entering the common area after about thirty minutes or so in the bedroom, dressing and primping; Sarah is ready."I'm going out." She looks stunning in a very beautiful, light blue evening gown. Her red curls are in a French twist at the nape of her neck. She wears a small string of pink pearls with little pink studs on her earlobes. Sarah grabs a wrap and handbag before heading for the door. "By the way, don't wait up for me." Sarah turns back with a wink and grin. She leaves without waiting for an answer.

Aaron and I rest on the sofa, and gaze at the window, as the sunsets. Already Aaron has turned on a few lights, so that we don't suddenly find ourselves sitting in the dark.

He keeps his arms around me. For a minute, I tell myself I must fight the need to be with him. The urge to jump out of his grasp slips away from me, as I begin to feel safe and warm, protected. We're not married, and I'm a widow. Besides, this isn't the shtetl. They leave, as quickly as they came.

My heart skips a beat, and begins to pound erratically. I feel the blood rush to parts of me that only Joe has touched. I feel warm and alive. It's good.

He picks me up without a word, and carries me into the bedroom. Laying me across the bed, he goes over to turn a few small lamps on. He shuts the door.

I untie the sash holding the Torah scroll to my body, and try to figure out a safe place for it. I decide it should be in the chair beside the bed. I know Aaron or I could reach it if something ... then Aaron's lips are on mine.

His arms are around me, and hold me so tight I almost can't breathe. Our breathing becomes heavier.

"Do you want me to stop?"

"No."

"Are you sure?"

"Yes." I reach up, and plant my lips against his. They melt together. I want him to make love to me, to feel him inside of me. He pushes me to the limits of my emotions. I know he isn't my husband, but the bond we have grown between us is strong. I missed him in Bangkok. When the Nazi was trying to rape me, all I could think of is that I couldn't let myself have another bad experience. They destroy me. I'm saving myself for Aaron.

He kisses a trail along my neck and face. I'm still wearing the Siamese clothes, so there is no easy way to slip them off, but Aaron manages. His hands are so gentle, and tender as they stroke my breasts.

He frowns when he spots the bruises on my back and legs. I tense up, waiting for him to say something about them. Without saying a word, he kisses them. I relax and let myself melt into him once more. We make love, and I believe I'm flying without wings.

###

When I awaken, my clothes are back on, and I'm wrapped

around the tiger once more. I feel the hardness of the scroll inside

the tiger, and know it's still here. I remember picking it up, and

huddling with it after Aaron got up to do watch.

Aaron steps in and smiles.

The sun shines through the window, and I know it's getting

closer to my fated camel ride.

"Hello."

"Hello."

"Did you get any sleep?"

"A little. I was just about to doze off when Sarah came in."

I chuckle heartily, as he shakes his head.

"She had a good time, huh?"

"Oh, yeah."

"Did you have a nice time?" I wink. *How brazen I have*

become, Mama would not be proud, but I can't worry about her.

She's not taking a camel ride to Safed, or is she?

"Yes, I did." Aaron strolls over, and gently kisses my lips.

"Me, too."

"Are you hungry?"

"Very much."

"Food is here. I just thought I would check on you, and let you know."

Getting up, I sash the tiger back onto my belly. I should probably use the necessary room before I do this, but in the short time that I've been attached to it, I've become fond of it. I want to feel it next to me. I will bathe after I eat.

We saunter into the common area where the food is already laid out on the table. Aaron and I eat, watching the sunrise. When we're done, I go to the bathroom and run bath water. I'm anxious to make sure that I'm clean before we start the next part of the journey. I'm sure it will be a while before I have a chance to bathe again. I'm happy, as we are nearly done.

"I have something for you." Aaron enters the necessary room. "We have to make sure you are properly covered on our trip." He holds up robes and a birka, head covering, for me to see.

I chuckle at his boldness. "You aren't Orthodox, are you?"

"No, why?" He puts his arms down and frowns.

"An Orthodox man would never walk in while his wife is bathing, even if they are husband and wife for many years."

He grins and shrugs. "He doesn't know what he's missing. These are the clothes that you need to wear." He holds them up again.

I nod. The head covering is nothing new to me. Every good, married Orthodox woman wears a head covering even if she's a widow. Only her husband is privilege to seeing her hair. Well, of course the children see as well.

"You will have to cover your face as well." He shows me the little lace eye openings.

"And if I didn't have green eyes and a big tiger wrapped around me, no one would know it's me. They might think me native."

"Actually, you will have to put tiger under the robes for this." We both begin to snicker over this comment, but we know it's true. It'll take some careful sashing to pull this part off.

After my bath, I begin to dress. I pray that I don't have to use the necessary room too quickly with all of these clothes on. I put on the clean Siamese outfit. Then we wrap the sash Master Chou gave me around the tiger. With it in place, Aaron produces a second one for extra security.

She's so snug against my belly that I wonder if this is what it feels like to be nine months pregnant. Then the first robe is applied, and then the second. The birka goes over my face. I stare at myself in the mirror to see if I can see myself. I notice nothing but my dark green eyes through the light lacing over the eyehole. It's impossible for me to see much of anything. I lift the veil off my eyes.

I turn to see Aaron also dressing in costume. He's wearing lighter colored robes, three of them. He dons the white keffiyah with a black rope, headdress. He looks like an Arab from a picture book I found in secular school. I don't recognize him.

"Are we ready?"

"Do we need to tell Sarah?"

"No, we must leave now. She knows where we're going."

I grab up my handbag, and we head out of the suite. Soon we're walking down the steps, with me a meter behind Aaron.

No one notices us, as we amble past them in the lobby or parking lot. I have to fight to keep from laughing, as I feel awkward. It doesn't take long to get to the airport. I try to peer out of the veiling, but still find everything so blurry. I wonder if I could live like this, with only a partial world to see when I walk down the street.

We go directly to the gate where a private plane is waiting for us. We aren't at the airport more than thirty minutes before we're on the plane. It's about the size of the clipper, but with more seats and fancier.

I want to ask questions, but we aren't alone. If we were in Saudi Arabia, as we will be soon; I wouldn't be able to do so in public. I decided to start practicing now.

####

The plane ride is smooth. Several oilmen from the United States are on the plane. They had decided to take a small side trip to India while visiting the Middle East. Their wives had given them a hard time about no gifts when they returned home. For some reason, these men thought the good gifts could be found in India.

I discover the birka gives me the ability to snoop without actually staring at someone. I listen intently to these strangely accented foreigners.

The ride is long, and torturous in this outfit. I thank HaShem several times for making me a Jew, and that it's only my hair that is supposed to be hidden. I'm anxious to get to Riyadh, and onward to Safed.

###

We arrive at the airport, which really isn't an airport. A landing strip is open for the planes to land on, and a building for people to wait. Inside the building are offices and necessary rooms, as well as a cafeteria. I think I heard someone from the oil company say his company built this stop just for him.

Aaron follows me to the necessary room, and waits patiently for me outside the door. This is one place I will be able to go to by myself while we're here.

When I stroll out, he smiles.

"They're ready for us," he whispers, as he passes a few inches from me.

I nod in response, as I know saying words might be frowned upon.

We walk outside into the bright sunshine, and see cars and camels. Some are getting into cars, and I envy them. While others are opting for the camel rides.

"Are you ready?" a man in full Arabian dress asks in French, as he walks over to Aaron. His colors are green and black with more white.

Aaron answers him in Arabic. They converse for several minutes before the man nods. He motions for us to come with him, with his right hand.

We trail behind him to the airport parking area. A group of people are standing with their camels. We're all dressed alike except for the colors of our outfits. I stumble over to the women, and try to blend in. I can't say anything as my accent will give me away. I realize after ten minutes that I don't know their language, but pray I can get by.

No one is paying attention to me. They seem to have their own worries to take care of. Soon we are being loaded up on the camels. The men grab the reins of their camel, and the camels of their wives, as Aaron does mine. We're off.

I attempt to peer at the big hairy beast under the veil, but it's almost impossible. His fur feels like that of a cow. His clip clopping reminds me of the elephants we saw in Delhi. The saddle is actually comfortable. Several skins of water hang off the horn where I place my hands for balance. Every once in a while the camel makes a noise from one end or the other. I have to stifle many giggles. Once we start moving, I try to lull into the movement without becoming sick. It isn't easy.

Someone in the front, an older man, is singing a song to the camels. It has a nice melody, and seems to calm them.

###

We travel as far as we can which isn't many hours, maybe six and then stop. The women build a fire, and then gather near it to cook the food. I try to help even though I don't speak the language. It's easy to understand that they aren't pleased that I'm here. I decide it's a language or cultural barrier, and ignore their hostility. They look right through me. At times it's as if I'm alone.

I was afraid that jade tiger would shift during the ride, but luckily this doesn't happen. At times my tucas goes numb, and I have to pinch myself hard to keep from laughing out loud. I'm sure there are high consequences for such offenses. So I pray that HaShem bestows patience on me to make it through.

We give food to the men first. When they are done, we are

allowed to eat what is left. We clean up, and then we're back on track.

At night, we stop and make camp. Everyone puts up their own tents. Luckily, Aaron and I share a single tent. We hold each other closely, and get very little sleep, but we're together.

This is how the trip goes for nearly five days.

###

We've just eaten and are cleaning up. The women's attitudes have become less hostile. They now let me help with unpacking, cleanup and packing. The women are placing two more bags onto the camels, and we'll be back on track.

I'm already sitting atop Adam. I named my camel Adam back on day one. He looks like an Adam, of the Earth. Several other women are also on their rides. Two men are standing next to their women, ready to help them up as well.

Out of nowhere, several robed men come riding up on horseback beside us, and start screaming something at the leaders. The men grow panicky, as they argue back and forth. I watch in horror. It looks as if the men on camels and the men on horses, might dismount and start fighting each other.

The others quickly mount their ships of the desert in preparation to run.

Without thinking, Aaron tightens the reins to my camel, pulling me closer to him. I'm only a meter from him.

Aaron asks the men several questions. They bellow something back in his direction.

Terror strikes my heart. *We're going to die. We're so close to Safed, I can feel it in my bones, but we're going to be killed here.* Just as these thoughts cross my mind, a band of thieves make their way from behind a large sand hill.

Five or six of them are riding down from the sand dunes, and we easily outnumber them. I don't know if we have any weapons. It's so difficult to see through the birka.

The women instinctively huddle up. I glare between them and Aaron. I wonder what I should do. By now my heart is beating so loudly that even if I understood their language; I wouldn't be able to hear over the sound of the blood whooshing in my ears. The palms of my hands begin to sweat, and I'm shaking.

The women scream, and I notice that I'm screaming with them. The men pull out guns in preparation for the raiders.

Everything happens so quickly, as the camel men roar at the men on horses. The raiders are now ten meters from us. They also have guns. Several take shots at us.

Impulsively, I lay down across the saddle so that they can't see my body. I hear the thud of someone getting hit with a bullet, and I pray it isn't Aaron. The body falls to the earth.

Several more gun shots ring out. Someone yelps, and drops to the ground.

I find myself saying the Shema, and any other prayers I can think of to ease my mind. I sense someone is moving my camel. I struggle to glance upward to see if it's Aaron. I see his camel's tucas, and realize he's safe.

More gunshots go off, and I stare at the other group just in time to see one of the women dangle off a camel. I lift my head and veil slightly so I can see if Aaron's all right. He is hunched over like me. He spots me, and winks in my direction. He motions for the veil. Sighing, I close my eyes and the veil. For a second, I strive to will this all away. When I look up, everything is still the same.

The women are still giving earsplitting shrieks like dying

animals. Some of the men are yelling, too, as we hear the thunder of horse beats tread away from us. It's quiet except for the distant thunder. No one stirs. We remain like this for five, maybe ten minutes, as if paralyzed in time.

I dare to sit up slightly. It's like living in slow motion. I gaze at Aaron, as he watches the rider turn around, and charge us once more. He's alone, and he has his gun ready to fire. It's aimed at me. The other men in the company strive to get between him and the group. Their camels can't catch up with the fast pace of a horse galloping full out.

Aaron plunges toward me off of his camel at the same time that the rider fires. I involuntarily yelp and shudder.

Thwump. The bullet hits the top of my shoulder, and knocks me off the camel. I land on my back with a thud. It's all I can do to keep from speaking. It takes my breath away, and leaves me limp. The pain is excruciating. It takes me a few seconds to realize that the bullet has hit me.

I believed it was a rock that hit me, but then he wasn't shooting rocks.

I struggle to sit up, but pain ricochets through my shoulders and chest. My tucas is awake from the fall. All my bruises scream out in pain. I reach down to make sure my precious cargo is safe, and find it well.

Blood flows from my shoulder, coloring my clothes a deep red. Wondering how far away civilization is right now, close my eyes to the pain. I wonder if we're still be watched by our people.

I listen to several more gun shots and thuds. I peep through the veil to see the man who shot me, lying on the ground in front of us, dead. Aaron's crawling toward me, he isn't hurt.

I know this is all happening in seconds, but for a minute it takes hours to get back to now.

Aaron holds me up, and removes the veil so he can give me a drink of water. The water feels good going down my throat. I'm suddenly very thirsty. He rips off part of one of his robes and begins to hold it tight against my shoulder. He hauls me up, and I squirm as if fire is racing up and down my back.

"It's okay. I want to see if the bullet went all the way through your shoulder."

I nod, as the suffering is so great that speaking is impossible. I hear the others getting off their camels, and tending to their wounded and dead. No one seems worried about protocol. They're only worried about surviving.

"We'll need to stitch you up. I don't think this is serious, but you may lose a lot of blood," Aaron says softly. He gently presses on the shoulder, but the bleeding doesn't stop.

"Are we almost home?" I gasp and choke for a few seconds.

"Yes." He provides me a few more sips of water.

The world begins to spin and then everything goes dark. I want to tell Aaron I love him, and to make sure the gift is taken home. But when I go to speak, nothing comes out.

Safed

Blinding pain in my shoulder, and chest awaken me. Gasping for air, I try to move to a better position. There is none. I grasp my stomach, searching for the tiger and scroll. They're still attached. The bouncing motions tell me that I'm moving again, but I'm unable to open my eyes.

"Kfira."

"Huh?"

"Kfira."

Maybe it's HaShem telling me I'm dead. Maybe I failed the task after all, and death is my punishment.

"Kfira."

No, it's a voice I recognize. It's Aaron.

"Aaron." I cough, and gasp for air.

"I'm right here."

Inching my eyelids open until they are little more than slits, I spot him sitting beside me.

"Kfira."

I hear moaning, and realize that it's coming from me. Tears flood my face, as I try to remember what happened after I was shot. Nothing.

"You're safe now."

Suddenly, I realize that I'm not wearing the birka anymore. I touch my face, and it feels swollen.

"You fell off the camel when you were shot. You hit your face on the side of a rock. It'll be okay in a couple of days. The Torah kept you safe and alive." This is said in a soft whisper.

"Where are we?"

"We're on our way to another air hop to catch a plane, and get you to go to Amman, Jordan. We can get you to a doctor there. Then, when they say everything is okay, we'll go home."

"How long have I been asleep?"

"Almost two days. When you were shot we weren't very far from the nearest village. Luckily, there were some British soldiers out and about. They wanted to see some of the sights they once patrolled, and they came across us. They agreed to bring us to the air hop."

"How many people died?"

"Four."

Coughing, I try to take a breath, but my throat is as dry as the desert. Every time I cough it sends little knives into my shoulder and back, making me wince and moan out loud.

"Here, let's get you some water." Leaning me up slightly, Aaron places something cold and wet against my lips.

I attempt to glance to make sure to let the water flow down my throat, but my eyes refuse to focus.

"You lost a lot of blood. You aren't bleeding now, but that's why we have to get you to Amman."

"Aaron, I'm so sorry."

"You have nothing to be sorry for. I'm the one who should be sorry. I thought this would be the safer route."

"Sometimes there's no safe route." Reaching out, I grasp his knee. He pours more cool water down my throat, and I try not to swallow too quickly. I sigh. Tears well up in my eyes, but I know if I cry now there'll be no way to stop the pain.

"Just try to get some sleep."

I let my eyelids close tightly. My thoughts turn to the others who died in the raid. My heart goes out to them.

###

When I open my eyes again, it's daylight and we're nearing an air hop. My eyelids cooperate with me and, I can see everything. I'm laying in Aaron's arms in the back of a truck. We're on top of a bed of sheepskins.

"Aaron."

"We're almost there."

"Help me sit up please."

With one hand behind my back, and the other grasping my arm, Aaron leans me forward.

"Oh HaShem." Moans of pain and anxiety escape my lips. It feels like every piece of my body is on fire. Sweat pours off my face and down my neck. I'm scared. I've never felt so much intense pain in my life.

"We're here," someone says from the front.

"Thank HaShem."

With Aaron's help we turn to see where here is. It's just like the small airfield we landed at when we came to Saudi Arabia. For an instant, I think we're at Riyadh again.

"We'll have you all tucked away as quick as a jiffy," the male voice says from the front. It's a British accent.

The truck pulls over, and the driver turns off the engine. Two men hop out. Both are wearing light colored slacks and shirts. Both are tall, and one is blonde while the other a red head.

The red head marches back to us. "How are ya going?"

"I think we'll make it."

"Thank you so much." I struggle to lift my hand to shake his.

"No worries, you'll be right as rain in the morrow. We just need to get you to the doc."

The blonde walks back "They're ready for them."

Aaron, the red haired guy and the blonde huddle around me.

"Why don't we pick her up, and carry her to the plane?" Red suggests.

"Sure, she can't weigh much," Blondie answers.

"Okay, on three; one, two and three." They each grab a corner of the pelt I'm laying on, and lift it up. Sliding to the edge of the truck, they let Aaron get off so that he can walk in front of the makeshift carrier. Almost running, they struggle with me all the way to the plane.

Their breathing quickens, and sweat pours off their faces and armpits. Once we get within three meters of the plane, two more men run out and take the other sides. Within seconds, we're inside. They put me on a small cot.

It's much more comfortable than the truck or the camel, but not a bed.

"You take care," Blondie says, he shakes my hand.

"Thank you."

"Thank you. I kind of feel like I did my good deed for the day," he says, with a hearty chuckle. Small laugh lines grace his eyes and mouth, betraying his true age of forty something.

"Well, gotta go see if we can rescue any more damsels in distress."

Red comes over next. "You have a good trip. Get well soon. I thought we were gonna have tie this one down when we found you two."

"Thank you."

Red shrugs and salutes, he turns and walks down the steps to leave.

"I hear someone needs a doctor here," a man from the doorway speaks.

"Yes, please," Aaron says, as he sits beside me.

The man walks in carrying a black bag. He stands over me, and looks at the temporary dressing that's holding my shoulder together. "You have lost a lot of blood."

"I'm going to look at you for a few minutes. Then we'll take off, and get you to a real hospital." He draws back the blood soaked bandage.

It's red and puffy around the stitches, swollen almost to the point of breaking them. It's black and blue all the way down into my chest. "Who did the stitch work?"

Aaron raises his hand.

"Nice job. I think it would have been all right, but since you two were in the desert when it happened, sand and whatnot probably got inside. It definitely looks infected." He lifts my arm, and rotates it.

The pain intensifies, making me claw at the cot. Heels digging into it as well. Aaron reaches over for my hand, but I refuse it for fear I might hurt him.

"It really doesn't look like anything is broken, but we should get you some new blood." He smiles. "I'll give you something for the pain." He pulls out a syringe and a little bottle. Drawing up the medicine, he plunges the needle into the bullet-wounded arm.

For a second or two everything is warm and fuzzy before everything goes dark.

###

"Kfira."

Bright lights are shining in my eyes. A cool sheet covers me. I reach down, and realize I'm wearing different clothes. I panic. *Where is tiger? Where is the scroll?* Jumping up, I nearly knock myself out when the pain hits. My eyes are wide open.

"Shh, it's okay. I have the tiger." Aaron holds the tiger up in front of my eyes.

I breathe in, and slowly exhale. Closing my eyes, I'm thankful that we're alive. I open my eyes once more, and glance a look around the room. We're in a hotel room, but it's different somehow. Medical equipment is in here. Something is in my arm that goes up to a bottle of water, some sort of tubing.

I gaze over at Aaron and see him grinning. He's laying his head on the tiger ever so gently. "What happened?"

"We got you to the hospital. They reopened the stitches, and cleaned out your wound. Then they pumped you with medicine, and gave you some sugar water. When you start eating, you'll get to go home."

Home. Ancient Torah scroll. Safed. Can it be possible to be so close now.

"We're in Amman, Jordan, which is actually pretty close to home. We may be able to just drive there."

Knock, knock, knock.

"Come in."

A young man walks in who looks a lot like Aaron. He's a little darker, and a little shorter with a couple of days growth of beard. I stare over at Aaron, and see he also has a couple days growth of beard. I almost laugh at these two.

"I just stopped in to see if you are awake," he says, with a very thick accent. "The wound is healing nicely. Now that you are awake, we need to feed you. We have to make sure that you take care of the baby."

"Oh yes." I turn to Aaron to clutch his hand. I'm ready to eat and go home. All of a sudden a frown crosses my face. I know I'm having a hard time understanding this man, but did he say baby? "Baby?"

"Baby, yes, you heard correctly. You're going to have a baby." Aaron squeezes my hand.

"But how?"

"Well, I will leave the explanation to your husband," the doctor says, with a chuckle. "I will have them bring you some food. Take it easy, as it will be difficult to eat for the first few times. If you need anything, let me know. I am Dr. Rahala."

"Okay."

He turns and leaves, as quickly as he came in.

I stare at Aaron, and frown again. *How long were we out on the desert? How long have we been traveling? At which time did I get pregnant?*

"You and Joe made a baby."

I don't know what to say. I know where babies come from and all that. After all I am twenty-five, but with all the danger around us I never gave it more thought than ... sitting Shiva for my Papa and Joe.

Tears flow from my eyes, and sobs rip from my throat. The pain in my heart matches the pain in my shoulder. Every gunshot, every dead body, every plane crash, and even the sight of the Kristallnacht fires roar before me. I can't stop weeping.

Aaron puts his arms around me, and holds me close. Tiger sits on the bed between us, but next to us to keep us safe. "Let it out. Let it all out."

I cry so hard that the bed begins to shake.

Someone walks in, and asks if everything is alright.

"Her father died," Aaron says, looking over at the woman.

"I'll give you two a few minutes, and then I'll give her

something."

I pull away from Aaron's embrace to look the young woman in the eyes. "No, that's okay. I would like something to eat." I wipe the tears from my face with the back of my hand.

Both Aaron and the woman pull handkerchiefs from their pockets to hand to me.

"Thank you." I take them both. I sob heavily several more times before I'm able to take in a deep breath. The pain in my shoulder isn't as bad as it was.

"Are you sure you don't need anything but food?"

"Yes."

The woman smiles at me knowingly. She leaves.

"What day is it?"

"December 21st, the first day of winter."

Funny, it doesn't feel like wintertime.

"Chanukah." I whisper the word.

"Yes, it's Chanukah. If all goes well maybe we can be home by the eighth night."

Aaron beams at me.

###

For the next two days the doctor checks my wounds, changes the dressings, and asks me how I am. The American nurse also changes my dressings, and brings me food. Occasionally we get to gaze out of the window, and see the rest of the world.

A few tall buildings block some of the view. Lots of people live here, but they are hard to see from so high up.

Aaron and I discuss the baby, and Chanukah. We both pray that we'll be home by the eighth day.

"How will we get home?"

"Car."

"How long were we in the desert?"

"Eight days."

"I must have miscounted, I thought it was five." I giggle.

"Well, I have to admit that riding a camel across the desert isn't all it's cracked up to be. Being passed out in the back of a truck with a bullet wound to the shoulder is not everyone's idea of a good time. I'm sure it was about eight days." He sniggers.

I nod.

"Ready to go again?" Aaron presses my hand. Then he pulls it to his lips, and kisses it softly.

"With you? Yes."

His eyes turn down, and a sly smile is on his face.

Knock, knock, knock.

"Hello."

"Hello," the doctor says, as he walks in. "Is someone ready to go home?"

"Can I?"

"I will check you over. If everything is looking good, yes. The nurse will assist me this time."

Just as he says this Nurse May enters the room.

They pull me into a sitting position. Then Nurse May holds the gown while the doctor looks over the wounds, back and front. He takes off the old bandages, and pushes slightly on the shoulder.

I wince, but the pain isn't as bad.

He redresses it, and helps Nurse May. "I think you can leave today. We can get you out of here in less than an hour."

"I can leave?"

"Do you want to stay?"

Nurse May chuckles, as well as Aaron.

"No. Send me home."

"You promise to watch your shoulder for redness? Eat properly? Be good to your man? Name the baby after me?"

"Yes, yes, yes and what?" I frown, and then smile, as I realize he's trying to be funny.

"It is a simple name. Mohammad Ishmael Arabarb Rahala." Everyone snickers.

"You get dressed, and we'll have you out in ten minutes." The nurse follows the doctor out.

Finally, we're on our way home. I wonder if I still have the piece of paper from the Jade Tiger with the address, but then realize that Aaron probably has it memorized. He's good like that.

Rubbing my eyes, I pull Jade Tiger toward me. I look her over once more for blood spots. It's something I have done constantly since I woke up here. I'm confused about the baby. I worry about how I will take care of it. Aaron assures me that the baby and I will be well taken care of, no matter what. Learning of the baby has not stopped the closeness that has built up between us.

I sit in the chair in my Siamese dress. Aaron tells me that I don't have to wear the birka here, and I'm thankful. He signs the release papers. They're in Arabic. Even though Jordan is a little more progressive than Saudi Arabia, I'm still a second class citizen.

"Let's get you home." Nurse May brings in the wheelchair and Aaron.

"Thank you." With their help, I get up, and slide into the chair with my tiger and handbag.

"You travel light for a woman," the nurse remarks.

"It's the nature of my life."

Aaron and Nurse May gab about the weather, and driving in the area. Soon, we're downstairs, and in the car.

As we turn out of the driveway, I pray that this is the final leg of the journey, and that the Torah will be safe soon.

###

It's a quiet ride over the road to Palestine. I have to remember to call it Palestine, at least until we get around more Jews.

"We must be getting close to the border," Aaron says, as the cars begin to slow down. I'm surprised to see so many people driving on this road. It's actually one of the more modern roads I have seen since the United States.

"Will we be able to pass through?"

"I don't think it will be a problem. I have the paperwork." He pats his jacket pocket. He's wearing a white linen suit. "We really need to get you some new clothes."

Belly laughing, I glance down at my clothes, and then open my handbag. No clothes in there now. "You don't think you will get tired of this ensemble, do you?"

"It looks nice on you but the maternity clothes will look even better."

We pull up next to the soldiers, before I have a chance to answer.

"Can I see your papers?" the British soldier asks. He is young, maybe eighteen with light brown hair and gray eyes.

Aaron hands them to him.

The man beams. "I have something for you." He walks over to his truck, and produces a small bag. Bringing it back over, he hands it to Aaron. "From the friends of Abraham."

"Thank you."

"Thank you." I lean over to see what's in the bag.

Aaron delivers it to me. Inside the bag are corned beef

sandwiches like the ones we ate from the New York City deli.

"Thank you so much."

The soldier waves us through.

Without thinking, I pull one out, and begin to nibble on it. I

figure if it's poisoned I will have made my delivery before it

takes effect.

"Are we hungry?" Aaron chortles.

"Uh huh."

It doesn't take long before we see a sign that reads "Safed, 15

kilometers". It's only minutes now. Not days. Not weeks. Not a

lifetime ago. Today, we'll be at the Shul, giving someone the

Torah scroll.

I finish off the sandwich, and wish I had something to drink. I

find a canteen of water next to my seat, and take a long drink.

Jade Tiger is still at my side.

The town looks small, but as we get closer it takes on a whole

new life. Many old buildings are scattered here and there, until

we get to the main section. People roam around, taking care of

the daily chores of life. It's a bright, sunshiny day.

We pull into a little area off from a large building. It's a large home, sitting off from the road. Several smaller houses are on either side, but they aren't very close.

"This is it?" From the looks of the front, it looks abandoned. It's a two-story building made of white plaster and such. A cedar tree is on one side, and a willow on the other. On the second floor is a balcony.

"Come on, let's go inside." Aaron races up the walkway, and the twelve steps to the porch.

Cautiously, I amble along. Clutching jade tiger in one hand, and my handbag in the other. As I ramble up the steps something hits me, I smell Mama's matza ball soup and lamb stew! Bounding up the last few steps, I throw open the door, and almost leap into the hallway.

"She's here! She's here!" Screams echo from all over the house, as people pop out from everywhere. Across the ceiling is a big sign in Yiddish saying Welcome Home. Mama, Esther, Minka, children and more, come and grab me tightly in a hug.

Tears and sobs escape most eyes and lips. Although they try to be careful with the hugs. I feel a twinge of pain in my shoulder, and shrink back slightly.

"Give her room everyone. She's healing from a gun shot wound." Mama pulls me over to her. "Today Kfira is a woman of valor. We have another surprise for you."

The Rebbe emerges from the kitchen, wiping his hands on a napkin. Everyone chuckles, as they realize he is already sampling the cooking.

"I never could keep you away from my food," Mama says, as she waves a finger at him.

"You're a good cook, woman. May all of your daughters feed their families so well."

Everyone laughs.

"Let us go into the den," Rebbe says, as he leads the way. He sits in an overstuffed, brown cloth chair. A smaller chair is beside him. "Sit."

I take the chair beside him. I hold my treasure in my hand.

He reaches out, and touches my hand. Something that just isn't done. "You have done a good thing. You have been braver than anyone could have expected. You saved most of your family. Now, we have the second oldest Torah scroll in the world

... here in Israel." He sighs, and looks around at everyone as if they are gold.

"There will be many blessings to happen for your family. Did Master Chou tell you the story of how the Torah came to be in such a far away land?"

"Yes, Rebbe."

"Good."

I embrace the tiger gently for a few seconds, and then hand it over to him. He takes it as if it's the largest baby he has seen. He hugs it to himself, caressing the ears. Then he produces a small knife from a pocket, and tears out the stitching that Master Chou made.

Within two minutes, the baby of a Torah scroll pops out from the jade tiger's stomach. Most Torah scrolls are tall, maybe a meter and a half to two meters before the dowels are attached. They're always heavy as well, but not this one. It's maybe a meter in length. He removes the sash.

Opening the page as I did, he sees the words and tears begin to flow from his eyes. He closes it quickly, so as not to smudge, and puts the sash back on. "This scroll was made small even though the first one, and the others are usually quite large. They thought if they made one smaller than the others that the chances of her surviving for thousands of years would be greater thus insuring the survival of the Jewish people. It would be easier to smuggle away from danger. Now that she is home, she will not leave again. She'll have to go into hiding but not far away. Never again."

We all nod.

"Maybe we should keep her with the tiger?" I ask.

With that, Rebbe places her back inside her safe place. "We can sew her back up later, but now its time to eat, and celebrate such a wonderful homecoming!"

"YEAH!"

They rush over for more hugs till the Rebbe strolls toward the dining area.

"We better go eat." Aaron takes my arm with tiger in the other. We head for the food because I'm famished.

Thank you for reading. I hope you enjoyed it.

Barbara
(lilcoyote2002@peoplepc.com)